"THERE IS HATRED AT THIS TABLE."

The fortuneteller swayed in her chair. Her eyes were closed but her hand rested on the Queen of Clubs. "A dark and rainy night...A man alone... Another man...Desperation! All is Darkness! Tragedy rules! Villainy triumphs!"

Judith and Renie almost banged heads trying to press closer against the door. They were steadying themselves when they heard the crash and the screams.

"The lights!" Judith called. Oriana immediately obeyed, bringing the chandelier up to full beam. Madame Gushenka was sprawled facedown on the table, one hand on the cards, the other clawing at the azalea's vivid blooms.

"Get back!" Harvey ordered, assuming his best operating theater-style. As the others moved away, he felt for a pulse. His sallow face sagged as his search for a vital sign grew more frantic. "My God," he exclaimed, "she's dead!"

"Dead? That's ridiculous!" screeched Oriana. "I paid her two thousand dollars! I want my money back!"

MARY DAHEIM

Just Desserts

A BED-AND-BREAKFAST MYSTERY

AVON
TWILIGHT

TO JMC:
If you haven't got a nickel,
then I haven't got a dime.

AVON BOOKS, INC.
1350 Avenue of the Americas
New York, New York 10019

Copyright © 1991 by Mary Daheim
Excerpts from *Just Desserts* copyright © 1991 by Mary Daheim; *Fowl Prey* copyright © 1991 by Mary Daheim; *Holy Terrors* copyright © 1992 by Mary Daheim; *Dune to Death* copyright © 1993 by Mary Daheim; *Bantam of the Opera* copyright © 1993 by Mary Daheim; *A Fit of Tempera* copyright © 1994 by Mary Daheim; *Major Vices* copyright © 1995 by Mary Daheim; *Murder, My Suite* copyright © 1995 by Mary Daheim; *Auntie Mayhem* copyright © 1996 by Mary Daheim; *Nutty as a Fruitcake* copyright © 1996 by Mary Daheim; *September Mourn* copyright © 1997 by Mary Daheim; *Wed and Buried* copyright © 1998 by Mary Daheim; *Snow Place to Die* copyright © 1998 by Mary Daheim
Inside cover author photo by Tim Schlecht
Published by arrangement with the author
Library of Congress Catalog Card Number: 91-91766
ISBN: 0-380-76295-1
www.avonbooks.com/twilight

First Avon Twilight Printing: June 1999
First Avon Books Printing: July 1991

AVON TWILIGHT TRADEMARK REG. U.S. PAT. OFF. AND IN OTHER COUNTRIES, MARCA REGISTRADA, HECHO EN U.S.A.

Printed in the U.S.A.

WCD   20 19 18 17 16 15 14 13

ONE

JUDITH GROVER MCMONIGLE thrust the phone away from her ear a good two feet, knocked her coffee mug off the kitchen counter, and booted her cat, Sweetums, into the open cupboard under the sink. At the other end of the line, Oriana Bustamanti Brodie was covering every note of the scale, beseeching Judith to change her mind.

"We're fumigating," Oriana wailed. "Carpenter ants. It smells. It's impossible. And Otto is counting on this weekend with the family!"

A disheveled Sweetums was eyeing Judith with open hostility. His orange fur bore traces of chili beans and apple peel. Any other cat would have ignored revenge for the sake of cleanliness. In Judith's opinion, Sweetums was as unnatural as he was filthy.

"I'm sorry," Judith said, for the third time, bringing the handset up to her mouth while she threw a dish towel onto the spilled coffee and began swirling it about with her foot. "I'm booked, have been since November."

"But you told me January wasn't a busy month!" Oriana had launched into her full-throated Act Four, Scene Three voice.

"It isn't," Judith agreed as Sweetums put a paw in the coffee, sniffed, and choked up a hairball. "Only two of the four rooms are taken, but you'd need all of them for your . . . family, right?" Somehow, "family" wasn't a word she readily associated with Otto and Oriana Brodie; "horde" sprang more easily to mind.

The sigh that heaved over the phone line possessed seismic force. "Otto will be sooooo disappointed." The mezzo-soprano voice that had mesmerized indiscriminating opera lovers in second-rate houses dropped several notches. "We would have paid extra for the short notice."

"Another time, maybe," Judith said pleasantly, if firmly, and replaced the handset as Sweetums slipped out through his cat's door into the back yard. As much as she hated turning guests away, Judith was relieved. The Brodies might be considered by many on Heraldsgate Hill to be prominent personages, given his wealth as a carpet-sweeper mogul and her fleeting fame in the music world. But Oriana's demands conveyed a hint of desperation which put Judith off.

Not that she had either the time or the inclination to indulge in speculation on neighborhood eccentricities. Widowed for almost three years, she had hurled herself into establishing the family home as a bed-and-breakfast known as Hillside Manor. At the moment, she barely had time to finish mopping up the mess left by the coffee and Sweetums before her mother came thumping into the kitchen on her walker.

"Where's my Tums?" she demanded, giving the walker an extra whack for emphasis.

"Up your nose," muttered Judith, grateful that Gertrude Grover was nearly deaf as a post. More loudly she said, "Try your housecoat pocket, left-hand side." She checked the Caesar's Palace coffee mug for cracks with one eye, while watching her mother with the other.

"Damn," breathed Gertrude, "how'd they get there?"

The telephone saved Judith from having to answer. It was Dorothy Dalgleish, calling from Pinetop Falls, a small logging community some fifty-five miles to the northeast.

"Oh, Mrs. McMonigle, I'm *so* sorry!" wailed Dorothy Dalgleish. "We're going to have to cancel this weekend. Homer is sick."

"That's a shame," said Judith with feeling, though more for herself than the ailing Homer. "I hope it's nothing serious."

"It's always serious with Homer," Dorothy responded with a touch of annoyance. "Bronchitis, this time. He *will* work out in the woods in the worst weather. But that's the life of a gyppo logger. You're on your own, with no big timber company behind you."

Judith could sympathize, at least with Homer's private initiative. "Tell him to take care. You, too. Mrs. Dalgleish."

"He will. *We* will," asserted Dorothy. "In fact, put us down for next weekend. If you can."

Judith could and did, filling Hillside for the first weekend of February. A glance at her reservation book gave her mixed pangs of satisfaction and apprehension. Since opening the B&B in May, she was already discovering a pattern to bookings: Weekends up through October were generally full; so were most weekdays during the summer. Business revived in mid-November, but dropped off dramatically after New Year's. St. Valentine's had been taken since early December, but there were a lot of blank spaces until April. Maybe she should add catering to her repertoire. Or try to book more wedding receptions. Perched as it was on the steep hill on a dead-end street, the big old house was ideal for romantic getaways and for visiting shoppers who didn't want the hassle or expense of a downtown hotel. Tourists, however, had yet to beat down Judith's door. Perhaps that would change if she could get listed in one of the national guidebooks. She'd made various contacts, from AAA to specialty publishing companies, but so far without any payoff. Patience, she told herself; patience—and the cultivation of a tough hide—had gotten her through eighteen years of marriage.

"Where's Mike?" Gertrude inquired, her pugnacious jaw thrust out above the gaudy green and red of her housecoat collar.

Judith was somewhat startled by the question. Her mother might be ornery, even absentminded, but she was hardly senile. "Away at school," she replied in a much less certain voice than she usually employed.

"Of course he's away at school," growled Gertrude. "What do you think I am, daffy?" She rummaged in her other pocket and pulled out a package of cigarettes. "I meant, where is he at school? I thought he was off on some half-assed field trip."

"Oh!" Judith ran a hand through her prematurely graying hair. "Idaho, some place. Priest Lake?" She knew, of course, but momentarily went blank. As a forestry major, her only son had already been on several field trips which seemed to focus on how much beer could be sneaked into one's backpack rather than how much knowledge could be crammed into one's skull.

"What are those damned fools doing at that university, teaching kids how to camp? No wonder education costs so much—they waste it on all those frills!" Gertrude plunked herself down in a captain's chair at the kitchen table and lit a cigarette. "And what's he going to do when he gets out? Grow into Paul Bunyan?" The question emerged in a cloud of blue smoke.

"Well, he's already dating Babe, the Blue Ox," Judith replied, recalling the Viking-like Kristin of Christmas past. A sports medicine major, Kristin had carried Judith's eleven-foot unsheared Douglas fir into the house with one hand. It was no wonder Mike had described his girlfriend as awesome. "I don't know, Mother, I just hope he ends up doing something he likes. He's got almost two more years, after all."

"Seems like he's been there for ten already," rasped

Gertrude as the phone rang again. "Face it, kiddo, he could turn out like his father. The closest Dan McMonigle ever got to work was when you put his ashes out in the toolshed."

With a baleful glance for her mother, Judith answered the phone in her professionally charming manner. The voice at the other end went on nonstop for three minutes, signing off in a flood of tears. Judith sighed and put the phone down. "The Hunicutts," she said. "Their second honeymoon turned into a trial separation. Damn."

"Wiped out, huh?" Gertrude stabbed her cigarette into an ashtray made out of a clamshell. Sweetums reentered the kitchen, growling menacingly at Judith as he made for his food dish just inside the pantry door.

"January is thin," said Judith, slamming the reservation book shut. "I wish I were." She gave her blue jogging-suited figure a disparaging glance, though in fact, she was a tall woman who could have easily carried another ten pounds without much detriment. Her hand strayed to a pile of bills in an English biscuit box. "Christmas seems like six months ago instead of barely one, except for paying for it."

Gertrude was unwrapping a fresh batch of Tums. "I thought you were going to close up for two weeks this month anyway and wallpaper the living room. Why don't you get off your butt and do it now that you've got the chance?"

Watching Sweetums lick his chops after polishing off his cat tuna, Judith eyed the packages of wallpaper that reposed in the back entryway. "I could. Or," she went on grimly, feeling not unlike Marie Antoinette heading for the guillotine, "I could call Oriana Brodie."

"I could call that fathead a lot of things, but she wouldn't much like most of 'em," said Gertrude, chomping on her Tums.

Judith acknowledged her mother's remark with a vague gesture, then opened the phone book. "I wonder why they moved back here from Palm Springs in the first place," she murmured. "I would have thought Oriana would have preferred something more posh than Heraldsgate Hill."

"Otto. The old fart always had a sentimental streak, according to your father, rest his soul." She waved a hand in a haphazard sign of the cross on her forehead. "Otto used to cry like a baby in poetry class, especially when they read Rupert-What's-His-Name."

"Brooke," supplied Judith, waiting for the phone to be answered at the Brodie residence four blocks away in distance, but a world apart in hard cash.

A breathless Oriana gulped her hello, explaining that she had been on her way between the main body of the house and the guest quarters over the triple garage. "It's the only part not being fumigated," she said. "Oh, my lungs! I shall have to give up practice this afternoon."

Judith was tempted to suggest that Oriana simply give up, period, but instead conveyed her message with forced enthusiasm.

"But how fortunate!" cried Oriana. "Otto will be ecstatic!"

Ecstasy as embodied by the porcine Otto Brodie struck Judith as a vision of Porky Pig hoofing madly away on his stout little trotters. To Oriana, she merely expressed pleasure and asked if any members of the party suffered from allergies. During the first month of her tenure as mistress of Hillside Manor, a superior court judge had been hauled away in an ambulance after eating crab dip. Judith had suspected that her son had substituted Sweetums's cat tuna, but discovered later that the judge had a violent seafood allergy and that his wife was furious with him for not inquiring as to the ingredients in Hillside's hors d'oeuvres. Since then, Judith had been careful about her guests' dietary eccentricities, feeling that the screeching arrival of aid cars and emergency vehicles might give Hillside a bad name.

"Allergies," mused Oriana, sounding not unlike Tosca mulling over the choice between surrendering to Baron Scarpia and jumping out the window of the Farnese Palace. "Otto has sinus, but mostly from dust and pollen. As for the others, I think not . . . but you must remember I haven't been stepmother to Otto's brood for all that long. Of course, Harvey is a doctor. As for the fortune-teller, she won't be dining with us except perhaps for dessert."

"Fortune-teller? Dessert?" Judith grimaced into the phone. "Actually, I do breakfast, not dinner . . ."

". . . promptly at seven-thirty, or Otto gets . . . unruly. And Harvey sulks, while Lance tends to wander off. Mentally, that is, and Guinevere is never on time unless you absolutely insist on punctuality for meals." Oriana had interrupted like an orchestra conductor giving instructions to a slightly dim-witted lead singer. Judith's protests died aborning.

Facing a hopeless task, she decided to take advantage of what appeared to be a good thing. "Roast beef is ten dollars a plate, salmon eight dollars, and chicken, ah, seven-fifty. I only do one entree per party. Which will it be?" she asked cheerfully. If Oriana expected dinner as well as breakfast, she'd damn well pay for it.

There was a pause at the other end. "We pay for the roast beef or salmon or chicken? I didn't realize . . ." A deep masculine voice rumbled in the background. "Roast beef," Oriana said quickly. "Cream puffs for dessert, if you will, and do make one for the fortune-teller." The phone clicked in Judith's ear.

"Cream puffs?" Judith shrieked into the handset. "I should have told her they'd cost another two-fifty each!"

"Cream puff, my foot," muttered Gertrude, lighting up another cigarette while Sweetums preened against her baggy stockings. "Otto's no cream puff, he's one tough customer. When he isn't bawling, that is. Hey!" She grabbed the walker and swung it at Sweetums. "Beat it, you mangy little fleabag!" Sweetums pounced; Gertrude retaliated with the rubber-tipped leg of the walker. Cat and contraption became an orange and silver blur.

Judith ignored the encounter; she was busy counting china. "My service for twelve has dwindled to eight," she said, more to herself than to her mother, who was still wrestling with Sweetums and the walker. "I wonder if the fortune-teller knows where to find odd lots of Wedgwood's Pembroke pattern?"

"Odd lots is right," her mother snorted as the war with Sweetums wound down to its inevitable conclusion. After Gertrude whacked the walker against the wall, an ear-shattering screech ensued. Sweetums abandoned the field and fled into the dining room, leaving behind a trail of fur. "Lots of odd ones in that Brodie family," remarked Gertrude, panting a little. "I'd search 'em before they left come Saturday noon."

Disinclined to argue, Judith looked at the art deco calendar on the refrigerator. It was Thursday; Saturday suddenly seemed far away. The house would be empty tonight, tomorrow would be taken up with grocery shopping and fixing the impromptu dinner. Judith's logical mind toted up the price tag to feed the brood of Brodies, plus a fortune-teller for dessert: A rib roast for eight would probably cost over fifty dollars, plus potatoes, vegetables, bread, and condiments. Maybe they'd expect liquor, too. It was possible that the impulsive figure she'd given Oriana was going to backfire. Especially with the cream puffs.

"What's the matter?" demanded Gertrude, seeing her daughter's worried expression. "Screw yourself again?"

Judith uttered a truncated laugh. "Well, nobody else has offered."

"Watch your mouth," snapped Gertrude, leaning on the walker and getting to her feet. "What kind of a girl have I raised?" With a show of indignation, she clumped out of the kitchen toward the back stairs. "Besides, if you're talking about romance," she rasped over her shoulder, "there's always that damned cat."

TWO

JUDITH HAD TO give the Brodie family their due: They arrived promptly though almost simultaneously at six-thirty p.m. Friday night, sporting luggage with various designer labels, the rain blowing in behind them. Judith's regular cleaning woman-cum-laundress, Phyliss Rackley, had called in sick. But a last-minute crisis had been averted when, as if in answer to a prayer, good old Cousin Renie had phoned not two minutes later, announcing that she had made the deadline for her annual report design, her husband had gone to a creative dream seminar for the weekend, the kids were away, and she was going to put her feet up and watch *Brideshead Revisited* on video, eat microwave popcorn, and drink six gallons of Pepsi. Judith demolished her cousin's own creative dream in ten seconds by asking her to fill in for Phyliss.

"Who are all these goofy people?" Renie demanded when she peeked out through the swinging kitchen door into the dining room between tosses of romaine lettuce.

Judith explained even as she tested the rib roast and

started the gravy. "Otto Brodie lives over on the Bluff, in that big old stone house with the topiary animal shrubs. He made his fortune in bombs during World War II, and then cleaned up—so to speak—with carpet sweepers. He's retired now, and that's his second wife, Oriana, who"— she paused long enough to grab the peppermill, grind it too fast, and sneeze—"was once an opera singer of some renown if little talent. Otto's two kids—if that's how to describe the Hulk and the Bulk—are Lancelot and Guinevere, his first wife, Minnie, being into King Arthur."

"Aha! The house with the blue baggie over it. Fumigating, which is why they're here, instead of there." Renie diced the tomatoes with verve. "Lance played pro football and Gwen writes dirty books, right?" She saw Judith nod from behind her Kleenex. "Don't blow your nose in the gravy, coz, it looks bad in the tour books. Gwen's been married about ten times and Lance's wife does something on TV. If I ever watched anything but PBS and sports, I'd know what it was. Lance I remember. He played wide receiver for the old Hollywood Stars and retired early with a bum knee or something. Out-of-Bounds Brodie, he was called, because he always ran for the sidelines."

"No wonder the Stars went kaput," commented Judith, smoothing out the lumps in the gravy with a wooden spoon. "Mrs. Out-of-Bounds, otherwise known as Mavis Lean-Brodie, is the anchor for KINE but is on vacation this week."

"That accounts for the brittle but sincere façade," said Renie, examining a cucumber. "I knew I'd seen her, but I thought she was the demo lady at Falstaff's Market."

Judith ignored her cousin's ignorance of the local media. "The little weasel is Otto's nephew, and he may look like an idiot but he's actually Harvey Carver, a big-shot surgeon at Norway General. His wife is the original Mrs. Do-Good, can't think of her first name, Nellie or Tilly or something like that. Check your PBS donation list."

"I did. They misspelled our name. How the hell can

you screw up Jones? Bill says it was a subconscious effort to fulfill his need for anonymous charity.''

"Bill is full of crap," said Judith, though not without affection. "I'd like to see him psychoanalyze this crew. I don't know why, but they make me nervous. I should have wallpapered instead.''

Renie leaned against the door, taking another peek at the assembled guests who had, to Judith's immense relief, brought their own liquor supply. Indeed, Otto appeared to be well on his way to what Oriana had delicately referred to as "unruly." Lance looked vaguely cross-eyed, or perhaps merely vague. Mavis was regarding her husband with benevolent disapproval, while Gwen twittered at her cousin Harvey in a voice that could only be described as jarring.

"Who's the dark-haired guy in the cheap suit?" Renie whispered, letting the door close discreetly.

"That's a very expensive suit, made cheap only by the wearer, whose arrival, I must say, certainly disconcerted both Mrs. Brodies and Mrs. Carver," replied Judith, leaving the gravy long enough to test the potatoes. "I take it they had not met him before and were expecting someone—or something—else. The ascot's a bit much, as is his name, Felix 'Dash' Subarosa, and he's Guinevere's current whatever. They're, er, engaged.''

"Really." Renie exchanged raised eyebrows with Judith. "Cute. Are they ready for the salad, or shall we turn them out in the back yard so they can graze?"

"Mother's already out there setting the cat on fire." She poured some of the potato water into the gravy and stirred like mad. "Actually, Mother is over at the Rankers's for the evening. They're watching old Nazi movies. You know how worked up Mother gets over Goebbels.''

"My mother still thinks his first name was George. Do the Rankers still fight like heavyweight champs?"

Judith scraped the sides of the of the gravy pan. "Not since the kids moved out. They haven't had a TKO since both of them threw Carl Jr. out the upstairs window." She sampled the gravy and nodded. "Not bad, just a bit thin.''

"I think the Rankers are fun," said Renie, giving the lettuce one last toss, "not to mention good-hearted. Okay, let's do the honors with the salad. Whatever happened to the rest of your Wedgwood? You're down to eight in just about everything except the dessert plates."

"Dan used to throw them at me," Judith replied without rancor. "Except for the soup tureen, which he threw at the TV set, missed, and sent through our picture window in the house on Thurlow Street."

"I always told you it was a rotten neighborhood," said Renie, as Judith began bearing salad plates out of the kitchen. "I'm so glad you're back on Heraldsgate Hill. You've got to admit it's a lot more peaceful up here."

"So far," Judith noted dryly, and wondered why the words stuck in her throat. Shrugging off the uncharacteristic sense of doom, she stepped into the dining room and immediately felt the old house wrap its arms around her.

Oak, darkened by age and numerous applications of varnish, lent the first floor of the house a sense of dignity. A small bay window curved out at one end of the room, though its view was limited to the Rankers's living room, where the drapes were now tightly drawn. An authentic Venetian chandelier hung from the ceiling over the oval table, and a breakfront crammed with four generations of bric-a-brac took up most of the wall opposite the kitchen door. The room opened up into the large living room at one end, and another, smaller door led into the entry hall, which housed a former coat closet converted by Judith into a half bath. A red azalea sat in the middle of the table, and two cyclamen plants, one white, one pink, reposed at either end of an oak and marble washstand that Judith used for bar service. The table linen was from Ireland, the crystal from Italy, the sterling an English heirloom from Grandmother Grover. As always, Judith felt a sudden rush of pride at her creation. All those risks she'd taken might still pay off. The old house had required a lot of work and it needed even more, yet she had managed by dint of a bank loan and her own labor to turn Hillside Manor into a cozy retreat. Indeed, it was more than that, though Judith herself could not have identified the intangible quality of hospitality that was due not so much to creature comforts as to her own innate knack with people.

"Feast time," she announced breezily, setting the salads down at each place. "It's a real treat for me to host a sit-down dinner for a change, especially for hometown folks." The lie was glib, the smile convincing. "Rolls coming up. Here," she urged, tapping the back of the Jacobean chair at the head of the table, "Mr. Brodie, this is your place, with your daughter-in-law on your right and Mrs. Carver on your left. Mrs. Brodie, you have the honor of sitting at the other end of the table, then Dr. Carver and your stepson, and we'll put Mrs., uh, er"—she faltered, not immediately recalling Guinevere's present married name—"Tweeks in the middle on this side, and Mr. Subarosa directly across, between Mrs. Lean-Brodie and the doctor. All right?"

It seemed all right to Mavis, Dr. and Mrs. Carver, Guinevere, Oriana, and even Dash, who, Judith noted, was not wearing socks despite the chilly January weather. Lance, however, looked uncertain until he got his cue from Mavis. As for Otto, he was staunchly clinging to a bottle of scotch and grinning lewdly at his hostess. Judith thought his hazel eyes weren't as unfocused as they should be, considering his apparent state of semi-stupor.

"Hey, I'll take my seat, but I'd rather have yours!" he chuckled, making a pass at Judith's backside with his free hand. "How about sitting on my lap? Isn't true you're the hostess with the mostes'?"

"Absolutely," replied Judith, deftly stepping out of Otto's reach, but bestowing a dazzling smile on the lecherous carpet-sweeper king. Experience had taught her that fast feet were as important in her business as a quick mind. "The mostest being dinner, most of which is still in the kitchen." She glanced at Oriana, whose full lips were pursed with practiced disdain. It was Guinevere, however, who hurtled to the rescue.

"Come on, Daddy," she said in a soothing voice, wrenching the bottle away and steering him into his chair. Guinevere was a big woman, taller than Judith and built along more Amazonian lines. In her early forties, she still exuded girlishness despite her size, and would have been pretty except for the garish makeup and overdone wool jersey jumpsuit trimmed with mink. "You mustn't keep us in suspense! We're all so excited to hear what the fortune-teller is going to say about our futures!"

"About your inheritances, you mean," growled Otto, finally sitting down with a large plop. Completely bald, he looked considerably younger than his seventy years, and though he was only average height, he gave the impression of being a big man in more ways than just girth. "I suppose you'd all be tickled pink if I fell in the salad with a heart attack right now."

"Daddy!" exclaimed Gwen, her china-blue eyes wide. "Don't say such things!"

"Harvey could always revive you," Oriana said with a touch of asperity, carefully arranging the gleaming rope of pearls which fell from her jutting bosom like a waterfall going over a cliff.

"Hunh!" snorted Otto, digging into his salad as Judith poured a California cabernet from a cut-glass decanter Gertrude had bought at a garage sale. "He's a surgeon, not a heart specialist."

"They're both doctors, aren't they?" Lance's mystification was genuine. Shifting in his chair, he tried to get his long legs into a more comfortable position. He was a handsome man in his forties, with wavy brown hair and hazel eyes very like Otto's, except not nearly so keen. His athlete's build had not yet started to crumble, despite the fact that Judith was sure he'd been out of football for some years. Given the height of both Brodie children, it occurred to Judith that the first Mrs. Otto must have been a tall woman. Harvey, the nephew, was of average height, slender of build and sallow of complexion. He had, however, surgeon's hands—long, deft, mobile. He was using them at the moment to tear up his romaine. Judith turned back into the kitchen. "The rolls," she said, vaguely panicked. "Where did I put them?"

Renie opened the oven and pulled out a bun warmer. "Here, we'll use this basket. Hand me a napkin. What's with Happy Families out there? Do I detect dissension?"

"You detect greed. I gather they're all here for Otto's pronouncement about his estate." Judith counted the rolls, then covered them with a monogrammed linen napkin. "Maybe the fortune-teller is really an attorney."

Back in the dining room, Judith observed that the conversation had taken a different turn, not necessarily for the better. Mavis, her fine features crimped into an expression of disgust usually reserved for reporting the most heinous of crimes, was lecturing Gwen. "I have never understood how you can refer to what you write as a novel. There is only one plot, only two kinds of characters, and the only verbs you ever use are 'throb,' 'moan,' and 'explode.' The covers all look alike, and the titles are exactly the same. In fact," she went on, oblivious to her sister-in-law's crimson cheeks and shaking hands, "there are only twenty-eight usable words for romances, and all those dreadful two-word titles are merely a variation on 'Love,' 'Lust,' 'Desire,' 'Passion,' and the remaining twenty-four."

"That's not true!" shrieked Gwen in her jarring voice. "I used three words in mine, and one of them was 'beast'!" She appealed to Lance for confirmation. "My first book, remember? *Beast's Beautiful Bounty.*"

Lance, as ever, looked blank, but Mavis was not put off. "That's because the drooling vegetables who read that sort of thing thought 'beast' was really 'breast.'" She tossed her short, smart blond coiffure in triumph.

Judith, nimbly avoiding Otto, handed the roll basket to Oriana. Dr. Carver's wife, whose first name Judith had finally remembered was Eleanor, looked up shyly from under pale lashes. Her gray eyes seemed to stray to Dash Subarosa, then wandered across the centerpiece to Gwen.

"I've read two of your books," she said in her breathless little voice. "I thought they were very nice."

"Oh, Ellie," exclaimed Gwen with a grateful sigh, "they *are* nice. Some people," she added with a malevolent glance at Mavis, "who haven't read them say they're just full of smut. But that's not true . . ."

"Smut?" Otto's ears twitched. "You kidding, Gwen? You've been writing smut all this time and haven't told your poor daddy? What have I been missing?"

"I gave you autographed copies of them," Gwen said in a vaguely offended tone. "I thought if you didn't read them, Oriana might."

Oriana's usually mobile face was wooden, her fork poised near her mouth. "I don't read much. I haven't the time, except for scores and libretti, of course."

"And all those damned beauty treatments at sixty dollars a crack. You get worked over more than my Rolls Royce, and the car's in better shape than you are, even if it is a 1950 model." He gave Oriana glare for glare, then turned back to his daughter. "Well, by God," he asserted, pounding on the table and making the china rattle so hard that Judith winced, "I'm going to read one when I get home! I like that part about 'thrust' and 'explode.' Hey, sweetie pie," he coaxed, reaching around a cringing Ellie to grip Gwen by the scruff of her neck, "which one's the hottest?"

"Now Daddy . . ." Gwen began in reproach, but stopped as Otto let go of her and put a finger to his nose.

"Damn!" he bellowed after a thunderous sneeze. "You got a cat around here?" His porcine face glowered at Judith.

"No cat in this house," Judith said truthfully. Sweetums had been expelled for the night, presumably to prowl the neighborhood for errant mice.

"Hunh," muttered Otto, searching his pockets. "Something set me off. Where's my inhaler?"

"Upstairs," replied Oriana, starting to rise from her chair. "I'll get it for you, I know where I put it."

But Gwen had somehow miraculously extricated her considerable bulk from between her brother and Ellie. "I'll take care of Daddy," she insisted. "Besides," she added with a seemingly innocent glance at Oriana, "my legs are younger."

"Sturdier, at any rate," murmured Oriana, her trained voice carrying at least as far as the entry hall. Although voluptuous, the present Mrs. Brodie was not a big woman, barely average in height, with a neatly tucked-in waist under her form-fitting black wool crepe. Coils of auburn hair were swept back from a clear brow, and a huge pearl dangled from each perfect ear. Her features were too irregular for classic beauty, but she possessed an undeniable amount of sex appeal even into middle age. Otto hadn't been quite fair to his wife. Given her alleged beauty treatments and perhaps the skill of a plastic surgeon, Judith had to extend the latitude of Oriana's age between thirty-nine and fifty-five, compromising on an arbitrary forty-eight.

Returning to the kitchen, Judith was about to comment on Oriana's state of preservation when the phone rang. The caller asked not for a reservation as she had hoped, but for Dash Subarosa. Opening the swinging door, Judith signaled to Gwen's alleged fiancé.

"Telephone, Mr. Subarosa. You can take it in the living room."

Dash evinced mild surprise, and excused himself while Ellie Carver giggled nervously and Mavis watched his departure with keen gray eyes. Dash moved with a feline grace that would have done credit to Sweetums, but somehow Judith half expected to see him leave an oil slick in his wake. Yet despite his faintly sleazy manner and the absence of socks, Judith had to admit that he was not unattractive. His curly black hair, the soulful black eyes, and that vaguely dissipated hollow under his cheekbones would no doubt intrigue a romantic soul such as Guinevere Brodie Tweeks. Hearing the extension picked up, Judith put the kitchen handset down. She headed back to collect the now-empty salad plates, but halted precariously in mid-step as Dash called out from the living room:

"Where's the phone? I don't see it."

"Maybe he stole it," Mavis said under her breath as she gave the butter a vicious stab.

Lance turned quizzical eyes on his wife. "If he stole it, he'd know where it was, wouldn't he, Mavis?"

Judith pretended she hadn't heard the exchange. Instead, she gestured at Dash: "The extension's on that little round table by the bookshelves." Still hesitating, she saw Dash pick up the phone and speak into it in a low voice. A glance at the table told her that not only was Gwen still gone, but Oriana's place was empty, too.

"Add snoopy to greedy," noted Judith, salad plates piled high in her arms as she reentered the kitchen. "Either Oriana or Gwen is listening in to Dash on the phone in the upstairs hall."

"Are you sure your mother didn't sneak in through the cat's hole?" Renie asked, slicing the roast and letting the juices run into the gravy pan. But of course she knew better; Aunt Gertrude's walker would have made a lively clatter coming into the house. Her room, along with the rest of the family's private quarters, was on the third floor, an old ballroom partitioned into three bedrooms, a bath, and what had originally been intended as Judith's office but had actually evolved into Gertrude's parlor-cum-TV sanctuary. The staircase to the upper floor led from behind a door that was marked Private and always kept locked when guests were staying at the B&B.

"Oh, hell," said Judith with a shrug as she drained the broccoli. "It's none of my business. I just hope they don't kill each other while they're here. I get the feeling they aren't exactly a close-knit crew. It's a pity their house was out of commission just at a time when—"

She stopped abruptly, startled by the black-clad figure emerging from the pantry area. Oriana, perched on suede Bruno Magli sling pumps, made a self-deprecating gesture, the sort which the Countess Almaviva might have

offered to her wayward husband in *The Marriage of Fi-
garo*.

"Forgive me for using your back stairs, Mrs. Mc-
Monigle, but I wished to speak to you privately and I
hadn't yet had the chance." She gave Judith a brilliant
smile, spared some of it for Renie, and turned confidential. "I felt it would be more thrilling if Madame Gushenka came in through the back door. She's due here at
nine." A glance at the clock informed all three women
that it was now five minutes to eight. "You have a dimmer
switch on your chandelier, I see. Could you turn it way
down after you usher her in?"

"Of course." Judith's attitude was equally confidential.
"Easier to see the crystal ball in the dark?"

Oriana was unruffled. "She uses cards, actually. You
have heard of her? She's quite the rage on the Hill these
days."

Judith had not kept up with current fads and fashions
among Heraldsgate's social set. A searching look at Renie
elicited no help. Her cousin merely lifted one shoulder and
stuck a serving spoon in the baby carrots.

Oriana was only too pleased to enlighten them both.
"Madame Gushenka moved to the Hill just before the hol-
idays. She's been sought out by all sorts of people, with
amazing results." She put a beringed hand on Judith's
arm. "Do you know that she told Rick Nordquist that his
profits would skyrocket before the year was out?"

"No kidding?" Judith struggled to keep a straight face.
Somehow, telling the owner of the region's largest department store that his sales would be up at Christmas was a
little like telling an Eskimo to wear warm mittens.

"Oh, yes!" Oriana was nodding solemnly. "She told
Coach Hackett at the university to beware of teams from
the sun, and that Jenny Doakes-Brenner should take a vacation from her talk show in the next six months or get
quite ill, and that the mayor should be on guard against
vested interests! What do you think of that?"

"I'm astounded," Judith answered, still with a straight

face, though it wasn't easy, with Renie practically rolling with soundless laughter against the wall, behind Oriana. "Gee, I wonder what she'll have to say tonight?"

Oriana's face suddenly hardened. "She'll say some things some people won't want to hear, I can tell you that. I'm not paying her two thousand dollars just to predict a rosy future." Apparently aware that her hostess was about to serve dinner, Oriana again shifted gears, from the haughty Turandot to the compliant Violetta. "Oh, the roast looks superb! Let me get out of your way . . . I've been interfering with progress!" She essayed an about-face on her high heels, heading back toward the pantry. "I'll return the way I left," she called over her shoulder. "By the way," she added, pointing at Sweetums's various culinary accoutrements, "I see you have a cat. I should have mentioned that Otto is allergic to them." Oriana made her exit with clicking heels and swaying hips.

Judith exchanged baffled looks with Renie. "I did ask."

"That's all you could do," replied Renie, presenting the platter of roast to Judith. The meat was layered a bit haphazardly, but done to perfection: just enough rare, medium, and well-done to satisfy the choosiest of eaters. In triumph, Judith entered the dining room at almost exactly the same instant Oriana came in from the entry hall. Dash and Gwen were both back at the table. Mavis was practically leaning back out of her chair, trying to draw Harvey into conversation about a recent news story she'd done on unnecessary surgical procedures. Meanwhile, Ellie was breathlessly recounting her latest successful fund raiser to a reasonably interested Otto. The mood was definitely more mellow, though Judith would not have called the gathering jolly.

"This," declared Renie after they had delivered all the food to the table, "is a group to tax even your vaunted prowess as a hostess. By the way, where are the cream puffs?"

Judith moved slowly but surely to the far end of the

cluttered counter and flipped over a tea towel like a magician uncovering a rabbit. *"Voilà!* Aren't they lovely?"

Renie's brown eyes widened. "They sure are! But only nine? What about us?"

"We don't count. Besides, I could only induce Mother to make that many."

"Your mother made them?" Renie's surprise was as genuine as it was short-lived. "I suppose she did. I keep forgetting that behind that steel wall of a walker lurks one of the great cooks of the Western world. But I still wish she'd made two more."

Judith checked the cream puffs for cat hair and cigarette ash, then re-covered them. "Are you that hungry?"

"I'm starved," said Renie, loading the dishwasher. "Right about now I could eat Otto."

"There ought to be some leftovers," Judith said none too certainly. As she plugged in the coffee maker, the phone rang again. This time it was for Lance Brodie. "What is this?" Judith demanded after she'd sent a mystified Lance off to the phone in the living room. "Nobody ever calls guests here."

"Why don't we get a pizza?" Renie offered, obviously less concerned with the popularity of Judith's guests than her own raging hunger pangs. "Jeez, they ate all the potato rolls!"

"Have some cheese. Get some Grape-nuts. Peel a carrot. Just shut up while I get the dessert plates out and put on the hot water. Oh, and get down the cups and saucers. You'll have to use one of the English bone china collection for Madame Garbanzo or whatever her name is. They're in the breakfront."

Renie looked mock-horrified. "You mean I have to go back out there with those animals? Otto tried to grab my leg when I put out the gravy boat."

"I have a feeling Otto is trying to pull everybody's leg. Or maybe it's Oriana." Judith gave her cousin a wry glance as she turned the heat on under the tea kettle.

"Actually," Renie recalled, "he was whispering sweet

somethings into my ear, about talking to the Madame before she goes into her act. I guess he wants to coach her a bit. I told him he could sneak in here by going up the main stairs and then down the back way by the pantry.''

Judith considered. ''It's his nickel. He and Oriana can form a tap dancing trio with the fortune-teller for all I care.'' Putting some of the dirty pots and pans in the sink to soak, she gave a little shake of her head. ''I've had an Irish wake, a bar mitzvah, a Cinco de Mayo fiesta, a divorce celebration for two couples who were switching partners, and a bunch of crazy Welshmen who came wearing necklaces made out of leeks. So why does this group make me edgy? They're probably not any screwier than our own relatives.''

''Hey, now you've got me worried!'' But Renie laughed when she said it.

Judith took heart from her cousin's good-humored response. ''You're right, I'm being sappy. I'd better get the extra cup and saucer. It's already after eight-thirty.''

Halfway through their meal, the Brodies had turned faintly maudlin. Lance, of all people, was relating an anecdote about his cousin which somehow showed that Harvey had always been inclined to medical practice.

''But I was worried because Harvey had taken all the arms and legs off our stuffed animals. So then Gwen said she bet she knew where Spot was because she'd seen Harvey playing with him and what do you know, sure enough, we found Spot all right, he was on the patio . . . and under the hedge . . . and in the driveway.'' Lance laughed, but the sound carried a note of pain. Several others professed varying degrees of mirth except Gwen, who clucked with sympathy, and Harvey, who looked embarrassed.

''I was only seven,'' he protested. ''I thought dissection was part of medical science. Besides,'' he added with a dark glance at his cousin, ''you always seemed too busy playing ball to care about your dog. Or anything else.'' Harvey's fine hands pleated his napkin into knifelike folds.

Gwen leaned across the table, her chin almost crushing

the azalea. "Harvey wasn't good at sports, you see," she explained to Dash, who was looking bemused. "He was always more of a student. He got wonderful grades."

Otto's small mouth turned down. "Lance's report cards looked like a tic-tac-toe game. Remember, son, how I tried to bribe you into studying by tearing down the old playhouse and putting in a basketball court?"

"That was *my* playhouse," said Harvey. "I used it for my laboratory."

"Harvey was always very scientific," said Gwen, again for Dash's benefit. "Not in the least like Lance and me. He was a real loner. And much quieter."

"That came from being orphaned very young," Ellie put in, showing a lot more spunk than Judith would have credited her with. "His father died in World War II and his mother just . . . pined away." The last phrase came out on a wispy little sigh.

"It was tragic, yet romantic," agreed Gwen. "Poor Aunt Irma just couldn't live without Uncle Jake. At least she had the comfort of knowing he died defending his country."

"What're you talking about, sweetie pie?" growled Otto, pouring more wine with a lavish hand. "Jake died of food poisoning at Camp Riley in Kansas and Irma had the clap. She couldn't live without him, all right, so she found about forty other guys who were all 4-F. And," he noted with a leer that traveled around the table, "for those of you who are too young to remember, I won't tell you what the 'F' stood for, at least as far as my sister was concerned."

"Otto!" remonstrated Oriana as Mavis's face tightened and Ellie put a hand over her mouth. "We're eating! Nor is this the time to air family scandals!"

"Oh?" Otto shot his wife a dry look that suggested he wasn't quite as drunk as he should have been, all things considered. "Funny, somehow I thought this was the time—and the place—for it. Ever occur to you that our house isn't the only thing that needs fumigating?"

Judith, who had been trying to squeeze in behind Ellie, Gwen, and Harvey to get at the breakfront while avoiding Otto's roaming hands, almost dropped the Royal Worcester cup with its pattern of pink tea roses. It rattled dangerously against the saucer, causing her guests to turn and stare.

"Excuse me," she apologized. "Dessert is coming. We'll clear those dinner things away right now."

Otto went for the last piece of meat and knocked over his inhaler in the process. "Get that contraption out of here!" he snarled at no one in particular. "I didn't need it in the first place! What's one little sneeze?" He swerved in his chair as Judith passed, catching her by the arm. "Clear the table, you bet, but if you want to earn your money, you could clear the air, too."

"So I could," Judith smiled, backpedaling into the kitchen. "Maybe there's some dust."

"Hell, no," grinned Otto wickedly. "The dust hasn't settled. Not by a long shot."

THREE

AN EXTRA CHAIR had been brought in from the living room to accommodate Madame Gushenka. Judith had set a place for her between Otto and Mavis, which pleased the daughter-in-law far more than the father-in-law.

"Awww—now we can't play kneesies any more," Otto lamented in mock despair. Mavis gave him a picture-perfect profile of displeasure.

Out in the kitchen, Judith ticked off her latest duties on her fingers: "I dimmed the chandelier halfway for now, more later, coffee and tea are ready, sugar and cream, forks and spoons are already on, let's take out the cream puffs."

Renie nodded in semi-military fashion. "Ever organized. You amaze me, coz. You were such a slob as a kid. Life with Dan sure shaped you up." Obviously resisting the urge to dip her finger in the cream puff filling, Renie hesitated, then marched into the dining room.

Her cousin was right: Being sole provider, nursemaid, housewife and mother had brought out Judith's un-tapped talents. She'd had no choice, or so it had seemed. She'd also not had the luxury of time to think, but only to do. Judith was reaching for another set of plates when a rapping at the back door caught her attention. For a brief moment, she thought she'd gone back in time to Hallow-een, then realized that the long black hair, the flurry of colored veils, and the shimmer of golden earrings she saw through the square window in the door belonged to Ma-dame Gushenka. The rain was still coming down, almost obscuring the stark branches of the three apple trees which were all that remained of the original Grover orchard. The wind was up, rattling the windows and shaking the bird feeder which had been placed well out of Sweetums's reach. The figure at the little window knocked again, this time more preemptorily. As Judith hurried to open the door, she half expected a black cat to slither in behind the fortune-teller.

"Meezus MigMonickal?" came a throaty voice through crimson lips. Not waiting for a reply, the seeress sailed past the pantry and came to a halt in the middle of the kitchen just as Renie returned.

"Oh!" cried Renie, her jaw dropping. "Oh, you're the fortune-teller! I hope," she added.

"Of course, of course," Madame Gushenka responded in a thick accent. "I am here for to tell the future. And eat delicious cream puffs." Her dark eyes lingered covet-ously on the plate Judith had been about to deliver to the dining room. "I tell you now, without the cards, those will taste marvelous!"

"About now I could eat the cards," muttered Renie, but stoically resumed her duties as Judith took Madame Gushenka's purple cape.

"And this," said the fortune-teller, thrusting a large brown handbag at Judith. "You keep. For now. Most im-portant. Where is safe place?"

The house's best security was a safe Judith had installed in her bedroom, but she didn't want to take the time or make the effort to go all the way up to the third floor. Nor could she imagine that Madame Gushenka was carrying anything of real value, except to herself.

"The freezer?" Judith suggested. She used it herself as a hiding place, especially when she forgot the safe's combination, which happened rather often. Her logical mind did not extend to numbers. "It's in the basement."

But Madame Gushenka was dubious. "Your pantry—it has flour bin?" She saw Judith nod. "Wrap in plastic grocery sack, put there, please."

It was Renie who acted on the instructions, returning with patches of flour all over her Notre Dame sweatshirt just as Judith came back in from the dining room. Madame Gushenka was smoothing her multicolored veils over the masses of black hair. A wig, Judith decided, and wondered how much of the fortune-teller was authentic. If Oriana's makeup was artful and Gwen's was overdone, Madame Gushenka's was outlandish. The crimson lipstick had been applied to reshape her mouth, the eyebrows had been darkened and plucked to give a slanted effect to her hazel eyes, and the green eyeshadow was extended almost to her temples to widen her long face. Up close, she appeared younger than Judith had guessed at first, perhaps no more than her early forties. One thing was certain, however: In her green and gold satin robes and flowing motley veils, Madame Gushenka wasn't just another pretty face.

"They're ready," Judith announced. "Renie, we've got five coffees and three teas. What will you have, Madame Gushenka?"

"Is coffee Turkish?" inquired the fortune-teller with a jangle of bracelets.

Judith shook her head. "It's Colombian."

"I have tea, then. No, I don't read leaves, just use a bag."

A noise from the pantry area startled all three women. Turning, they saw Otto, poised pigeon-toed on the threshold of the kitchen, a finger at his lips.

"Madame . . ." he began in a pale imitation of his usual bluster.

"Gushenka," rumbled the fortune-teller, who was taller than Otto by a good two inches. "What you want? I prepare for Big Moment."

Advancing into the kitchen, Otto held his hands out, signaling for quiet. "I don't want them to know I'm here," he whispered, "because I've got something I'd like you to say to sort of, well, you know, put the fear of God into . . ." Within three feet of Madame Gushenka, he stopped abruptly. His little eyes widened, then narrowed as he rocked on the balls of his feet. "Skip it," he said gruffly, and wheeled out of the kitchen, his exit much faster then his entrance.

The fortune-teller rolled her eyes. "Funny man! Does Madame Gushenka frighten him? If he had hair, it would fall out!" She threw back her head and laughed, a frankly triumphant sound.

Wincing, Judith fought down the tide of uneasiness that had begun to rise again. "Maybe after he saw you, he figured you knew what you were doing," she offered.

Madame Gushenka shot her a dubious glance. "Maybe he saw I could see through him, eh? Often what happens to those who scoff." With a toss of her head, she pulled out a single veil from behind one ear, draped it across her nose, and secured the other side with a jeweled clasp. "There! Element of mystery, at least until I'm eating cream puff." She spoke through the green veil, which fluttered at every syllable, while her expressive eyes narrowed in apparent concentration.

"One more cup of tea coming up," chirped Renie, delving into one of four canisters shaped like toadstools. Having already squeezed the first three cups out of a single bag in one of her rare attempts at economy, she was faintly resentful. "Go ahead," she said to her cousin, "I'll bring it all out after Madame Gushenka sits down."

Feeling vaguely like a White House press aide about to announce the President of the United States, Judith swung open the dining room door. "Ladies and gentleman, Madame Gushenka!"

Already into the cream puffs, the Brodie clan looked up expectantly. In the dim light, Judith could see Oriana's triumphant smile, Ellie's nervous fidgeting, Harvey's frown, Mavis's skepticism, Lance's blank face, Gwen's high color, and Dash's curious gaze. Otto had not yet returned to his seat. The lace curtains fluttered in the draft at the bay window. Somebody, probably Ellie, clattered a fork against a plate. Lance's chair creaked under his weight, and Dash did his best to suppress a cough. It was Oriana who broke the uneasy silence, her hands clasped at her bosom.

"Dear Madame Gushenka, we are so thrilled to have you join us! Let me introduce everyone!"

"Pah!" sneered the fortune-teller, with a swish of veils. "I know them all! Secrets cannot be concealed from those who have the Power!" With vigor, she attacked her cream puff, forestalling further conversation.

Judith almost smacked Renie with the swinging door. "Sorry. I didn't know you were spying. Where did Otto go?"

"Otto?" Renie cocked her head to one side and made a haphazard effort to brush the flour from her sweatshirt. "The can, probably. Shoot, I got flour all over your floor. It's even on my shoes."

"Never mind, I'll sprinkle some catnip on it and Sweetums can lick it off later. He's much cheaper than a mop. In fact, he sort of looks like a mop." She paused in the act of returning the cream carton to the refrigerator. "How much of a phony do you think Madame Gushenka really is?"

Renie shrugged. "They're all phonies. Fortune-tellers, I mean. Though in this case, maybe the Brodies are, too. Still," she went on quite seriously, "Bill has a theory that some people are so sensitive to others and so perceptive that they can actually see—"

She stopped as Ellie came diffidently through the door.

"This is so strange," she said in a whisper. "Really, it's given me a headache. Do you have any aspirin?"

Judith had, in a bottle on the windowsill along with her vitamins and assorted over-the-counter remedies. Ellie gratefully swallowed two tablets, then insisted on helping Renie take out the coffee. Judith hurriedly filled up the dishwasher, dumped in some detergent, and turned on the switch. Renie came back for the tea, with Mavis at her heels.

"Excuse me, I have to take out my contacts. They're new and they're just killing me." Mavis slipped a case out of the pocket of her Chanel suit and leaned over the sink.

"There's a bathroom in the entry hall—" Judith began, but Mavis interrupted as if breaking in with a news bulletin.

"Harvey's in there," she said, standing storklike on one foot. "Throwing up, no doubt. This entire evening is such bilge. I think I'll do a feature on charlatans when I get back to work." She straightened up, turned around, and blinked several times. "Ah! Thank God! I can't see, but at least I'm not in pain. Here," she said in her crisp voice, "let me help with the tea."

Renie started to demur, but juggling four cups was admittedly beyond her. At the cupboard, Judith was getting out liqueur glasses for after-dinner drinks.

"Smoke 'em if you got 'em," she announced to the dining room, having at the start given up trying to ban tobacco at the B&B. If she couldn't get her own mother to quit, she certainly wasn't going to try to reform her guests.

Otto, who was now back in place, responded by lighting a long, dark cigar, while Dash extracted a gold cigarette case from his suit jacket and Mavis produced a package of unfiltered Camels. Ashtrays appeared and dessert plates disappeared. Otto brandished his own bottles of Courvoisier, Drambuie and Strega, pouring with his customary generous hand, while the guests waxed eloquent on the subject of cream puffs.

"They are wonderful, aren't they?" beamed Judith. "Gertrude of Grover Gourmet does them for us."

Oriana pounced, requesting Gertrude's phone number. Judith put her off by promising to look it up in the morning. Noting that everyone had turned expectant and somewhat wary eyes toward Madame Gushenka, Judith dimmed the light switch as far down as it would go without shutting off. The guests seemed to tense. Madame Gushenka bent her head briefly, then, with a dramatic gesture, displayed a deck of cards and carefully cut it into three piles.

"Past," she intoned, pointing to the thick stack on her left. "Present," she continued, indicating the middle batch. "And," she breathed, dropping her husky voice and tapping the top card on her right, "the future!"

Dash was leaning on his elbows studying not the cards, but the card reader. Gwen giggled and poked Harvey in the ribs. "How exciting! It's just like the gypsy in my third book, *Passion's Trumpet!*"

"The readers thought it was 'strumpet,' " murmured Mavis, ignoring Gwen's umbrage and Oriana's glare.

"Pipe down," commanded Otto. "The Madame here is starting the show."

She was indeed. Judith withdrew discreetly, but was not surprised this time to find Renie up against the door. Judith joined her and switched off the kitchen light. "Atmosphere," she whispered. "I turned the living room lights off, too."

"Then turn off the dishwasher," said Renie. "I can't hear a damned thing."

Judith complied. Madame Gushenka's throaty voice vibrated through the old oak:

"There is hatred at this table . . . deceit . . . fraud . . . terrible troubles . . ." Feet shuffled under the table. Outside, the wind blew over the Rankers's garbage can with a startling crash. Several of the guests jumped, but Madame Gushenka was unmoved. She played the pause like a harp, letting her self-imposed silence hang on the air with the portent of a dirge. "Sunshine. The distant surf. Palm trees." The fortune-teller swayed in her chair as if moving with the tropical breeze. Her eyes were closed but her hand rested on the queen of clubs. "A woman, half crazed she is, abandoned . . . The pen is mightier than the cord—or is it? She who tells all, knows too much . . ."

At the door, Judith and Renie raised their eyebrows at each other, then shrugged. Except for the wind and the occasional rattle of cups and glasses, the dining room was very quiet. Madame Gushenka resumed speaking, her voice coming more rapidly and slightly higher-pitched.

"A baby, crying for its mother . . . Like Snoozing Beauty, a spell is cast. The years go by . . . The baby is grown woman, betrayed and deprived . . ." Chairs creaked as their owners shifted about uneasily. "Another girl-child, born to comfort, yet accursed, too, she is, until saved by a prince with sword so sharp . . . She reigns first in the valley, then ascends to the mountains. All pay homage—will she pay the piper?"

"Weird," breathed Renie.

"Wacko," whispered Judith. But both cousins couldn't help becoming enmeshed in Madame Gushenka's web of words.

"The cock crows at dawn." The fortune-teller's voice was growing deeper, more ominous. "A great man does not wake . . . until too late."

Someone snorted. Judith thought it was Otto. She was sure that a snicker of disbelief had come from Mavis. The stifled gasps could have emanated from either Gwen or Ellie—or both. From the kitchen, it was hard to tell.

"A dark and rainy night . . . a man alone . . . another man . . . desperation! All is darkness! Tragedy rules, villainy triumphs!" The throaty voice surged with feeling; the swinging door seemed to shudder. More gasps, a couple of curses, and the clatter of cutlery indicated that the audience was much affected. Renie's brown eyes had grown very wide, while Judith pulled on her lower lip and frowned.

"She's pretty good at what she does," remarked Judith in an undertone. "I wonder if Oriana thinks she's getting her two grand worth?"

Over the flutter of unsettled noises, Madame Gushenka was speaking again: "Far off, bleak, isolated. A handsome bird in a concrete cage." Her voice rumbled into the very depths of her chest, then suddenly brightened. "There is music, too. Such pretty notes! Or are they? Greed, deception creep onto the stage." The tone had changed again, now overtly sinister. "Wrongs not righted, the past swept under cover, while over the ocean, a crowd roars, then goes silent. Disaster strikes! The night goes black, the sky is empty, hush . . . hush . . . ssssh . . ."

The last utterances had slowed, then begun to fade away. Judith and Renie almost banged heads trying to press closer against the door. They were steadying themselves when they heard the crash, the screams, and the sounds of chairs being overturned, crystal shattering and china breaking. Even as Judith fumbled for the kitchen light switch, the dining room sounded as if it had erupted into a stampede. Renie threw open the door.

The illumination from the kitchen showed a scene of utter confusion, with everyone clustered around the head of the table. Lance was struggling with something or someone, Ellie was whimpering and clutching at Harvey, Gwen was verging on hysterics, Oriana was deathly pale despite her makeup, Otto was swearing like a sailor, Dash was trying either to help or to hinder Lance, and Mavis was shrieking for order.

"The lights!" called Judith, and was amazed when Oriana immediately obeyed, bringing the chandelier up to full beam. Gwen stared at the blaze of shimmering crystal as if hypnotized and Lance stepped back, revealing Madame Gushenka, sprawled face down on the table, one hand on the cards, the other clawing at the azalea's vivid blooms. Her black hair spilled onto the Irish linen, and the brilliant veils seemed to have wilted like weary petals.

"She's out like a . . . light," said Lance, peering up at the chandelier.

"It must be a trance," Oriana said, but her usually confident voice was uncertain.

"Get back," Harvey ordered, assuming his best operating-theater style. "Give the poor woman room to breathe." As the others, including the distraught Ellie, moved away, Harvey felt for a pulse, first at the wrist, then at the neck. His sallow face sagged as his search for a vital sign grew more frantic. "My God," he exclaimed. "She's dead!"

FOUR

"DEAD? THAT'S RIDICULOUS!" screeched Oriana. "I paid her two thousand dollars! I want my money back!"

Mavis checked her watch. "Nine fifty-five, I can still make the eleven o'clock news." She started for the phone in the living room.

"Hold it!" Judith shouted. "We've got to call 911 first!" She whirled on Harvey Carver, who was still looking grim. "Can you . . . Is there any possibility of . . . you know, what do you call it, not artificial respiration, but . . ."

"CPR?" Harvey sadly shook his head. "Not at this point. It's been—what, over five minutes since she collapsed? I'm only guessing it was a heart attack, though it could have been an aneurism. But you're right, call 911 at once."

"They're on the way," said Renie from the kitchen door. She gave Judith an apologetic look. "I told them to turn off the sirens and not to use the flashing lights. I mean, there's no hurry, and I didn't see any point in, uh, calling attention to, er, um . . ."

"To the fact that this guest house can be fatal to your health?" Judith retorted with bitterness, and was immediately embarrassed. Fortunately none of her guests was paying any attention. Harvey was now tending to Ellie, plying her with brandy. Dash had escorted Gwen into the living room. Otto was arguing with Mavis about her intention of informing KINE-TV.

"What's the big deal, dollface? A heart attack, a stroke—that's news? For all we know, she had a fatal disease. Hell, it isn't like any of us had ever met the woman before." He saw Oriana's eyelashes droop and jabbed a stubby finger in his wife's direction. "Except you, my little pizza! You met her, right?"

"No! We corresponded by letter and talked on the phone! In fact, it was an accident that I got in touch with her in the first place. She dialed our number by mistake." Dabbing at her mouth with a lace-edged handkerchief, Oriana slumped back into her chair, a remorseful Marguerite in the last act of *Faust*. "I feel terrible! Awful! Accursed!" She offered no resistance when Otto hauled her to her feet and led her along with the others into the living room.

Oriana in the throes of guilt held no appeal for Judith at the moment. Shaken as well as stirred, she took a deep breath and remembered Grandma Grover's family motto: *Keep Your Pecker Up*. Apparently Renie was dredging up those same late-Victorian words of wisdom, for she was holding the coffee carafe in one hand and Otto's bottle of Drambuie in the other.

"Why I don't I just mix them together?" she asked, more than half serious.

"Bring it out into the living room. I'll get their cups and whatever's left of . . . Jeez," whispered Judith, "this is terrible! I'm not used to having a dead body at the dining room table!"

"After twenty-odd years with Dan, you came close," Renie replied.

Judith's baleful glance was tinged with irony. That Daniel Patrick McMonigle had been an ill-tempered, lazy, self-ish, and generally impossible person was inarguable. Judith knew that the union remained a mystery to friends and family—with the exception of Renie. Yet Dan had been a good father, in his way, and he was no dummy. His death of heart failure at forty-nine hadn't shocked anyone. A seriously overweight man with a half dozen chronic illnesses didn't exactly shine on the actuarial tables.

In the living room, the Brodies were clustered on the twin beige sofas and matching armchairs arranged around the big hearth. The fire that Judith had set off just before her guests' arrival was sputtering fitfully. Judith was about to put on another log and offer sustenance when the doorbell rang.

The room was suddenly full of men in blue and black, moving with practiced precision. At the makeshift bar, Renie was pointing to Madame Gushenka's body and trying to answer a series of questions from one of the medics.

"The fact is," explained Renie when she came a-cropper over how the fortune-teller had looked before her collapse, "I was in the kitchen. With Mrs. McMonigle."

Judith had joined her cousin and the emergency crew in the dining room, leaving a curious and edgy group behind her. "I'm Judith McMonigle," she said, aware that her usual outgoing warmth was fraying around the fringes. "One of the guests is a doctor. Perhaps you should speak with him."

A crewcut medic whose nametag read Kinsella nodded, then let Judith lead him into the living room. "This is a sad occasion for all of you," he began, letting his pensive blue eyes roam from face to face. "I understand there's a doctor on the premises." Either by instinct or experience, Kinsella's gaze rested on Harvey Carver.

"I'm a surgeon," said Harvey, keeping at Ellie's side, but withdrawing the protective arm from around her shoulder as if to symbolize his sudden change in status from husband to professional. "Harvey Carver, chief of surgery at Norway General."

"Well." Kinsella's horsey face registered respect. "An honor, Dr. Carver. You're highly regarded in the medical community." He paused to let the compliment sink in, but Harvey merely inclined his head. "You pronounced the deceased dead, I gather," said Kinsella.

"Yes." Harvey frowned. "We thought she'd fainted," he explained in his dry voice. "Or, given her calling, gone into a trance." He spoke with a trace of embarrassment. "She was a fortune-teller, you see."

"So we guessed," Kinsella said with a straight face. "Exactly what happened, Doctor?"

Harvey tugged at his right ear, looked to Otto for support, found only disgruntlement, and plunged ahead. "She—Madame Gushenka, I think it was—had been reeling off a lot of strange, disconnected gibberish about the past. Then she grabbed at her chest and fell forward." He pulled at his chin, working over his reconstruction of the scene. "That was it."

From the armchair nearest the hearth, Mavis waved a hand in protest. "No, no, Harvey. It's a good thing you never went into journalism. Her voice began to fade, she sort of choked, and then she grabbed her throat and *then* her chest." Accurate reporting job finished, Mavis sat back smugly.

"I thought it was a fit," said Gwen, clinging to Dash's hand. "Epilepsy, maybe. I researched epilepsy for *Fits of Fancy*. I write books, you see," she added with a tremulous if coy smile for Kinsella.

"Her readers thought it was 'tits,' " murmured Mavis.

From the archway between the dining and living rooms, one of the other medics called to Kinsella. He excused himself to join his colleagues for a brief consultation. Judith was standing by the little table with the phone, a bowl of potpourri, and a framed photograph of Gertrude and Donald Grover on their honeymoon. She strained to overhear the whispered discussion, but failed to catch more than a few meaningless words.

"Okay," said Kinsella, striding out of the dining room. "What did Madame Gushenka eat and drink tonight?"

Apparently feeling the burden for the fortune-teller's demise, Oriana spoke up: "She ate a cream puff and drank some tea. That's all, unless she nibbled on something in the kitchen." The sharp gaze she threw at Judith was accusatory. "I must confess, I knew nothing of any allergies on her part, inasmuch as I was acquainted with the woman only by reputation."

Judith did her best to ignore Oriana's insinuation. "Madame Gushenka didn't eat anything before she got to the table. If she had any allergies, they weren't to cream puffs or tea, since she expressed great enthusiasm for the former and requested the latter herself. Why," she inquired pointedly of Kinsella, "do you ask?"

Kinsella didn't reply at once, but looked first to his fellow emergency personnel and then at his audience. "From a preliminary examination of the body, we're inclined to rule out heart or other natural causes. We can't be sure until we get the medical examiner's report. But for now, it looks as if death was caused by poison. Our next step is to call in the police. I'm sorry, but we'll have to treat this as a homicide."

FIVE

NO GREATER FUROR could have been caused by Medic Kinsella's announcement if he'd declared himself a PLO terrorist with intentions of shooting the lot of them on the spot. Gwen fell into Dash's arms, Ellie burst into tears over the awkward protestations of Harvey, Oriana began shrieking denials at the top of her ample lungs while Otto threatened her with the fireplace shovel. Mavis tried to battle her way to the phone but was restrained by both Lance and Kinsella.

"Keep the line free for us just now," ordered Kinsella. "Stay put, all of you, until the police get here."

Lance, limping slightly from the evening's exertion, was steering a bellicose Mavis back to the armchair. "Don't get Dad mad," he urged. "Remember, this is the night we're all supposed to be *nice.*"

Apparently, Oriana wasn't constrained by any cautionary advice. Rounding on Harvey, she shook a fist in his direction. "You're some doctor! I hope you diagnose your patients more accurately! I'd hate to see your malpractice insurance rates!"

Harvey froze, his sallow face turned to ash. "I'm a surgeon, not a medical examiner. I haven't seen a poisoning case since I was in med school at UCLA."

Judith, who barely noted the battling Brodies, had also become quite shaky and needed to lean against the little table for support. Her whole world, built with such hard work and cold cash, seemed to be crumbling. She could already see the quotes in the guidebooks:

"Hillside Manor—Avoid due to homicidal mania."

"Skip this particular establishment unless you're dying for a good time."

"Sleep like the dead here. You won't be the first."

"If you thought the crab dip was bad, wait until you taste the cream puffs!"

Renie sidled up to Judith, who knew her cousin could read her mind exactly: "Look at it as positive publicity," counseled Renie. "People are morbid. You'll be famous, and thus, rich."

"Bunk," muttered Judith, trying to rally. "I'll be finished, and thus, broke."

Renie's further attempts to soothe her cousin were thwarted by the arrival of four uniformed policemen. "Lieutenant Flynn is on his way," announced one of them, a stolid black man with a walrus moustache.

Judith blinked. "Flynn?"

The walrus moustache barely moved when the policeman spoke. "Joe Flynn. Homicide. Very sharp."

"Oh." Judith didn't dare look at Renie. "Joe Flynn," she echoed in a voice that sounded dangerously giddy. *"Joe Flynn!"*

Renie had purloined Otto's Courvoisier when the medics weren't watching. "Drink this," she whispered, sloshing brandy into an empty glass from the little bar. Judith obeyed and sat down on an armless rocker, a relic of Grandma Grover's era.

Across the room, Otto was bickering with Oriana. "That's not my tea, I had sugar in it. Mine's the one with the fruity-looking flowers. Where the hell did it go?"

"That was Madame Gushenka's," Renie put in, a hand steadying Judith's rocker. "It's still on the table, but I don't think we'd better go into the dining room just yet."

"Bull," contradicted Otto, "that was my tea. Oh, hell," he exclaimed, throwing up his hands, "I'd rather have a stiff scotch anyway."

Ever obliging, Gwen made a rush at the bar, but was stopped by the firemen at the archway. "Please, Daddy needs a little something," she begged, all fluttering eyelashes and rippling wool jersey.

But the stalwart men in uniform could not be coerced. Kinsella and the others were conferring over the body, checking forms, and using the phone in the kitchen. Dejected, Gwen backpedaled straight into Renie, who was holding the almost-empty brandy bottle aloft.

"Here," offered Renie, "let Daddy polish this off. It's his, anyway." She gave Gwen a genuine smile, reminding herself that no matter how bizarre the Brodies might be and how disastrous the evening had become, Judith was still the hostess and needed all the cousinly support Renie could muster. And when Joe Flynn showed up, Renie would have to be prepared for just about anything. Like nuclear war, but not as nice.

At the moment, however, Judith was trying to appear benign. She couldn't prevent her gaze from sliding in the direction of the entry hall, and the rocker moved in jerky spasms, but otherwise she hoped she was exhibiting a calm exterior. Inside was another matter: What, she wondered, would he look like after over twenty years? Would he even recognize her? Did he know her married name? Would he give a rat's ass? She swallowed more brandy and braced herself as the front door swung open.

For Judith, the years rolled back at a dizzying pace, to bouffant hairdos, stiletto heels, and the Good Wool Suit; to picnics on the Ship Canal Bridge, the sun coming up at the city zoo, and driving a sports car on the pedestrian overpass at the university; to sourdough bread flown in fresh from San Francisco, Moscow Mules made out of lab alcohol, and root beer floats at four a.m.

What Judith actually saw was a red-haired, middle-aged man with a receding hairline and just the hint of a paunch. His shoulders were still broad, the charcoal-gray suit was impeccable, and the green eyes still held those gleaming gold flecks. Magic eyes, she thought, and felt her stomach hop, skip, and jump. At the moment, those eyes were registering the entire tableau, the cluster of Brodies, the medics hovering over the body, the police and firemen on the alert. At last, Joe Flynn's gaze came to rest on Judith McMonigle.

"I'll be damned," he said without inflection, "it's Jude-girl."

"And Renie," said Judith, grabbing her cousin as if she were a lifeline. "Remember Renie, Aunt Deb's daughter?"

"Sure." Joe Flynn put out a hand, first to Judith, then to Renie. His smile was as easy as ever, the charm was still intact, if frayed around the edges. "Damn, it's been a while. Not exactly the time or place to catch up, though." He glanced around, exhibiting a professional demeanor. "Where can I get some privacy to interview everybody?"

Summoning up her natural resiliency, Judith moved toward the entry hall. "The front parlor has two doors: one here," she said, flipping on a torchère lamp, "and the other one goes back into the living room."

Joe nodded his approval. It was much smaller than the main parlor, but large enough for intimate parties. The stone fireplace was flanked by converted gaslights with an eighteenth-century hunting print over the mantel. The furniture was solid oak, from the pedestal table to the armoire which housed Judith's overflow of linens, books, and tapes. Closing the door to the living room, Judith pulled two chairs covered with her mother's petit point up to the table.

"Shall I light a fire? Get more chairs?" she asked, and

inwardly cursed herself for sounding like a twittering ninny. "Make some coffee?"

"Hang from the chandelier?" Joe Flynn's green eyes twinkled, and Judith flushed like a schoolgirl. She'd actually done that once, in a semi-drunken stupor at what had then been the city's most elegant—and staid—hotel. But Joe was already back to business, taking out a small spiral notebook and a red ballpoint pen.

"Price can help me," he said, and called for the policeman with the walrus moustache and taciturn expression. "I might as well as start with you and Renie. Price, get Mrs. . . . ." He stopped and turned to Judith. "What's her married name? I assume she's married, she was engaged the last time we—I saw her."

"Renie was always engaged," said Judith dryly. "At one point, she was engaged to three guys at once, all with the same first name."

Joe shrugged one broad shoulder. "Kept her from making tactless mistakes, anyway. Which one did she marry?"

"None of them," answered Judith, speaking more naturally now, almost as if she were picking up the threads of a conversation from almost a quarter of a century earlier. "Somebody told her she ought to see a psychiatrist because she must be nuts to keep telling men she'd marry them and then break it off. Renie said shrinks were a bunch of bunk, but finally, on a dare, she went to see some grad student at the university. After the first session, they got engaged. They've been married for over twenty years." She looked up just as Renie entered the room with Officer Price. The foursome arranged themselves at the table, looking like bridge players in search of a tally sheet.

Joe folded his hands over the slight rise of his stomach and nodded at Price. "You take the notes for now. First things first," he continued, looking back at Judith. "Full name."

"Mine?" Judith sounded startled, but Joe's half smile urged her on. "Judith Grover McMonigle. Widow." Joe's expression didn't change. "Owner of Hillside Manor B&B

since a year ago January after I bought it from Mother, Aunt Deb, and Uncle Al. Mother lives here and so does my son, Mike, when he isn't away at school. I have the proper licenses and I'm up to code. No, I have no idea who Madame Gushenka really is, and I still can't comprehend that she was murdered. I think the medics have made a mistake."

Joe, however, hadn't seemed to follow Judith's statement to its conclusion. "So Dan died." His voice held an undertone of awe. "What did he do, poison himself in one of his ill-fated restaurant ventures?"

Judith's mouth turned prim. "That's not funny under the present circumstances. He blew up."

"No kidding?" Joe was grinning, much to the consternation of Officer Price, who had viewed the entire exchange with veiled curiosity.

Judith's attempt to look disapproving lost ground. "He weighed four hundred and three pounds when he died. He hadn't worked in six years, and we were living in a rental out on Thurlow Street. I was working days at the local library and nights at the Meat & Mingle. Life was hard, times were tough, my feet were killing me. What else do you need to know?"

"Gee," remarked Joe, "and all this time I thought you were shacked up with that Dutch drug czar on the Costa Brava."

"He dumped me in Rome," said Judith, only half lying. "When do I get to ask the questions?"

Joe sobered. "Later." Scowling, he looked over at Price's notes. "If you don't know who this fortune-teller was, who would?"

Judith straightened a lacy doily in the middle of the table and shrugged. "Oriana Brodie, I suppose. She hired her."

"Brodie?" Joe's red eyebrows shot up. "As in carpet-sweeper Brodie?" He saw Judith and Renie nod in unison. "Damn! Then I did recognize the TV star and the ex-jock." He let out a big breath and clicked the ballpoint pen several times. "I suppose that'll mean a lot of pressure from all sides. Did I hear somebody say another one of them is some big-shot doctor?"

Judith gave Joe a commiserating look. "Harvey Carver, Norway General. His wife's the Duchess of Do-Good. The Brodie daughter writes romance novels under the name of Guinevere Arthur. And Mrs. Brodie used to be an opera singer."

Joe drummed his fingers on the oak and let out a low whistle. "Why couldn't I get stuck with one wino bashing another over the head with an empty bottle of rubbing alcohol?" He turned to Price. "If the medics are done, get the body out of here. I want the medical examiner's report as soon as possible. And," he added as Price headed out of the little parlor, "tell the guests they can go wherever they want—as long as they don't leave the house."

Renie was running a hand through her short brown curls. "I don't get it. The fortune-teller is supposed to be a minor celebrity on the Hill. But this crew didn't know her. Not even Oriana, right?" She appealed to her cousin for confirmation.

Judith nodded. "There was supposed to be some big announcement—by Otto, I guess—about how he was going to divvy up his estate. I don't think they ever got that far, though."

"Money, the eternal motive," said Joe in an undertone, getting to his feet. "But that doesn't seem to have anything to do with your fortune-teller. First, we find out who she was. Did she bring a purse?"

"Purse." Judith momentarily went blank. "Oh, it wasn't a purse, it was sort of a satchel thing. It's in the flour bin."

"And your guests' coats are in the cat box," Joe deadpanned. "It all makes perfect sense." He paused, rubbing the back of his neck. "Okay, let's go find this satchel. She ought to have some I.D. in it."

Judith led the way, but Renie lingered behind, ostensi-

bly studying the yellow and black tape which now cor-
doned off the dining room set. The body had been
removed, along with many of the items that had been on
the table. A glance into the living room revealed Otto and
Oriana, still in front of the fireplace, arguing. Harvey was
browsing among the crammed bookshelves while Ellie
leafed nervously through a gardening magazine. The rest
were nowhere to be seen.

In the kitchen, two firemen were poking about, though
whether they were checking for evidence or inspecting the
wiring, Judith couldn't tell. She nodded politely as she
showed Joe into the pantry. It was the classic well-stocked
larder, right down to the old-fashioned cooler where she
kept extra butter and other semi-perishables. The room
was small and cramped. Judith resisted the urge to turn
around and confront Joe Flynn in relative privacy.

"Here," she said, pulling out the door to the flour bin.
"It's in this grocery bag."

Except that it wasn't. The bag floated free in her hand,
and Judith let out a little cry. "It's gone!" She stared at
Joe, reminding herself not to let those green eyes mes-
merize her. "Did your men find it first?"

Joe looked grim. "I doubt it." He whirled out of the
pantry, surprisingly nimble of foot.

But none of the emergency personnel knew anything
about a satchel in a flour bin. After a brief discussion with
Kinsella and one of the firemen, Joe surveyed the kitchen
and pantry area. He bent down to study the dusty white
patches that Renie had left behind her. "I take it somebody spilled flour when you ditched the satchel?"

"It was Renie. She got it all over herself. As you may
recall, she's a bit awkward."

Joe looked up and grinned at Judith. "She sure couldn't
dance like you could, Jude-girl. You could make sparks
fly with your feet."

And with other things, Judith thought with a pang. At
least with Joe. She turned away, speaking briskly: "Can
you get footprints out of those flour patches?"

Joe considered, still kneeling and rubbing at his round chin. "Maybe. The stuff's pretty well scattered around, though." He straightened up, but not before he'd carefully dusted a few white specks off his well-polished loafers. "Who else knew Madame Gushenka had a satchel?"

"Nobody." Judith's nervousness returned, though not for precisely the same reasons. "Except Renie, of course." She saw Joe's jaw tighten, and suddenly realized that she and her cousin might be under as much suspicion as their guests. The idea was as incredible as it was unsettling.

"What about access?" Joe was already studying the kitchen door, the back stairs, and the steps that led to the basement.

"The back porch runs the width of the house," Judith explained, "with French doors leading into the rear of the living room. Anybody could get to the pantry from any direction, including by going up to the second floor via the main stairway off the entry hall and then coming down again by the back stairs."

"You don't keep your doors locked?" Joe asked with raised eyebrows.

"Not until everybody goes to bed," Judith replied, aware that she sounded faintly defensive. "Guests are free to go outside or anywhere else, except for the family quarters on the third floor."

"Great." Joe let out a long sigh, then went to the swinging door to formally dismiss the medics and the firemen. When the phone rang, Judith jumped, then dove across the room to answer. To her consternation as well as relief, it was Gertrude.

"What's going on over there?" she rasped. "I've tried to call three times, but the line was busy. It looks like all hell's broke loose. You kill somebody off with your god-awful lumpy gravy?"

"No," snapped Judith. "It was your soggy cream puffs. Luckily, only one death has occurred so far." Before Gertrude could pepper the phone line with invective, Judith tried to explain what had happened in the past hour. A subdued Gertrude listened with relative restraint, and even agreed to Judith's suggestion that she spend the night with the Rankers.

"It's almost eleven o'clock now," Judith said in her most appeasing manner. "It's going to be a zoo around here for a while, and if Arlene and Carl don't mind, I can send over your night things."

Gertrude went off the line, presumably to confer with her host and hostess. A moment later, she was back, sounding older and wearier than usual. "Hell of a note. Dead bodies at the Grover dinner table! Wouldn't have happened in *my* day." She expelled a grunt of disdain. "Don't forget my Tums, I ran out. And my hairnet. Oh, yeah, some bed socks, but not those silly things with the pom-poms." She paused, ostensibly running through her mental checklist. But when she spoke again, Gertrude's voice was back to its normal aggressive rasp: "Am I getting daffy or did I see Joe Flynn going into the house?"

Judith took a deep breath. "Yes. And yes."

"The bastard," said Gertrude, and hung up.

SIX

JOE WAS GOING over the sequence of events with Judith and Renie when the phone rang again. This time, Renie raced out of the little parlor to answer it on the table in the living room. Only Otto remained, brooding into his Drambuie. The fire was now blazing cheerfully, the flames giving his bald head an extra sheen.

"Sorry," said Renie to an unknown male voice, "there's no Wanda Rakesh here." She shot Otto a surreptitious glance as she put the receiver down and headed back to the front parlor. Before she reached the door, the phone rang again. Otto looked up with beady-eyed annoyance while Renie went into reverse.

"No, there's nobody here by the name of Wanda Rakesh," insisted Renie. "What number are you calling?"

The voice at the other end was just as persistent. "Wanda's my sister. She gave me this number herself. Are you sure she's not around? She's doing some cornball fortune-teller routine."

Renie's hand froze on the receiver. "Oh, *that* Wanda

Rakesh." She felt Otto's little eyes boring into her. "Well. Uh, what's your name?"

The faraway voice was growing impatient. "Lester Busbee. Hey, what's going on? Is Wanda there or not?"

"Not," gulped Renie. "Mr. Busbee, there's been some trouble. Did your sister use the name of Madame Gushenka?"

"She could call herself the Wizard of Oz for all I know," snapped Lester. "What's this about trouble?"

Trying to ignore Otto, who had now risen out of the chair and was trotting toward her with a menacing air, Renie struggled for the right words. As always, she wished she could resort to pictures; self-expression for Renie came much easier visually than verbally. "A woman calling herself Madame Gushenka showed up tonight as a fortune-teller." She paused, turning away from Otto, who was hovering at her elbow. "Unfortunately, she, ah, passed away during the seance. Or whatever. I'm sorry."

"Sorry! Jeez Louise! Listen, you nitwit," roared Lester Busbee, "my sister is strong as an ox! It couldn't have been her! Where are you? Where is Wanda?"

Renie gave Judith's address, but was considerably more vague about Wanda. "Well, I'm not sure . . . I think there was an ambulance . . . The morgue?" The word echoed obscenely. Otto blew his nose like a trumpet. "Where are *you*, Mr. Busbee?" asked Renie, cringing.

Lester Busbee's temper seemed to be deflating as he faced grim reality. "I'm in a town called—what?—Cedar River. I've driven up from L.A. and my car broke down." His voice quavered slightly. "It won't be ready until noon tomorrow. How many hours away am I?"

Renie calculated. "About three, if the freeway's not too crowded. Get off at the Heraldsgate exit, then turn left at the first light. Drive safely," she added. If Lester Busbee was indeed the brother of Madame Gushenka, Renie realized he needed a lot more sympathy than she had shown thus far.

Lester hung up without another word. Having disposed

of one obstacle, Renie was now forced to confront another. Otto was wiping at his nose and scowling. "Who's Wanda Rakesh?"

"I don't know," Renie answered evenly. "Do you?"

"Never heard of her." He spoke decisively, but avoided Renie's scrutiny as he stuffed the handkerchief back in his pocket. "Where's my inhaler? I left it on the dining room table, but it's gone. That blasted cat hair is getting to me again."

Renie went as far as the yellow and black tape would permit, but saw no inhaler. "The police took some of the stuff from the table. They must have made off with the inhaler, too." She offered Otto a genuine look of apology. "I have some Diphenhydramine in my purse. Would that help?"

But Otto clearly preferred to suffer, though not in silence. "Hell, no, I don't take secondhand stuff. I suppose that lamebrained nephew of mine doesn't have anything with him except a scalpel and a saw." He was winding up for a full-fledged diatribe, but was interrupted by Officer Price, who asked Otto to bring his wife in for questioning.

"My wife?" bristled Otto. "That moron doesn't know anything! What about me?"

Price remained implacable. "You're next, sir. But Mrs. Brodie hired the deceased, correct?"

Otto sputtered and grumbled, but trotted off upstairs to fetch Oriana. Renie returned to the parlor, where Judith and Joe were going over a plan of the house. It was not clear whether Joe was studying the layout for purposes of the investigation or to admire Judith's accomplishments.

"Four bathrooms," he was saying, a blunt finger pressed against the crude drawing Judith had made. "The plumbing bills alone must have set you back a bundle."

Noting their absorption, Renie hesitated. The last time she'd seen her cousin and Joe with their heads bent together, it was over a map of Mexico for the vacation they'd been planning for six months. Renie had hoped they'd get married first, but even in those days, she wasn't about to criticize. Two weeks before the trip, Joe did get married. But not to Judith.

With an apologetic clearing of her throat, Renie presented the news bulletin from Lester Busbee. Joe made notes, and Judith went for the phone book. "There's no Rakesh listed," she said, scanning the page. "Of course this directory is almost a year old now."

"I didn't know her as anything but Madame Gushenka," declared Oriana, standing on the threshold with Officer Price in tow like an Egyptian attendant waiting on Princess Amneris. "Here," she said, her high heels rapping their way across the hardwood floor, "this is the note I got from her confirming our date." She tapped at the saffron envelope. "Crabtree Street, where all those apartments are toward the bottom of the Hill."

"I'll send someone down there to check that place out," said Joe, who promptly dispatched Officer Price to get a couple of men with a search warrant. Waving the note and envelope at Judith and Renie, Joe asked if they knew the address.

"The 800 block," mused Judith. "I think so, it's an older building, four, five stories, maybe. Uncle Al's barber used to live there."

Joe put a hand to his own high forehead. "Uncle Al still got his hair?"

"Most of it," replied Judith, "but not all his marbles. He's taken up martial arts."

Joe didn't seem surprised, but Judith was used to people showing a lack of astonishment when it came to the Grover clan. She was, however, taken aback by his abrupt dismissal. "You and Renie get lost for a while," he said, pocketing Madame Gushenka's letter. "I have to talk to Mrs. Brodie and the others in private."

"Just a moment," interjected Oriana with a flounce of pearls. "Do I need an attorney present?"

"No, no," soothed Joe, revving up the Irish charm. "We're just on a fact-finding mission. Now the way I understand it, you heard about this fortune-teller from a friend of yours who hired her to . . .''

His voice died behind the closed door. In the dining room, a uniformed policeman was using a hand vacuum to gather up possible evidence in the vicinity of the fortune-teller's chair. Judith and Renie looked at each other, then marched in step to the kitchen. ''I wonder if he does windows,'' Judith mused, suddenly aware that she was very tired.

Renie's needs ran in a different direction. ''Murder or not,'' she declared, ''I'm still hungry.''

Judith glanced around the counters. ''There's a bit of roast left in the pan. I'll turn on the oven to heat it up. See if there's any salad in the fridge. I'm going to clear away the coffee table.''

Back in the empty living room, she turned off all the lights. The fire was still burning cheerfully, and Judith was grateful to whoever had been kind enough to put on more logs. Sitting on the cushioned window seat across from the flickering hearth always soothed her soul. She propped up a couple of thick embroidered pillows and tipped her head back. The big bay window looked down on a small rose garden and the laurel hedge that separated Hillside Manor from the dizzying planes, angles, and sheets of glass that made up the architect's house next door. Luckily, the Ericsons were gone for the weekend. Unlike the Rankerss, who had known the Grover family for almost thirty years, the Ericsons were relative newcomers and young enough to be closed-minded.

Rubbing at the back of her neck where a headache was just beginning, Judith tried to collect her thoughts. At least her mother was settled for the night. Renie would no doubt stay over. The Brodies appeared to be stuck, on orders of the police. Judith wondered if Oriana would demand a refund. She also wondered if the press had been alerted, either by Mavis or through the regular media channels. That idea made her grit her teeth: Renie was too sanguine about negative publicity; Judith could already see the For Sale sign in front of Hillside Manor.

Below in the garden, the carefully pruned rose bushes stood like stalwart soldiers, resisting the rain and wind. Heavy clouds hung low over the city, nestling against the curve of the bay where the midnight ferry was making its run into town. Judith loved her city, her old neighborhood, her family home. She had made great sacrifices to marry Dan McMonigle, all for naught, except for Mike. Miraculously, she had gotten everything back. But perhaps it was only a temporary miracle, about to be snatched away by ugly circumstances she could not have foreseen in her wildest dreams. There was only one way to save Hillside, not to mention her own reputation, and that was for Joe to solve the case as quickly as possible. Surely he must be a first-rate homicide detective. She had to rely on him to get her out of this grisly dilemma.

A strange little laugh burbled up out of Judith's throat. For all she knew, Joe Flynn was the biggest clown in the police department. She had relied on him twenty years ago and had been left holding more than just her flight bag. She didn't know Joe anymore; she didn't know if he was married, a father, an Elk, or a transvestite.

The worst part was that she didn't care what he had become. Joe was still Joe. Judith swore to herself, then at herself, and got up as a noise from the far end of the room caught her attention. Peering into the gloom as the fire began to die down, she saw two figures huddled close together on the other side of the French doors. A man and a woman, she realized, behaving in at least a semi-intimate manner. The man turned just enough so that she could recognize his profile: Dash Subarosa. No doubt he and Gwen had decided to defy the rain and catch a breath of fresh air. Judith was about to tiptoe over to the coffee table and retrieve the cups and saucers when it occurred to her that the woman was much too small to be Guinevere Brodie Tweeks. Pausing in mid-step, Judith squinted at the small square panes of glass.

The woman in Dash Subarosa's arms was Ellie Carver, and as far as Judith could tell, Mrs. Do-Good was doing a lot better than might have been expected.

"You won't believe this!" Judith exclaimed in a stage whisper as she hurtled through the swinging door. "Ellie is out on the back porch necking with Mr. Sleaze!" She stopped dead in her tracks, oblivious to Renie's gaping reaction. "What's that smell? Are you baking a boot?"

"I was just going to check," said Renie, reaching for the oven door. "We must have left something in there. A pan, maybe."

Black smoke curled out of the stove, sending both women reeling in the direction of the dishwasher. Waving her hands, Judith ran to the back door and threw it open, but the smoke alarm went off anyway. Out on the porch, two pairs of feet stampeded down the back steps. Joe Flynn flew into the kitchen and made a face.

"What's on fire?" he yelled over the screech of the alarm.

Renie was poking at the oven with a meat fork. "Oh, dear," she gasped. "You won't believe this, but . . ." The alarm stopped, leaving her voice pitched at high volume. "But," she went on, several notes lower, "I think we just roasted the evidence at 350 degrees."

Smoke was still pouring out of the leather satchel as Renie dangled it from the steel fork. In the doorway, Oriana was clutching at her pearls and emitting a series of shrieks. Judith was at the sink, pouring water into a kettle, but Joe had grabbed the fire extinguisher from the wall by the refrigerator.

"You may be up to code, but you aren't up to snuff with your emergency reactions," he shouted at Judith.

"Don't you dare spray that thing all over my kitchen floor! Stop it, you're going to zap Renie!" Judith dove in front of Joe and threw the kettle of water onto the satchel which her cousin had dropped unceremoniously at her feet. "There! The enemy has been subdued."

"Oh, good," remarked Renie, "only my shoes got wet." She looked again. "Eeeek! The flour I spilled has turned to paste! I'm glued to the spot!"

At the kitchen door, Oriana had been joined by Otto and what appeared to be the rest of the guest list. Judith noted that Dash and Ellie had taken up the rear. Over the twittering of Gwen, the cries of Oriana, and the vague murmurings of Lance, Otto bellowed the obvious question: "What the hell's going on now in this loony bin?"

Before anyone could answer, Sweetums streaked through the open back door, flew across the kitchen, and splayed himself against Otto's pantsleg. "Owr!" yelled Otto, swatting at the cat. "Get this ugly furball out of here!"

Judith charged after Sweetums, slipped on the wet floor, and had to be steadied by Joe. "Thanks," she gasped, feeling his hands at her arm and waist.

"Take a deep breath," cautioned Joe, still holding on to Judith. He waited a moment, the magic eyes resting on her startled face.

"I'm okay," she said, but her voice was shaky. Not, she realized, from the near fall, but from Joe's touch. She cursed herself and broke free, all attention riveted on Otto, who was still trying to pry Sweetums loose from his pants.

"He likes you, Daddy," said Gwen. "Nice kitty, come see Gwenny. Gwenny woves kitty-witties."

With a spate of apologies, Judith finally broke Sweetums's hold and carted his hissing form back out through the kitchen. "You'll be cat soup tomorrow," she muttered, slamming the door on his yowling face and securing the cat latch as well.

Renie had managed to get herself unstuck and was mopping up the floor while Joe dispersed the Brodies, except for the irate Otto. "Look at the tears in this seven-hundred-dollar suit! I should have brought my Doberman along! Booger shreds cats into confetti! I'm covered with fur! I'll probably go into a coma!"

"How about the front parlor instead?" suggested Joe, steering Otto out of the kitchen. "If you wait there, I'll be right along. Mrs. McMonigle is just making more coffee.''

"Mrs. McMonigle is making mayhem, if you ask me," grumbled Otto, but complied with relative docility.

Joe made sure that Otto was out of earshot, then turned to Judith and Renie. "Put the coffee on and let's see that satchel."

"It's locked," said Renie, then looked again. "It's not locked. Somebody pried it open."

Joe gave Renie a patronizing look. "Of course. What did you expect, they just wanted to braise it for fun?"

A quick search showed some melted cosmetics, scorched store coupons, a ruined hairbrush, and a wallet which was surprisingly intact. "It's Wanda Rakesh, all right," said Joe, studying the California driver's license. "Doesn't look a lot like Madame Gushenka, but it's her."

Judith and Renie stood side by side, scrutinizing the face that smiled back at them. According to the license, Wanda was forty-six years old, five foot eight, a hundred and forty-five pounds, and lived in Culver City. Her hair was brown, her eyes were hazel, and she was nearsighted. She had probably been a pretty woman, at least in her youth, though given the distortion of California Highway Patrol photography, it was hard to tell. Judith took another look at the smiling face and shuddered.

"Just think, she came in here three hours ago, all full of phony nonsense and bright shiny beads . . . and now she's dead. Why?"

Joe was still rummaging in the satchel, extracting hairpins and Band-Aids and paper clips. "Check the rest of the wallet. It seems as if she was a nurse at St. Peregrine's Hospital in L.A. Credit cards, too, mostly for California stores. I wonder what else was in here?"

"What do you mean?" Judith asked, flipping through the plastic holder with its passports to poverty for Visa, MasterCard, Bullock's, Robinson's and several oil companies.

"I mean," said Joe, digging even deeper into the

charred satchel, "that whoever filched this thing must have thought there was something incriminating in it. Not her identity, though. If that had been the case, he—or she—would have gotten rid of the wallet." He gave the two women a sidelong glance. "There's no checkbook, you'll note."

"You mean," said Renie, trying to piece his logic together, "whoever found the satchel wasn't trying to destroy it, they just wanted to ditch it in a hurry?"

Joe nodded. "The oven was the best place, I suspect. Whatever they took out of here is somewhere else in this house. Or has been . . ." He stopped, his hand still inside the satchel. "Hello? What's this?" Very carefully, he pulled out a Polaroid picture which had been stuck in the recesses of an inside pocket. The edges were curled and the color had faded, but despite the youthful faces, there was no mistaking the two people who beamed at the photographer into the camera.

Judith let out a little shriek. "Wanda and Dash?"

"Or Dash and Wanda. In love, it would appear, judging from the arms wrapped around each other." Joe turned the picture over. "Just '1969.' That's all it says, but that's plenty."

"Enough to arrest him?" Judith asked eagerly.

"Hardly." Joe put the satchel in yet another grocery bag. "But it *is* evidence. Just about anybody could have sneaked into the pantry and even the kitchen in the past couple of hours. At least after the murder. That trail of flour no doubt led the way, just like Hansel and Gretel's birdseed."

"Bread crumbs," corrected Judith absently. She gazed at the floor, noting that most of the flour had been tracked up, spread around, or absorbed. In any event, it was virtually gone. She turned back to Joe. "Could you get any prints?"

"Footprints?" Joe shrugged. "We tried. To be frank, I think the firemen tramped through most of it. Sometimes we seem to work at cross purposes." He looked faintly rueful, then squared his shoulders. "Now I'd better talk to Otto before he busts a gut."

"Wait!" Unthinking, Judith put a hand on Joe's arm and brushed aside the thought that it seemed to fit there. "Dash was out on the back porch with Ellie Carver just now. I saw them embracing. Sort of."

"Sort of?" The red eyebrows lifted as Judith's hand fell away. "Ellie?"

Judith nodded emphatically. "They suggested intimacy. And then they ran off after I opened the back door."

"Dash must be pretty dashing," mused Joe. "I'd better run him through the computer downtown." With the garbage bag swinging from his hand, he strolled out of the kitchen.

"Here," said Renie, pouring out the first of the coffee. "It looks like a long night."

Judith took the mug and stared with unseeing eyes at the smoke-smudged oven door. "It looks to me like a short career. I wonder if I can go back to the library?"

Pouring out her own mug, Renie didn't answer right away, but when she did, her voice was unusually somber. "I don't know about the library, coz, but you know what they say." Her anxious brown eyes met Judith's bleak black stare over the coffee mugs. "You can't go back. Not ever."

SEVEN

THE PROCESSION OF guests pounded up and down the main staircase until almost two a.m. For the first hour, Judith and Renie finished cleaning up from dinner, trying to find comfort in routine. The lights went out at the Rankers's, the wind died down, the rain slowed to a drizzle and Sweetums made occasional raucous forays at the back door. Resisting the temptation to let the cat in, Judith ignored his indignant yowls. She also resisted the desire to talk about Joe.

Renie didn't ask. Raised virtually like sisters, the cousins could almost read each other's minds. Eventually, Renie knew, Judith would talk, would pour it all out in her wry, self-deprecating manner. But not yet. Judith put away the Wedgwood instead, and spoke of murder.

"Dash Subarosa knew Wanda Rakesh," she remarked, stacking saucers. "But maybe he wasn't the only one. It's possible that Otto recognized her and that's why he high-tailed it out of the kitchen." She paused and made a face. "One broken goblet, two smashed dessert plates, plus I'm missing at least two cups and saucers. The police must have taken them. Do you suppose they think that's how Madame Gushenka was poisoned?''

Renie slumped into a kitchen chair, her brown curls wilted, dark circles under her eyes. ''Let's bury Madame Gushenka, I mean that name, and call her Wanda. I'll bet the accent was phony, too.''

''Probably. It sounded like an Early Espionage Movie.'' Judith closed the cupboards and joined her cousin at the dinette table. ''What do you suppose was in the satchel? And where is it?''

Renie shrugged and brushed crumbs off her bedraggled Notre Dame sweatshirt. They still hadn't eaten anything except for some stale cookies and limp crackers. ''The police can search their rooms, I suppose. Which means the missing whatever may have been destroyed.''

''How?'' asked Judith.

Renie reflected. ''The living room fireplace? Where else could you burn anything? You didn't start a fire in the parlor.'' Her eyes grew very wide, and she slapped both hands on the table. ''That's it! Somebody put more logs on the fire! Or was it you?''

''Not me.'' Judith pulled on her upper lip. ''When, I wonder?''

''I noticed it when Wanda's brother called. Otto was the only one left in the living room.'' Renie frowned, trying to be more specific. ''You and I were in the parlor with Joe. Your mother had just called. When was that? Around eleven?''

''Yes. I looked at the grandfather clock and hoped Mavis had missed the news deadline. The trouble is, we don't know if Otto was in the living room the whole time.''

''The way he was drinking, he probably wasn't,'' said Renie. ''He must have had to go to the can at some point or other.''

Judith's shoulders slumped. ''So that doesn't help. But I'm willing to bet that whoever started up that fire also burned what was in the satchel. Somehow, I don't see the Brodies as being domestically inclined.''

''True.'' Renie cast about in her mind for some helpful

scrap to buoy her cousin's spirits. "The police may have found something at Wanda's apartment."

"I wonder if Joe would tell us," mused Judith.

Renie wondered, too. For some time, the two women sat in silence, sipping their coffee, the ticking of the old schoolhouse clock in the background, the sound of feet overhead and out in the direction of the entry hall. Renie was about to suggest that they ask the police if it would be all right if they went to bed for a while, when tense voices floated down from the back stairs.

"Who?" mouthed Renie, practically falling off her chair in an effort to catch the words.

Judith listened intently and was rewarded with a few well-projected syllables. "Oriana." She got up as quietly as possible from the chair and tiptoed to the hallway that separated the pantry from the back stairs. Plastering herself against the wall between a stack of old newspapers and a carton of soda pop, she tried to make out the other voice.

It was Oriana whose words Judith first caught. ". . . tantamount to blackmail! Where's your sense of family?"

The reply was definitely masculine, but as inaudible as it was unidentifiable. Judith judged that the pair was right by the first landing, a scant ten feet away. Oriana was speaking again, but this time she had lowered her voice. All Judith could hear was something about "once in a lifetime" and "stabbed to the heart." The latter phrase sent a shiver down her spine. Judith considered dashing back to the relative safety of the kitchen, but felt compelled to try to hear more.

The other half of the duo wasn't cooperating, however. Again, the male voice was too muffled. Judith heard the shuffling of feet. Oriana's high heels had started up the stairs. Judith darted a glance around the corner. She saw just a glimpse of a man's black shoe, gray trousers—and no socks.

The grandfather clock had just chimed two-thirty when a bleary-eyed Joe Flynn returned to the kitchen with Officer Price in his wake. "Personally," said Joe, collapsing onto the chair vacated by Renie, "I'd like to arrest all eight of them for impersonating human beings. The only possible real person among them is Lance, and he's so dumb that when I asked him for his address, he said it was an expensive one."

"Maybe it's an act," offered Judith, pouring out the last of the coffee for Joe and Officer Price. "Dare we ask what you found out?"

Joe drank the coffee with the compulsion of an addict. "Sure. Nothing." He sat back, stretched out his legs, and kicked off his loafers. "Well, almost nothing. Dash admits he knew Wanda. In fact, he was married to her for a couple of years. But he swears he didn't even recognize her in that getup and hasn't seen her in twenty years."

"Do you believe that?" Judith didn't. It was just the quick, easy solution she wanted so badly.

Joe shrugged and looked at Price. "What do you think, Woody?"

A seemingly careful man, Woody Price tipped his head to one side and fingered his moustache. "I think it's too much of a coincidence that Wanda Rakesh should show up under the same roof as Dash Subarosa. But that doesn't make him a murderer. If I were going to guess—but that's not my job."

"Try it," urged Joe. "Just for once. Anything goes at two-thirty a.m."

Price shrugged his compact shoulders. "Okay. I think it's more likely that Dash and Wanda were in this together and somehow the wrong person got killed." He raised his heavy, dark eyebrows at his superior, waiting for an opinion.

After draining the mug, Joe set it down and rested his chin in his hand. "That's possible. But who was the real victim? And why? Who sat next to Wanda?"

Judith's answer was swift: "Otto on one side, Ellie on the other. All three of them had tea. I think."

"Are you sure?" But Joe didn't wait for an answer to his own question. He stood up and yawned. "I'm calling it a night. I'll check in downtown, then get a few hours' sleep and be back here around nine." He gave Judith a sleepy smile. "You do breakfast, right?"

"Didn't I always?" she said in a voice so low that only Joe heard.

He did not, however, react, except for the faintest flicker of the green eyes. "We might have the medical examiner's report by then. Come on, Woody, let's go." He started away from the table, realized he wasn't wearing his shoes, and slipped them on, reminding Judith of the confrontation between Dash and Oriana.

Joe showed only mild interest. "Come the dawn, it'll probably turn out to be the crux of the whole case. Right now, the rest of that crew could kill each other and I'd put them on hold."

"Oriana did mention someone being stabbed," said Judith doggedly.

"Well, that isn't my case," noted Joe, hands in pockets as he half lurched for the door. "I'm leaving some men on duty, two out, two in. Everybody stays until I get back." He paused, a hand raised in salute, and looked straight at Judith. "You two had better stick around. From an official point of view, you're both suspects."

Judith and Renie gaped at him. "That's absurd," retorted Renie. "You know damned well Judith didn't bump the poor woman off—and I got hauled into this crapshoot at the last minute!"

Joe cocked his head to one side. "Maybe so. But let's face it, ladies, from the chief's standpoint, since this is a poisoning case, you two could be voted most likely to succeed. You did prepare all the food, right?"

"Mother made the cream puffs," said Judith through tight lips. "Why don't you haul her in? You could always handcuff her walker."

With a rueful shake of his head, Joe raised his hands in a helpless gesture. "She's not beyond suspicion, to be frank. Hey, what I think doesn't count. The homicide squad works with facts, not sentiment." His expression turned faintly sheepish. "I'm just one cog in a big wheel, and I've got to do my job. After all, I have a wife and children to support." On that note, Joe left the kitchen with Officer Price at his heels.

"Damn!" exclaimed Judith, clutching at the refrigerator. "I should have seen that coming! Damn, damn, damn!"

"Oh, it's too stupid!" ranted Renie, gathering up the coffee mugs with a great clatter. "What did you do, shoot your face off to Joe about how you wanted to get a bumper sticker that said No Autopsies after Dan died?"

Judith shot Renie a contemptuous look. "Don't be an ass. I didn't mean that, I meant the wife and children. Who," she demanded bitterly, "was I trying to kid?"

One policeman was posted in the living room on the sofa, the other upstairs in a wicker chair in the hall. The outside men stayed in their patrol car, parked discreetly in the Ericsons' empty driveway. Judith and Renie had turned out all the lights downstairs except for a Tiffany lamp on an end table near the fireplace. They were on their way to bed when the front doorbell buzzed.

Judith swore, then trudged wearily across the entry hall. Yet another policeman stood under the front porch light with a big manila envelope in his hand.

"Lieutenant Flynn?" he inquired.

Judith stared at the envelope, then at Renie. Joe and Price had been gone less than ten minutes. "I'll give it to him," said Judith, dredging up a bright smile and putting out her hand. "Thank you very much."

She closed the door firmly and threw the dead bolt. "Dumb cluck," remarked Judith under her breath. Cautiously, she peeked into the living room. The officer on the sofa had nodded off. Judith slipped into the half bath off the entry hall and grabbed a towel, which she draped over the envelope. Without another word, Judith and Renie went upstairs. The policeman on duty in the wicker chair glanced up from his copy of *Field and Stream* and nodded in a halfhearted manner.

The two women kept going down the hall, past the four guest rooms and two baths, where silence now reigned. They ascended the short flight of steps behind the door marked Private at the far end of the hall, and came out into a small foyer. The walls were lined with bookcases crammed with hardcovers and paperbacks alike. As a librarian, Judith had eclectic tastes: Classics, sci-fi, romance, biographies, mysteries, popular fiction, and serious works sat spine-to-spine under the eaves. The only other objects in the little foyer were a big Boston fern and Gertrude's favorite painting of the Sacred Heart. Judith avoided Jesus's probing gaze and opened the door to her bedroom.

"Will we get arrested for this?" asked Renie, flopping onto Judith's goosedown comforter.

"I hope so," said Judith, unwinding the string that held the envelope closed. Fingering the contents, she frowned. "I thought this must be the coroner's report, but it's something else." Carefully, she dumped the contents on the bed next to Renie.

On the surface, the items seemed innocuous enough: three smaller envelopes, several newspaper clippings, a couple of snapshots, and an eight-by-ten glossy of what looked like a Word War II glamour girl.

"Who's this?" queried Renie, trying to decipher the inscription without her glasses. "She looks familiar. Is it Barbara Stanwyck?"

Judith shook her head. "No. This stuff must have come from Wanda's apartment. The name on the back is Gloria St. Cloud." She studied the photograph closely, taking in the dark, shoulder-length hair; the wide, sensuous mouth; the big, dark eyes; and the thin straps of what probably was an evening gown. "Gloria St. Cloud looks familiar because she's Wanda's mother. Listen to this. 'To Baby Wanda, my rising star. Love, Mommy.' " She shoved the photograph under Renie's nose. "What you recognize is a resemblance to Wanda, especially the eyes."

Renie was pensive. "She must have been an actress. I never heard of her. Is there a date?"

"No. But the photographer was located on Wilshire Boulevard in L.A." Judith picked up the two snapshots. "Here's Mom looking not nearly so hot." She tapped the photograph with her forefinger. "Is that Wanda? The kid must be about ten or twelve."

"Shoot," said Renie, "they're a blur to me. There's a boy who looks a little older, I can see that much, and another couple. What kind of building is that they're standing in front of?"

Judith looked at the back of the photo. "No writing on this one. That car on the right looks like the one my dad bought after the war. A '49 Chev, remember?"

"Black, four-door, no running boards. My dad bought a blue Nash. He ran over a cow with it."

"He always drove kind of fast," Judith commented, still staring at the snapshot. "It's Southern California. Spanish architecture and palm trees in the background."

Renie dug into her purse, which was about the size of a ten-pound potato sack. After a great deal of shuffling and rustling, she produced a pair of bent red-rimmed glasses. "Gloria must be in her thirties here, but her glitz is gone. I wonder if the teenaged boy is Lester Busbee."

"Who?" Judith plumped up a pillow behind her back. "Oh, the brother. Could be. Do you think the building is a hotel?"

Renie considered. "It looks too . . . formal for a hotel. See any resemblance between Wanda and the other couple?"

"I don't know how you see anything, those glasses are so scratched and gummed up. How do you work in them?"

Renie glared at Judith through the maligned spectacles. "I get some of my most innovative graphic designs right off the lenses," she declared, then sat bolt upright. "Palm trees! Madame Gushenka—Wanda—mentioned palm trees! What did she say?"

Judith put a hand to her head. "Oh, hell's bells, she

said so much! Abandoned women and children and fraud and deceit and jails and snails and puppy dogs' tails! I'm too tired to think.''

"Right.'' Renie's spurt of enthusiasm flickered out, though she forged ahead and picked up the third photograph. "This one's in color, if faded. Doctors, nurses, including Wanda at about—thirty-five? I'd guess the building behind them here is a hospital.''

Judith concurred. "A Catholic hospital. There's a statue in that niche above them. Which saint?''

"Vitus. He looks like he's dancing,'' said Renie.

"Can it, coz. He's levitating. Didn't Joe mention St. Peregrine's?''

"I think so. Hey, look.'' Renie held the photo up close, then at arm's length, and pointed to one of the doctors. "Is that Harvey with a moustache?''

Judith looked closely at the white-coated man who stood in the back row, not quite behind Wanda. "Clean your glasses, goofy. This guy's a leprechaun, not a weasel. The one next to him looks like Uncle Al.'' She flipped the picture on top of the other two. "Let's see what's in these envelopes.'' None of them was sealed. Two were legal-sized; the third was mauve stationery with Oriana Brodie's name and address printed on the back. The letter carried the same imprint. "Boring,'' said Judith. "It's just gush, confirming the date for tonight. Whatever ammunition Oriana gave Wanda to use in needling the rest of the family isn't in here. She must have done that by phone. Unless Oriana's lying and she did in fact meet Wanda before tonight.'' She tossed the single sheet to Renie, who was perusing it when they both heard someone shouting from the street below.

"What now?'' groaned Judith, flying to the window and pulling up the mini-blinds. Down in the darkness, three figures were wrestling on the sidewalk next to the laurel hedge. "I'm going to see what's happening,'' she said, racing for the door.

"Me, too!'' called Renie, right behind her. On the second floor, a sleep-befuddled Otto was shielding his eyes from the hallway light and muttering. Ellie Carver peeped out from behind the door at the far end of the passage just as Lance stumbled from his room in his underwear. Judith deduced that the policeman on duty had apparently gone downstairs to investigate, since his fishing magazine was lying in a heap under the wicker chair.

The rain had stopped. Overhead, the clouds were drifting slowly out to sea. The night was cold and damp, making Judith shiver under her mohair sweater and flannel slacks. She and Renie bounded along the front walk, then turned right in the direction of the Ericsons'. The struggle was already over, with one policeman holding Mavis Lean-Brodie by the arms, another insisting that she shut up, and a third searching through her shoulder bag.

"Listen, you idiots," railed Mavis who had changed from her Chanel suit into blue jeans and a huge fisherman's knit sweater, "I have a job to do! Freedom of the press! The Constitution! The people's right to know!"

"You can tell them over the phone, Ms. Lean-Brodie," said the officer, who had been trying to outshout Mavis. "You can't leave Hillside Manor until Lieutenant Flynn says so."

Mavis kicked at the sidewalk with her tennis shoe. "Fascists! I'll sue! KINE will sue! The network will sue! I can't put together a story like this over the telephone!"

But the officer who held Mavis was now propelling her back toward the house. Judith and Renie stepped aside to let them pass. Mavis ignored them, as if they were a pair of fire hydrants affixed to the parking strip.

"Nazis," she muttered. "Censorship, that's what it is—"

Her diatribe was interrupted by the policeman who had been going through her purse. "Hold it." He stood up, the shoulder bag dangling from one hand, something dark and shiny in the other. "Excuse me, Ms. Lean-Brodie, but do you always go after your news stories with a Smith & Wesson .357 magnum?"

Mavis's fine features were twisted with rage as she made

one last futile effort to break free. "You bet I do, turkey! I've got a carry permit, too! I bought that gun after I was nearly killed covering the Indian clam-digging riots!"

Judith nudged Renie. "Let's wait until they're all settled down before we go back inside. I don't want to see Lance in his underwear again."

"Why not?" asked Renie innocently. "He's the Brodie with the beautiful body, except for that scar on his knee."

"Knee?" Sadly, Judith shook her head at her cousin. "It wasn't his knee I noticed. I guess I've been a widow too long."

To Judith's relief, the house had grown quiet again when they went back upstairs ten minutes later. In the little foyer, Renie leaned against the wall and rubbed at her eyes. "Coz, I'm beat. I'm even beyond hunger. Would you hate me if I went to sleep in your mother's bed for a couple of hours?"

"Do it," said Judith. "You look like something Sweetums dragged in."

Renie needed no further encouragement. With a wan smile and a weak wave, she tottered off to Gertrude's aerie under the eaves. Judith fought back an overwhelming urge to give up for what was left of the night. But having purloined police evidence, she knew she had to make the most of her small advantage. She also realized with a pang that she and Joe were not necessarily playing on the same team.

With a heavy sigh, she opened the first of the legal-sized envelopes. The single sheet of paper revealed a photostat of a birth certificate issued by the City of Los Angeles, dated February 7, 1943. The infant girl's given name was Wanda Marie. Her mother's maiden name was listed as Gloria Ramona St. Cloud.

In the space after "Name of Father," the typed letters spelled out *Otto Ernst Brodie.*

EIGHT

FOR THE FIRST time since Medic Kinsella had stated that Madame Gushenka, AKA Wanda Rakesh, had not died of natural causes, Judith felt a faint sense of encouragement. Wanda, Otto's daughter, born out of wedlock, perhaps a secret to everyone, maybe even to Otto—no wonder the fortune-teller had rattled on about women and children. But what, Judith mused, had happened to Gloria St. Cloud? If she'd been in the movie business as the glossy glamour-girl photo indicated, she'd never become a household word.

Had Otto met Gloria in Los Angeles or someplace else? Was it a wartime romance or a one-night stand? Where had Otto been in the spring of 1942? Judith was bursting with questions, trying to figure out a logical way to get answers.

But there was still the other envelope. She opened it hurriedly and extracted yet another photostat, this time of a marriage certificate for Gloria St. Cloud and Otto Brodie. Apparently, they had been married before Otto took Minnie as wife. There it was in black and white, five p.m., June 13, 1942, in the City of Las Vegas, County of Clark, State of Nevada, Justice of the Peace Elwood F. Sturbridge officiating.

Judith fell back against the pillows. Wanda wasn't illegitimate. In fact, she had been a co-heir to the Brodie fortune, along with Lance, Gwen, and probably Harvey. As Joe had said, money was the eternal motive. But who—besides Otto—knew about Wanda? Or had Otto been aware of his elder daughter's existence? Judith thought back to the little scene between Otto and Wanda in the kitchen. Something about Madame Gushenka had put him off. Was it the unexpected recognition of his firstborn child?

Judith could only speculate. It appeared that there had been a quickie Nevada marriage, no doubt followed by a quickie Nevada divorce. Judith shook out the envelope: If Wanda Brodie Rakesh had brought copies of her birth certificate and her parents' marriage license north, she must also have had the divorce decree with her. But the envelope was empty. All that remained were the newspaper clippings. Judith was puzzling over the omission when a tentative knock at the door startled her. Renie, of course, unable to sleep and lapsing into uncustomary politeness.

"Come in," Judith said eagerly, then let out a little squeak of astonishment as Ellie Carver slipped into the room. In their haste to repair to the family quarters, the cousins apparently had forgotten to lock the private door behind them.

Judith did her best to toss a couple of pillows onto the police evidence, but Ellie didn't seem to notice. "I was afraid you might be asleep," she said, pulling her blue velour robe close. "I couldn't settle down."

"Have a seat," said Judith, indicating a chintz-covered armchair and arranging herself on the bed to conceal any remnants of Wanda's mementos. Patiently, she waited for Ellie to speak, but her guest was nervously fidgeting with the ties of her robe, gray eyes darting around the cozy room with chintz comforter and wallpaper to match the chair.

"I feel so silly," she finally said in a tremulous voice. "But I must explain, if only because if I don't, you might say something to the police and they'd get the wrong idea." The color had risen in her pale face as she wrestled with the words that sprang from her private demons.

"About what?" asked Judith with a bland smile. She was used to confidences, even from strangers. Whether behind the desk at the Thurlow Ridge Public Library or behind the bar of the Meat & Mingle, Judith would find herself the recipient of the most intimate secrets.

Ellie looked away, as if she expected the alabaster statue of the Virgin Mary on Judith's dresser to answer for her. The bedroom was very quiet, with only the sound of a red-eye flight coming in low under the storm clouds.

"You saw us outside," Ellie said at last in her breathless voice. When Judith didn't immediately respond, Ellie strove to clarify. "Dash—and me. On the porch." The pale lashes dipped; her hands clasped her knees.

"Yes." Judith shrugged. "It's none of my business."

Ellie lifted her chin. "This is a murder case. What everybody does is everybody else's business. There's a killer loose under your roof. Aren't you afraid?"

Judith blinked. She was, but not for the reason Ellie was indicating. Indeed, it had never occurred to her to consider herself—or anyone else—in danger. But that was a foolish reaction. "You're right," conceded Judith, suddenly aware of how cold the house had grown since she'd turned the furnace off. "It's such an incredible idea, I don't think I've taken it all in."

"Well, I have." Ellie had regained her composure, showing a hint of the steel that allowed her to prod patrons, coerce committees, and untie purse strings. "It's a horrible thought, but it's got to be faced." She frowned and shook her head, as if staving off weakness. "The police mustn't be misled. If they get sidetracked, they'll never find the murderer. That's why I wanted to explain about Dash. Years ago," she continued, swallowing hard, "we . . . went steady." The gray eyes dared Judith not to mock her. "I haven't seen him since I was a freshman at UCLA. My parents didn't approve." Her small mouth tightened, registering disapproval of her parents.

"I see." Judith thought she did. That Dash Subarosa should appear at Hillside Manor along with one ex-girlfriend and one ex-wife seemed somewhat unbelievable. Almost as much, she reminded herself, as Joe Flynn showing up after twenty-two years. "You didn't know who Gwen was engaged to?" Judith asked.

Ellie gave Judith a faintly patronizing look. "Dash and Gwen had been out of the country. They met in Mazatlán, I think. All I knew was his name." Ellie put both hands at her small bosom and took a deep breath. "Dash Subarosa isn't his real name, you see."

"Oh. That's a relief." Judith turned penitent. "I'm being flip, I must be tired."

Ellie absolved her with a nod. "Dash—I'll call him that since everybody else does—has had a rather rocky life. His father, Dukes Frascatti, was in the construction business in the San Fernando Valley. There were some questionable doings, indicating that Mr. Frascatti wasn't quite what he seemed." She spoke primly, now perched on the edge of the chair. "That was why my father disapproved of the romance. Like father, like son, Poppa said. It was very unfair of him, of course. Rico was just another carefree college student when I met him."

Obviously, Rico was Dash, once removed. "I suppose he had a reason to change his name," Judith remarked casually.

"Naturally." Ellie's eyes grew wide. "He explained all that to me tonight. The association with his father plagued him. To make his way in the world, he became Felix Subarosa, nicknamed Dash by a kindly professor of medieval English. Even though Mr. Frascatti passed away some years ago, Rico had already established himself as Dash."

Briefly, Judith searched her conscience and found it sleeping soundly. "Did he marry Wanda Rakesh as Dash or Rico?"

Had she asked if Ellie knew there was a ten-foot python around her neck, Judith could not have elicited an expression of greater shock. "Where did you hear that?" Ellie was gripping the arms of the chair, all but falling onto the carpet. "How did you get such a peculiar notion? What kind of rumors are the police spreading?" But behind the bravado, her face was crumbling like wet clay. "Is this all a frame-up, just because Rico's—Dash's—father was a little shady?"

"Actually," said Judith calmly, "Dash told the police about Wanda. I assume he also told you. The question is, *when.*" She let the word fall with ominous intent, then mentally kicked herself. Ellie could be a murderess. If she'd killed one person already, she wouldn't hesitate to try for two.

But Ellie had retreated into the chair, not quite cowering, but clearly jarred. "He told me when we were on the back porch. I swear to you, I haven't seen him in twenty-five years."

"That happens," said Judith, the irony lost on Ellie. Her weary gaze roamed around the room, taking in the comforting familiarity of the Spanish armoire that housed her TV and stereo, the dressing table with its old-fashioned flounce of chintz, the walk-in closet with her limited wardrobe and priceless Storybook Doll collection. "Did Dash also explain how he knew Oriana?"

This time the question definitely flummoxed Ellie. "Oriana? You must be mistaken. Unless, of course," she added dubiously, "Gwen had introduced them on a previous occasion."

"I gathered none of the family had met Dash until tonight," said Judith. "In fact, now that I think about it, all of you Brodie ladies seemed—how to put it?—disconcerted by his presence."

"*I* certainly was," Ellie admitted. "So much so that I can't remember how the others reacted. Except I did think Lance seemed . . . befuddled when he was introduced to Dash. But then Lance is often befuddled." She frowned, her hands again working at the ties of her robe. "But Mavis wouldn't have been put off! Nothing disconcerts that hard-bitten creature!"

Judith considered. "Maybe not Mavis. At least, not as much." The truth was, she couldn't be sure of what she'd seen. The incident had been so unimportant at the time.

Ellie was getting up, arms crossed, rubbing her hands up and down her sleeves as if she were very cold. "I must get back to bed. If Harvey wakes, he'll wonder what's happened to me."

Judith glanced at the digital clock next to the bed. The numbers were just changing to 4:21. She hadn't been up this late since Mike had pneumonia in fourth grade. Hoping that Ellie would be too immersed in her own problems to notice the items on the bed, Judith dared to get up and see her visitor out into the foyer.

"By the way," she asked Ellie, "when did Dash give up socks?"

Ellie paused at the private door. She was a full head shorter than Judith and had to crane her neck to look at her hostess. A tiny smile played at her lips. "In college, I guess. It made him different—and daring."

And stinky, thought Judith, but kept her mouth shut. It seemed to her that, given Dash's background, he didn't need any embellishments to cut himself from the herd.

But Ellie was speaking again, now very serious and with an air of dignity. "Dash wouldn't have come here to meet Wanda. He's having second thoughts about Gwen." The gray eyes took on a sudden glimmer of life. "Rico—Dash—has never cared for anyone but me." On that note, Ellie slipped across the threshold and down the short flight of stairs.

This time, Judith remembered to lock the door.

The newspaper clippings were almost too much for Judith. At first glance, they seemed to have no bearing on the case—or Wanda Rakesh: a pair of short articles about a man with amnesia, a gossip column, and a brief story about a hit-and-run accident, all from L.A. papers. The amnesia victim had been found by a chicken farmer near Chino, then had disappeared a day later without being identified. The gossip column featured a world-class model, a temperamental actress, a bigamous producer, and a jet-setting socialite.

Judith paused over the last snippet:

> *Cynthia O'Doul is back from Europe and rarin' to go on the annual Tiara Ball for St. Perry's Hospital. The scintillating Cynth is still laughing at her husband, the well-known Beverly Hills surgeon, Dr. Jack O'Doul, who not only forgot to meet her plane, but insists he forgot she was in Europe! Oh, Doc, you're such a cut-up!!! Where've you been operating lately? Just kidding, we know you'll both put the sparkle in the Tiara next month at the Bel-Air Hotel . . .*

The date was October 26, 1979. The stories about the man with amnesia were from the same week, October 23 and 24. Either Dr. O'Doul was an absent-minded surgeon—or an amnesiac. Judith couldn't imagine why Wanda would have kept the clippings together unless there was an important link. She had worked at St. Peregrine's Hospital—St. Perry's to the chatty columnist—perhaps as far back as 1979. But what did a decade-old incident have to do with the Brodie family?

The last article was also about a surgeon, Stanley Edelstein, forty-two, who had been killed in a hit-and-run accident outside of Star of Jerusalem Hospital in November 1981. "Edelstein," the news story ran, "had gone off-duty at 10 p.m., some 20 minutes before the tragedy. A Los Angeles Police Department spokesman said it was possible that heavy rains obscured the unknown driver's vision. The victim was already dead when two hospital workers found him sprawled over a manhole."

Some faint memory stirred in Judith's tired brain. But nothing came into focus. She read through the final paragraph: "A native of Houston, and a graduate of UCLA's Medical School with an undergraduate degree from Baylor University, Edelstein had interned at St. Peregrine's Hospital. He joined the staff of Star of Jerusalem in 1980. Survivors include his mother, Thelma, and a sister, Rachel Pierpont, both of Houston . . ."

Edelstein, like O'Doul, had been on the staff of St. Peregrine's. But so what, Judith asked herself. Maybe they were the doctors in the snapshot with the nurses. Maybe Wanda had a crush on both of them. Maybe she was a clipping freak. Maybe Judith should take a break.

Judith decided to take a shower. The clock showed five a.m. It was too late for a nap: Judith always got up at six to start breakfast for her guests, should any of them be early risers. The hot water and British National Health soap she swore by revived her a bit. She took more time than usual with her makeup and donned a bright red turtleneck sweater and black slacks. She nodded approval at the mirror. Her color scheme was symbolic—red, to show that she was undefeated by tragedy; black, to signify that she was mindful of murder in their midst. Resolutely, Judith descended the stairs and prepared to face the new day.

The policeman on the second floor was alert, drinking coffee from a thermos, with three glazed doughnuts on a napkin at his side. Someone was in the shared bathroom at the far end of the hall: one of the Otto or Lance Brodies, Judith reasoned.

Hurrying down to the kitchen via the back stairs, she turned the lights on to fend off the morning gloom. To her consternation, the dining room table remained off-limits. She couldn't possibly seat more than six around the kitchen table. Maybe her guests wouldn't all show up at once.

Sweetums was clawing frantically at the back door. Judith let him in, stuck her tongue out at his infuriated face, and fed him a lavish breakfast. For a moment, she stood on the back porch, breathing in the cool, damp air. Fog had settled over the city, drifting among the apple trees, creeping up the driveway, playing hide-and-seek with the

Rankers's house. A car started up across the street, a dog barked, the paper boy aimed, fired, and missed. Scooting down the back steps, Judith hurried to the front of the house where she retrieved the morning edition from a rhododendron bush.

"Hey, Dooley," she called softly as she tried to make out the boy's form in the fog, "you didn't try out for basketball, did you?"

"Archery," replied Dooley emerging on the walkway. "I'm real good."

"I'll bet," said Judith, unfolding the paper and holding her breath as she scanned the headlines.

"Anybody else get whacked during the night?" Dooley asked, his fair hair sticking up at various angles.

Judith stared at Dooley. The relief of not finding Hillside Manor on page one fled. "How'd you know?"

Dooley shrugged his thin shoulders and grinned. "Mrs. Rankers called my mom last night. Got her out of bed, but I was still up reading a spy book. It's all about some mean Bulgarians."

Judith sighed. No doubt Arlene Rankers had called everybody but Mavis's producer at KINE-TV. Even if the murder hadn't made the morning news, Arlene's Broadcasting System—or ABS, as it was known in the neighborhood—had probably already alerted most of Heraldsgate Hill.

"Poisoned cream puffs, huh?" queried Dooley, his jug-handle ears all but bending forward. "Cyanide? Strychnine? Curare? You'd be surprised, there are all kinds of poisons in the stuff you keep around the house. Look at the labels, I'll bet you don't pay attention to most of the warnings they put—"

"Whoa," she said, holding up a hand. Despite her dilemma, she had to smile at Dooley, who often showed a propensity for offbeat knowledge that was unusual in a fourteen-year old. As far as Judith was concerned, his secret weapon was safe from most other teenagers: Dooley was a voracious reader. And, when warmed up, quite garrulous. "No word yet. When it comes down, Arlene will be the first to know."

Dooley wasn't impressed. "She doesn't know everything. She didn't even see those guys out in the back yard last night."

"What guys? The police?"

Dooley gave Judith a condescending look as he juggled his bag of newspapers. "Naw—this was before the cops showed up in the Ericsons' driveway. About one o'clock. I was, you know, just going to bed."

"You need more sleep, Dooley, especially when you have to get up so early on the weekends," Judith said in her mechanical mother's voice. "What did they look like?" She glanced up at the Dooley family's Dutch colonial which was perched behind the Ericsons' architectural madness. The fog obscured both houses, but Judith knew that Dooley's bedroom had an excellent view of Hillside Manor and its garden. Only last summer, Gertrude had pitched a fit when she discovered Dooley's telescope had caught her in the altogether.

Dooley was reflecting, enjoying his moment in the spotlight. "Well . . . there were three of them, two who came up the drive, probably from a car parked down the street. The other dude came out from around the front of the house. He was big, you know, walked sort of odd."

Lance, thought Judith, and tried to remember what she'd been doing at one in the morning. Cleaning up in the kitchen while Joe interviewed her guests, as near as she could recall. "They just . . . talked?"

"The first two guys did most of the talking. Then they went away and the one with the funny walk went back in the house." Dooley chewed on his lower lip, clearly trying to dredge up more information. "The dude from your house acted like maybe he was being chewed out. He sort of . . . slunk, you know."

Judith remembered the phone call to Lance. Perhaps he had arranged to meet someone at Hillside Manor. It might be quite innocent. The call had come long before Madame

Gushenka had arrived. "You have a good eye, Dooley," said Judith, starting back up the walk. "I ought to hire you as a detective."

To Judith's surprise, Dooley actually blushed. "I'm staying on the lookout," he murmured. "It's sort of my hobby."

"Keep that telescope lens clean," said Judith with a wry smile. "and learn to read lips." Waving through the fog at Dooley, she hurried back around the house and into the kitchen. To her amazement, Lance Brodie was sitting at the dinette table in a big plaid bathrobe, a steaming towel on his left knee.

"Good morning," chirped Judith, remembering to act like a hostess. "I'm just getting breakfast under way. Hurt your knee?"

Lance smoothed the folds of the towel and grimaced. "It's an old injury," he explained in his vague voice. "The fog makes it worse. The damp from the fog. Or *in* the fog."

Talking to Lance was a lot like talking *to* fog, Judith thought uncharitably, but presented a sympathetic exterior. Indeed, she couldn't help but feel sorry for the poor man, with his gimpy leg and faded dreams of gridiron glory. A dark stubble grew at his chin and along his jawline; his eyes looked faintly hollow, as if he'd spent the night listening to Mavis rant about freedom of the press.

"I'll put the tea kettle on so you can soak that towel again," she said, already plugging in the coffee maker. "You played for the Stars, didn't you?"

"They folded," Lance said without expression. "They went broke."

Judith was filling the tea kettle at the sink. "It's been a while," she said, sounding almost as vague as Lance. She wondered if his condition was contagious. "By the way, did you see anyone in our back yard last night?" She purposely made the question ambiguous.

"Did I see anyone?" Lance's face was blank. "I guess I did. Nobody you'd know," he added, suddenly gloomy.

Turning the heat on under the tea kettle, Judith searched her brain for the appropriate queries which would pry the truth out of Lance. "A neighbor said they were . . . odd."

"Odd." The word seemed to stick on Lance's tongue. "No, not really. Stubborn. Like"—he gazed around the kitchen, his eyes coming to rest on Gertrude's Democratic Party donkey atop the refrigerator—"a mule," Lance concluded.

"Stubborn friends can present problems," sympathized Judith, setting out the makings for buttermilk pancakes. "They are friends, I take it?"

"No." Lance shook his head, then reconsidered. "You mean to me, or to each other?"

Judith ground her teeth as she cracked eggs into a big blue bowl. Abandoning subtlety in the face of Lance's literal mindset, she plowed ahead. "I mean, why did they come here if they weren't your friends?"

"That's a good question." Lance actually seemed pleased, especially since he had an explanation: "They came about Club Stud."

Judith might be insulated from the local social whirl, but even she had heard of the sports-oriented chain of disco-nightclubs up and down the Coast. She had not, however, associated them with Lance Brodie. Until now. "You have an interest in Club Stud?" she asked, slicing ham into thick pieces.

Lance nodded. "I own them." He looked faintly puzzled by the statement. "Now. Before, I had a partner, Calvin Tweeks. We played together for the Stars. Then he married Gwen."

"Calvin Tweeks." Judith matched up the name with a Sunday afternoon TV image of rugged bellicosity, tearing apart the opposition by merely breathing on them. "The nose guard?" She saw Lance gesture in the affirmative. "He was a great player. I didn't realize your sister had been married to *that* Tweeks."

"She's been married to a lot of guys," Lance said matter-of-factly. "It's hard to keep track."

The tea kettle whistled. Judith poured water into a plastic basin, took the towel from Lance, soaked it, and gingerly handed it back. "Speaking of weddings," she said, trying to sound casual, "what year were your parents married?"

To a keener mind, the question might have seemed odd, even cheeky. But Lance evinced neither curiosity nor resentment. "Gosh, let me think . . ." Judith girded herself for the effort, half expecting to hear wheels grind and motors whir. "I was born in 1945 and Gwen in 1948, so they must have been married in 1944."

Judith didn't try to cope with Lance's rationale, but took him at his word. The date made sense; even if Otto's divorce from Gloria hadn't been of the quickie variety, it should have gone through by '44. "Was your father in the service then?" she asked, hoping to sound guileless.

Lance shook his head. "Oh, no. He was deferred because of his allergies. And he was in the defense industry. He got extra ration book coupons for sugar and butter." There was a note of pride in Lance's voice as he boiled World War II down to the Brodie dinner table.

"That sounds very important. He must have done a fine job. Did he travel a lot?" Judith winced, aware that Lance's speech patterns were contagious, too.

Lance considered, rearranging the towel on his knee. "I don't remember much about the war. I wasn't alive then. But I know he went to Hollywood because he got Betty Grable's autograph."

A few more blank spaces were being filled in, Judith told herself. But she sensed that Lance was a blank for further information about Otto's wartime past. She changed the subject, hoping to catch Lance off guard, if it were remotely possible that he was on guard in the first place. "Were those men you met last night your new partners?" she asked, again trying to sound casual.

To Judith's surprise, Lance turned evasive. "In a way." He paused, flexing his leg. "That heat helps. The knee feels better. After more than ten years, you'd think it would stop hurting.'' He stared at the towel as if he expected it to apologize.

"Did Calvin Tweeks sell out his share of Club Stud when he and Gwen broke up?' inquired Judith, her eyes on the pancake batter.

"Yes,'' replied Lance, carefully putting the towel by the sink. ''He felt it wouldn't be right for us to go on being in business together. Not family anymore. Calvin's a very deep man.''

"Of course,'' said Judith. ''That's understandable. But it's a shame they couldn't make a go of the marriage. Still,'' she continued, remembering that Calvin Tweeks had been the son of a black Alabama sharecropper, ''even in this day and age, interracial marriages can be difficult.''

"That's true,'' said a somber Lance. ''They had their problems. Bound to, I guess. That's what happens when a Presbyterian marries a Southern Baptist.''

NINE

JUDITH WASN'T SURPRISED that Gwen arrived almost immediately after Lance went back upstairs to shower and shave. Wearing a gaudy kimono that could have been entered in the color sweepstakes with Madame Gushenka's veils and Gertrude's housecoats, Gwen sailed into the kitchen like a giant beachball caught in a wind.

"Coffee, thank heavens!" exclaimed Gwen, clasping her hands together as if in prayer. "I hardly slept a wink! This is all too awful! That policeman upstairs watches me so suspiciously, I know he thinks I did it."

"You had a motive," Judith said offhandedly, though her eyes studied Gwen's reaction closely enough.

The china-blue gaze grew very wide, but Gwen was more thrilled than offended. "You've heard? Isn't it too unbelievable? And Ellie, besides!" She put a hand to her mouth and giggled. "Dash does get around. Don't you just love a man with a past?"

A past, maybe, thought Judith, but not a whole damned family. Putting her personal reservations aside, she noted that Dash had confessed to Gwen as well as

Ellie and the police. Judith poured coffee for both of them as they sat down at the dinette table. Cozying up to Gwen in an attempt to create an intimate kaffeeklatsch atmosphere, Judith put on her most sympathetic smile. "It must have been a shock. You didn't know about Wanda—or Ellie—before last night, I take it?"

"Not about Ellie! Who would have guessed?" Gwen was quite agog, a willing victim of Judith's confiding manner. "But Wanda—well, I knew Dash had had an unhappy marriage and that she was a nurse. I don't remember that he ever called her by name. They were together only a year or so." She inclined her head, her face wreathed in doleful commiseration.

Through the kitchen window, Judith could see the fog nestled between the houses. It was lighter now, the sun coming up over the mountains to the east of the city. An ordinary winter morning, she reflected, but marred by extraordinary events at Hillside Manor.

"Dash is certainly an attractive man," remarked Judith with what she hoped was an appreciative tone of voice. "Where did you meet him?"

Gwen took a sip of coffee and donned a coy expression. "It was really quite touching. I was by the pool at my hotel in Mazatlán last fall. All of a sudden, this gorgeous hunk sort of sidled up to me. I could feel the animal magnetism," she breathed, speaking more softly, with her eyes focused somewhere in the direction of Judith's sink plunger, "and my pulses throbbed with excitement. I turned"—the china-blue eyes grew enormous—"and there he was, all bronzed skin and taut muscles! He asked if I were Guinevere Arthur." She paused to give Judith a demure glance. "Of course, I generally prefer to remain anonymous, especially on vacation, but this, my dear, was no ordinary fan!" Gwen leaned back against the chair, her face aglow at the recollection. "He had a copy of my latest book—they'd had them for sale at the hotel gift shop—and he wanted it autographed!" She beamed at Judith, as elated as if she'd won the Nobel prize for literature.

"How . . . interesting that a man would read that particular genre," Judith remarked, choosing her words carefully.

Gwen gave Judith a knowing look. "You'd be surprised, my dear," she drawled. "However," Gwen continued more briskly, "in Dash's case, he had a special reason. My last book was about a circus juggler who had been stranded in the wilderness—I called it *Without His Balls*—and Dash had known someone dear to him who'd been with the circus. So my novel had real meaning for him." She gave a shrug of her wide shoulders. "That's how we met. It was very romantic."

To Judith's logical mind, it was very calculated. Had Dash hit on Gwen because he thought she was rich, or had he a more devious motive—like Ellie? But could Dash have known that Guinevere Tweeks was related to Eleanor Carver? Judith found it unlikely, but not impossible.

Gwen was rattling on about nights under the stars, and mariachi bands, and tequila for two. Judith listened with half an ear, until Gwen said something that made her stop short: ". . . friend wasn't a juggler, actually, but a fortune-teller. Oh!"

Judith stared at Gwen, who had put a hand to her mouth again. "I never thought of it until now! He must have meant Wanda!"

"She must have moonlighted when she wasn't being a nurse," Judith said as she poured more coffee.

But Gwen was frowning. "No—whoever it was had traveled as part of a circus family. I gathered she was very young, a child in the beginning. In fact, now that it's all coming back to me, it was a sad story, a little girl raised by foster parents. They went from town to town, except for the winter, and never had a real home. When she got older, she ran away. Dash joked about that, saying this was the only person he'd ever heard of who had run off to un-join the circus." Gwen giggled. "Dash is very witty."

And I'm Elvis, thought Judith. But to Gwen, she offered a smile that indicated she was deeply impressed. "If that was Wanda, I wonder what happened to her, uh, real parents.''

"Dash might know," said Gwen, but she sounded dubious.

Judith knew what had become of Otto; she was trying to puzzle out the fate of Gloria St. Cloud when a noise at the front door caught her attention. She excused herself, got up, and hurried through the dining room and entry hall. The policeman who had been on duty in the living room was already there, opening the door to Joe Flynn and Officer Price. Behind them on the sidewalk, a contingent from the media stood in a swirl of fog, cameras and tape recorders at the ready.

"Don't worry," Joe said to Judith as he breezed across the threshold, "I told them that if they bothered you, I'd have them all arrested for dangling their modifiers in public."

Judith wasn't completely assuaged, but was so relieved to see Joe that she disregarded the media gathering under the maple tree. "I've got a lot to tell you," she said under her breath, leading him out to the kitchen. "But I'm not saying a word until you tell me a few things."

"Such as?" inquired Joe, nodding to Gwen, who was still ensconced at the dinette table.

"Later," murmured Judith, her eyes darting in Gwen's direction. "Coffee? Pancakes? Ham? Eggs?"

"Please. Orange juice, too. Powdered sugar instead of syrup, and the eggs aren't over easy but—"

"—cooked in one-sixteenth of an inch of water with the lid on," finished Judith. "The effect is the same, but the yolks don't get broken because the eggs don't have to be turned over." She stood by the stove with her hand on the griddle, giving Joe a gimlet eye. "The fact is, you learned that trick from my mother."

Leaning against the door between the kitchen and the dining room, Joe grinned sheepishly. "I'd forgotten that. For twenty-some years, I've claimed it as my own invention."

"Did you teach it to your wife?" Judith didn't look up from basting the griddle with bacon fat.

"Get serious," responded Joe. "The closest Herself ever came to cooking was when she set my Yves St. Laurent tie on fire."

"Hmmm." Judith let the subject drop. Gwen was wide-eyed, trying to make sense out of a conversation that was clearly not typical between detective and suspect.

Joe and Woodrow Price headed off to confer with the policemen who had stayed inside the house. Judith began cooking in earnest as she heard sounds overhead indicating that other guests besides Gwen and Lance were astir. Wielding frying pans, coffee cups, juice glasses, and silverware, she wished that Renie was among them. Unfortunately, her cousin was the type of high-energy person who could go like a whirlwind and accomplish ten things in the time it would take somebody else to do two—but once she stopped and took a deep breath, she collapsed like an old umbrella. Judith would be lucky if Renie woke up before ten.

In the next half hour, ham was fried, eggs were cooked, pancakes were flipped, and juice was poured. The coffeepot made the rounds several times as Gwen, Lance, Harry, Dash, and Otto breakfasted around the Grover kitchen table. Dash seemed unperturbed by the night's revelations, Harry looked as if he'd just finished up a ten-hour bilateral hip replacement, and Otto had gone from ornery to surly.

"Damnedest bunch of horse-pooky I ever heard," he grumbled into his soft-boiled eggs. "Stuck in this old barn while these damned fool policemen screw up. None of 'em probably ever arrested anybody for anything more dangerous than jaywalking."

"Now Daddy," cooed Gwen, offering her father more ham, "try to think of this as an adventure! Like one of those mystery books where everybody is trapped for the weekend in an English country mansion."

Judith didn't wait to hear Otto's reply, but pushed the tea wagon out into the front parlor where Joe and Officer

Price were waiting. Blowing an errant strand of hair from her eyes, Judith dished up pancakes for Joe, and toast for Price. She had just set out a small crock of boysenberry jam when Renie stumbled into the room, looking like she'd been run over by a Metro bus.

"Finally wake up?" Judith asked casually, well inured to her cousin's early morning state of physical and mental wreckage. "Coffee?"

"Snrphm," said Renie, bleary-eyed. Judith noted her sweatshirt was on backward.

"That means," Judith translated for Joe and Price, "that she would certainly enjoy a steaming cup, with just a wee bit of sugar." She gave her cousin a cloying smile. "Isn't that right, little Renie?"

"Frgcu," muttered Renie, moving toward the table.

"I won't bother translating that one," cooed Judith, pushing the tea wagon aside and sitting down. They were crowded around the little pedestal table: Joe, dapper in a navy blazer and gray flannel sacks; Officer Price, a stolidly reassuring presence in regulation blue; Renie, showing signs of emerging from her stupor; and Judith, seemingly composed except for the telltale shifting of her chair. "Now, gentlemen," she said, "tell us all or I'll have the Rankers bring Mother home."

Joe evinced mock horror. "If I made a threat like that, you'd charge me with police brutality. To be honest, I can't tell you a lot because the M.E. isn't finished yet." He paused to swallow about half his coffee all at once. "It's pretty screwed up. There was cyanide in Wanda's tea and Otto's inhaler was laced with Nembutal."

"Jeez!" exclaimed Judith, wondering if Joe knew about the father-daughter connection. "You mean somebody wanted to get rid of both Otto and Wanda?"

"We don't know," Joe said, the green eyes apparently frank. "Who else would use Otto's inhaler but Otto? As for Wanda's tea, it's unlikely that she drank enough of it to kill her. In fact, the lab people figure that even if she'd downed the whole cup, it wouldn't have been a lethal dose.''

''Any amount of cyanide sounds lethal to me,'' Judith murmured. ''But why two poisons?''

Joe polished off an egg and eyed Judith with a strange little smirk. ''Three. Wanda died from some poison other than cyanide or Nembutal. For one thing, she didn't use the inhaler, and again, it probably wasn't a fatal amount. So either we've got a rank amateur loose, or a random poisoner.''

''Wait.'' The croaking voice emanated from Renie, whose eyes had finally opened all the way. ''After dinner, Otto said something about having the wrong cup. He'd ended up with the English bone china, the one that was meant for Wanda.''

Joe and Officer Price both stared at Renie. ''How'd that happen?'' asked Joe.

Renie and Judith exchanged fretful looks. ''I took out the tea and coffee,'' Renie began, then stopped short. ''I had help, actually. Ellie and Mavis.''

''Ah.'' Joe's red eyebrows lifted slightly. ''Now how— and when—did they both get so domestic?''

''Ellie needed some aspirin,'' Judith said, striving to get the sequence of events in order. ''That was after Wanda had started her routine. No, she'd joined them at that point, but was eating dessert. Ellie said she found it all very bizarre and had gotten a headache. Then she offered to take out the cups.''

''And Mavis had to remove her contacts,'' Renie chimed in. ''She helped serve, too.'' Her brown eyes clouded over. ''I can't honestly remember whether I gave Otto and Wanda their cups or not.''

Joe was rummaging in his black leather attache case. ''Here,'' he said, pulling out the diagram they'd made the night before of the table arrangement. ''Otto was at the head, with Wanda on his right, then Mavis. Ellie was at his left. It would have been pretty hard for anybody else to get at the cups. Unless someone came into the kitchen earlier.''

"Otto and Oriana did," said Judith, "but I'm not even sure I had the cups out then. And the extra one came from the breakfront in the dining room.''

"I'm pretty sure I gave Wanda the floral cup," Renie muttered, more to herself than the others. "But maybe I gave it to Ellie to carry out. Or Mavis." She mulled for almost a minute while Joe and Price studied the diagram with Judith looking over their shoulders. "Damn," Renie admitted, "I honestly don't remember."

Joe's expression was patient, if pained. "The cup itself may have been a genuine mistake—but the cyanide was intentional. The question is, who was it meant for—and who put it there? What did Ellie and Mavis drink?''

Judith reflected. "Ellie had tea, Mavis, coffee. But Mavis carried out the tea. Or some of it." She sought confirmation from Renie. "Right?''

"Right." Renie blinked. "I think.''

A muscle tensed along Joe's jawline. "You'd both be terrific on the witness stand. A pair of minds like oatmeal mush." He chewed his pancakes and studied the diagram again. "We're pretty limited to four people, the two who helped carry out the cups also being the same pair who were sitting at that end of the table.''

"I take it you're not eliminating Wanda?" asked Judith.

"Somebody else already did," Joe pointed out, but he wasn't smiling. "No, it's possible that Wanda came here for the sole purpose of killing someone at the dinner party. Either she screwed up, or somebody got to her first. But not," he cautioned, waving his fork, "necessarily the victim she'd had in mind.''

"Nembutal's a sleeping drug, right?" queried Judith, pouring the last of the coffee for Joe and Officer Price while Renie held out her empty mug and put on a pitiful face. "But how do you get hold of cyanide?''

The question hung on the air as a crash emanated from the kitchen. Judith jumped up, but Renie was closer to the door. "I'll subdue the guests. I have to get more coffee anyway."

Woody Price had also gotten up. "She forgot the pot," he said. "Maybe I'd better go see what's going on."

Joe nodded to his subordinate, then grinned at Judith. "Your mother probably parachuted into the pantry." He didn't miss a beat: "You always looked terrific in red."

"A good thing," murmured Judith, feeling the color rise in her cheeks. "Joe, I've pulled a rotten trick." She took a deep breath, then suddenly relaxed. "No. I haven't, actually. A delivery came for you last night after you left, and I put it in my room for safekeeping."

The red eyebrows lifted. "Then, while it was being closely guarded by your trustworthy self, you looked through whatever it was to make sure there had been no mistake and/or that everything was intact. Is that about right?" he asked in an ironic tone.

"Well, of course." Judith turned wide dark eyes on his amused face. "Scooters, the delivery service I use, once brought a cake from Begelman's Bakery for an eighty-fifth birthday party I hosted. It was supposed to be for the Ericsons' Aunt Bea, and her name was written in cursive, only Duncan, the delivery boy, fell off his bicycle coming up the hill, and part of the 'A' in 'Aunt' came off on the lid, so it looked like a 'C'. I was mortified," Judith recalled with a little sniff of remorse. "Naturally, I've checked everything that comes through these doors ever since." She gave him her most virtuous smile.

"I should think so!" Joe matched her, phony for phony. "Now that I understand all that historical background, I think I'll dispense with asking what happened to Aunt Bea and ask instead," he continued, his voice rising, "what the hell you found in the goddamned envelope from Wanda's apartment?"

Leaning back in the chair, Judith assumed her usual unruffled manner and relayed the contents as concisely as possible. Joe listened without comment. When she had finished, he drummed his fingers on the table and stared off toward a tapestry Judith had stitched while she was expecting Mike.

"So Wanda might have had a motive for killing Otto," remarked Joe after a long pause. "And, if they knew who she really was, all of them could have had money as a motive for killing her. Except Otto, of course, who may have just wanted to keep her a deep, dark secret." With a certain amount of longing, he glanced at his empty coffee cup and stood up. "All we've gotten out of the L.A. Police Department so far is that Wanda had no record and that she worked at St. Peregrine's from 1953 until November 1 of last year, mostly in surgery. Come on," he gestured at Judith, "let's have a look."

Their progress through the entry hall was impeded by a glimpse of Officer Price and Harvey, who were wedged in the dining room door holding Lance between them. "He fell," said Price. "Just a twisted knee. Dr. Carver checked him out. We're putting him on the sofa." Cautiously, he and Harvey bore Lance's considerable weight toward the living room just as Ellie and Mavis appeared on the staircase.

"What's happening?" yelled Mavis, leaning on the banister.

Lance craned his neck, offering his wife a pained smile. "I tripped. I fell. I hurt my good knee."

"Oh, great," groaned Mavis, dashing down the stairs and leaving Ellie in the dust. "Lance, I can't leave you alone for a minute! You're worse than our children!"

The living room had been vacated by the downstairs policeman, who had presumably been dismissed along with his upstairs colleague. Judith started to get an icepack from the refrigerator but was forestalled by Otto, with Gwen plastered to his side. "This place is hexed," he asserted, scowling at Judith. "I want out of here while I'm still in one piece!"

Joe intervened. "Not quite yet, Mr. Brodie. We still don't have the M.E.'s official report. It'll probably come through this afternoon."

"The hell it will!" exploded Otto. "By then, at least two more of us will be dead and the rest half maimed! I want my lawyer!"

"What's all that?" shrieked Mavis, oblivious to her father-in-law's demands. Having been reassured by Harvey that Lance merely needed to keep off his feet for a bit, she was at the dining room bay window, her head stuck through the lace curtains. "Look!" she yelled, "it's half the local press corps, including Daphne Huggins from KINE! That bird-witted bitch wants my job! I'll kill her!" She whirled about, hanging onto the curtain like Salome down to her last veil. "Why the hell are they all over at the next-door neighbor's?"

Judith joined Mavis at the window, curtain and all. The fog was lifting and the Rankers's front porch was in clear view. Radio, TV, and newspapers reporters were clustered on the broad steps while Arlene Rankers regaled them with all the aplomb of a seasoned stateswoman. Behind her, Gertrude leaned on her walker and exuded great clouds of blue smoke.

"Oh, damnation!" breathed Judith. "Arlene will give them sixteen kinds of misinformation and Mother will end up as Lucrezia Borgia!"

"She looks more like Catherine de Medici," said Renie, who had finally come from out of the kitchen where she had been cleaning up after Lance's tumble. "Hey, look, my sweatshirt's on backward!"

"So's your brain," snapped Judith, then immediately turned repentant. "Sorry, coz, let's go upstairs with Joe and Officer Price. You've missed out on a lot by sleeping your life away."

"But I was just going to get some breakfast," protested a crestfallen Renie. "Can't it wait?"

"No." Judith caught Joe's eye as he gave up his battle to keep Mavis from going outside to confront Daphne Huggins. Dragging Price away from Otto's nonstop verbal abuse, Joe followed the two women up to the family quarters.

Judith fumbled with the key she always wore around her neck along with her Miraculous Medal. "I could have sworn I locked this," she breathed, turning the key a second time. Even as she crossed the foyer, her heart sank. It came as no surprise that when she opened the door to her bedroom, she found that Wanda's personal effects were gone.

Joe was on the verge of apoplexy. "You are an idiot!" he exploded, his face crimson. "How could you pull such a stupid stunt?"

For the first time since shedding a few perfunctory tears for Dan, Judith felt like crying. "You weren't here, you'd just left for downtown, I thought . . ."

"I didn't mean taking the evidence in the first place," Joe roared, pacing the room like a bull at a Sunday corrida. "I meant leaving the goddamned door unlocked! Who knew you had this stuff besides"—his flashing eyes rested on Renie—"the other idiot?"

Judith gulped while Renie coiled as if to pounce. "Ellie was here," Judith said, "but I don't think she noticed . . ."

Officer Price got up from a kneeling position at the outer door. "Sir—I'm not sure, but this lock may have been tampered with."

Joe whirled around on his heel. "Oh, yeah?" he said sharply. He went to the door, bending down, hands resting on flannel-clad knees. "Check for prints, Woody." He looked up at Judith and Renie, somewhat calmer now. "Don't touch anything."

But the cousins were practically tripping over each other as they charged the dormer window to investigate the source of sudden commotion from down below. In the middle of a circle formed by the visiting press, Mavis was applying a headlock to Daphne Huggins. Daphne retaliated by grabbing Mavis around the knees. The week-night and the weekend anchors for KINE-TV went down in a heap on the Rankers's front lawn.

Mavis's Calvin Klein shirt and slacks were damp with

grass stains. Daphne's Anne Klein blazer and skirt had lost their crisp cut. The women rolled about on the ground, clawing, scratching, and kicking. Their media colleagues teetered on the fringe in mixed attitudes of shock and fascination. At last, two uniformed policemen, a TV cameraman, and the crime reporter from the morning daily broke up the Battle of the Kleins.

Mavis's threats and Daphne's curses bounced off the dormer window like so much buckshot. "I hope the rival stations got that on tape," Judith said with feeling. "Maybe it'll push Hillside Manor into the background."

But the matter at hand was still uppermost in Joe's mind. "I'll talk to Ellie first. Meanwhile," he said to Price as they headed downstairs, "check out the amnesia case and that hit-and-run in L.A. Give Woody the dates, Jude-girl."

Wincing at the long-ago nickname, Judith dispensed the information to Officer Price. Returning to the kitchen with Renie, she found that order had been restored, the dinette table was vacant, and the old school clock stood at nine. Dash sauntered in just as Renie was putting some ham on to fry for herself.

"Quite a morning, huh?" he said, a master of understatement, with his hands in the pockets of his yellow linen slacks. "Some night, too. I suppose I'm at the top of the suspect list." Despite his words, he seemed remarkably cheerful.

"You certainly get around," Judith responded, setting a place for the newest arrival and relying on shock tactics. "Wanda, Mrs. Carver. Mavis, too, I gather. You didn't marry that one, did you?"

Dash was unperturbed by Judith's direct approach. "I didn't have to." He actually winked. "It was a fair trade. I had something she wanted and she had something I wanted. We swapped." He shrugged under his green polo shirt.

"Really," said Judith, pouring juice and coffee. "What was that?"

"I don't suppose Mavis is keeping any secrets right

now," said Dash with the hint of a furrow on his tanned brow. "She was a reporter on the *Daily Bruin,* the UCLA student newspaper. She wanted a 'scoop,' as they used to say. So I scooped her. About ten, twelve times. She'd never been scooped before. I think she liked it." His smile was ingenuous.

"I hope the, uh, story she got was worth it," remarked Judith, wrestling the frying pan away from Renie and breaking eggs for Dash. "She must have been a real aggressive reporter even then."

"She was." Dash sniffed the homey kitchen air which somehow murder had not sullied. Or, Judith thought irrelevantly, grease defies even death. "That ham smells great," he said. "Sunny-side-up on the eggs. Can you make the pancakes silver-dollar size?"

Ignoring the grinding of Renie's teeth, Judith complied with half a dozen spoonfuls of batter around the griddle. Out in the entry hall, Mavis's irate voice erupted over the soothing noises made by Gwen and Lance. Storming upstairs, she vowed to call everyone at KINE from her producer to the chairman of the board. Dash listened with a little half smile, then shook his head.

"A real firecracker under that cool exterior," he commented. "Truth is, she's wound up too tight. I guess she always was, which is why she married Lance."

Dash's perception caught Judith off guard. Perhaps there was more to the man than sleazy charm and no socks. "What was the story?" she asked, flipping pancakes and making a face at the whimpering Renie.

"The '66 Rose Bowl. UCLA versus Michigan State. The Bruins should have lost by ten, not won by two. But some people can't be bribed." Dash seemed oddly dismayed by the idea.

"Basic integrity," said Judith, setting Dash's plate in front of him.

"Basic stupidity," retorted Dash with a baleful look at Judith. "Some people are too dumb to bribe."

Before Judith could react, the kitchen door swung open,

revealing a tremulous Ellie. "Oh! Ri— Dash!" She put a hand to her flat chest. "Excuse me, I was just going to get a little something."

"Here," said Renie, who had returned to the stove, "take my ham, my eggs, my—"

"Oh, no," protested Ellie. "Just toast, please. And coffee. I have no appetite." Her face flushed. "I've just spent ten minutes with that cagey police detective. He actually grilled me!"

"About what?" inquired Dash, pulling out a chair for Ellie.

"I'm not sure," she said, apparently bewildered. "Something in Mrs. McMonigle's room." She glanced up at her hostess. "Pictures? Clippings? I told him we'd only chatted. I don't think he believed me."

"Now, Ellie," soothed Dash, "you're the most sincere woman I've ever met. Flynn's a cop, he likes to make people squirm. Believe me, I ought to know."

Across the table, their gazes met and held. The spell was shattered by Mavis, still rumpled, but outwardly composed. "Dog-eat-dog," she averred, barely acknowledging Dash and Ellie. "Oh, thanks!" she said, grabbing Renie's plate. "I timed that just right. How'd you know I like sugar instead of syrup on my pancakes?"

Renie debated decking the most recent breakfast thief. The punchout with Daphne Huggins might have sapped Mavis's strength, but she was four inches taller and ten pounds heavier than Renie. And Renie was debilitated by hunger. With a sigh of resignation, she stood on her tiptoes and reached for the Shredded Wheat.

"Well, Dash," said Mavis, "police spokespersons tell me you knew the dead woman. Intimately."

"That's the best way to know most women," Dash replied with a sly grin.

"Skunk!" Mavis flared, caught Ellie's wide gray gaze, and clenched her teeth.

Ellie stopped nibbling on her toast. "What are you talking about?"

"What do you care?" snapped Mavis. "What I'd like to know is what name Dash—or Rico here—used when he married Wanda."

"That's an easy one," Dash responded, setting his empty plate aside. "Artie Allegro. Nickname Ankles, for obvious reasons." He pushed back his chair, placed one sockless leg over his other knee, and wiggled his foot. "Get it?"

"Keep it." Mavis curled her lip over her coffee cup. "You took that one after doing five-to-ten in Soledad, right?"

The chilling look Dash gave Mavis was so fleeting that Judith almost thought she'd imagined it. "Two and a half. I got out early for good behavior. And I was framed," he added with dignity. "Guilt by association. It can happen," he observed with a glance at Ellie.

"It happened twice." Joe Flynn was in the kitchen, holding the swinging door behind him. "Conspiracy, racketeering, bribery, fraud, everything but forgetting the words to the 'Star Spangled Banner.' After Soledad, three years in San Quentin. A parole violation for an unscheduled trip to Europe. Who was your travel agent? The Mafia? I'll bet they booked you into Sicily."

Judith had to admit that Dash's self-control was exemplary. He regarded Joe much like one fraternity brother ragging another. "Northern Italy only. Milan, Florence, Lake Como. Some shrines, of course. You ever been, Flynn? The Irish are hot for shrines. When they sober up, they get all weepy."

"Shrines!" blurted Judith, oblivious to Joe's rising ire. "The last time Joe was in church, he got sick and threw up in the collection basket!"

Joe glared at Judith. "I had the twelve-hour flu. And how the hell do you know the last time I went to church?"

"Prison!" exclaimed Ellie, already having dropped her toast in her coffee. "Oh, Dash, were you really framed?"

"Like a Rembrandt, and just as deserving," Mavis put in viciously. "I'm surprised he's not still there."

"Don't tell me Herself got all three of her other marriages annulled!" railed Judith, facing Joe with hands on hips. "What did she do, take the Pope out for drinks?"

Joe was livid, his eyebrows bristling, the gold flecks striking dangerous sparks in the green eyes. "Put a cork in the personal crap! This is a murder investigation, Mrs. McMonigle!" He stopped, aware that the others had interrupted their wrangling to listen. Except, it seemed, for Renie, who was stuffing her face with Shredded Wheat and making chewing noises that sounded like an army marching on gravel. Joe gripped Judith's arm. "I'm the one getting the annulment," he said in a voice both low and fierce. "Herself can get stuffed."

TEN

JUDITH'S DARK EYES had grown very wide. Under the red sweater, her heart gave a lurch. She had a terrible desire to laugh out loud, but just stood there in the middle of the kitchen and wondered why she felt as if an enormous weight had been lifted from her shoulders.

Then, as reality set in, she recognized that whether Joe and his wife were separated, divorced, annulled, or in quarantine had nothing to do with her. The only thing that really mattered when it came to Joe Flynn was that he should wrap up his murder investigation and blow away the clouds of doom that hung over Hillside Manor. And, if he couldn't manage to do that quickly enough to save Judith's reputation, then she intended to do it for herself. With a lift of her chin, Judith took a step backward. Joe dropped his hand.

"Good luck," she said lightly. "The archdiocese has tightened some of the loopholes in canon law." She had no idea what she was talking about, but it sounded good.

"I've got some loopholes of my own to close up," said Joe, his color back to normal as he moved briskly to the phone on the wall. "I'm going to jack up that M.E. He's taking too long."

Everything was taking too long for Judith. Hurriedly, she wiped her hands off on a dish towel and excused herself to her guests. To her relief, the living room was empty, Lance apparently having limped upstairs with Harvey's help. Judith sunk down on the window seat next to the bookcase and pulled out an almanac. She had just flipped to the index when Renie appeared, dollops of milk on her sweatshirt and an anxious expression on her face.

"Are you okay?"

Judith started to shrug off her cousin's concern, then took a deep breath. "Yeah, I think I am. I just had to escape for a couple of minutes. I keep feeling as if I'm riding a carousel that's out of control." She cradled the almanac against her bosom. "It's not just Joe . . . It's this whole mess. Every time somebody says or does something, instead of answering questions, new ones are posed. I need time to think, to sift everything through my mind." She paused, pressing her lips together and glancing out the window at the rose garden. The fog had finally cleared off, with patches of blue sky breaking through the glowering gray clouds. "It's quiet right now. Let's go upstairs and brainstorm."

Unimpeded for once by their guests, the cousins reached the sanctuary of Judith's bedroom under the eaves. Kicking off her shoes, Judith flopped down on the bed and was sorely tempted to stretch out for a nap. She had been up now for over twenty-seven hours. It occurred to her that along about five a.m. she had gone beyond the point of giving in to fatigue and had advanced to the stage where sheer nerve takes over.

Renie was sprawled in the chair where Ellie had perched a few hours earlier. "Well? What does the almanac reveal? I hope it's more specific than Madame Gushenka."

"Football," muttered Judith, flipping to the latter part of the thick volume. "Rose Bowl games . . . Here it is,

1966, UCLA 14, Michigan State 12.'' She looked up from the fine print. ''You remember that game?''

''I sure do,'' said Renie with unexpected gusto. ''Don't you? Cousin Sue and Ken had just bought their house on the other side of the lake and she won five hundred dollars in a football pool. She bought that god-awful cut-velvet settee and those lamps with the safari shades.''

Judith grinned. ''Really hideous. And the house turned out to be an ex-brothel that smelled so bad they had to move out three months later.''

Renie nodded in amused reminiscence. ''That was after they tried to fumigate the place and the neighbors' goat wandered in and died of cyanide poisoning because he got into the—Oh, good grief!'' Renie's brown eyes locked with Judith's black gaze. ''The fumigating material had cyanide in it! Do you suppose that somebody got hold of the stuff they're using at the Brodies and popped it into the coffee cup?''

Judith thought for a moment. ''I don't know. I'll have to ask an expert. Like Dooley.'' She put the almanac aside and straightened up the rumpled comforter. ''What about the UCLA connection? So far, Ellie, Lance, Mavis, Dash, and Harvey have all gone to school there. We know Ellie and Dash were from the L.A. area. Maybe Mavis is, too.''

''She's very L.A.,'' said Renie, with the typical disparagement of a native Pacific Northwesterner. ''Aggressive. Ambitious. Hard-working. Not to mention being in what some would call a glamour job.''

''Right. Easy to check out. But how did Lance and Harvey get there?''

''I know that,'' said Renie brightly. ''Harvey did his undergraduate work at the university here, then went on to med school at UCLA. And Lance won a football scholarship. He majored in art because it was the only subject he could spell.''

''What about P.E.?'' Judith didn't wait for an answer to her own facetious question. ''How did you find all that out?''

''Actually,'' replied Renie, tucking her feet under her, ''I sort of pieced it together from remarks made while

Harvey was hauling Lance out from under the dinette table. Somehow, the subject came up, so I asked Ellie about it just now.''

''All of a sudden this place looks like a Bruin reunion,'' mused Judith. ''Who do we know who went to UCLA?''

''Cousin Marty did, for a while,'' replied Renie.

Judith looked askance. ''Marty went everywhere, including Alfred U.''

''He made that up,'' insisted Renie.

''No, he didn't. It's in New York. Anyway, he'd be too young for this crew.''

''We could call Westwood,'' Renie suggested.

''And ask what? If the dean of students at UCLA remembered how Dash and Harvey and Mavis and Ellie got along on campus?'' Judith gave her cousin a withering look. ''Besides, it's Saturday. Nobody would be around.'' She stopped, some shard of memory pricking at her brain. ''There was something—somebody—else . . . Dr. Edelstein, that's who. His obituary said he'd gone to UCLA.''

''Gosh,'' pouted Renie, ''I'm feeling left out. I knew I should have gone away to school.''

Judith ignored her cousin's lament and frowned. ''I'm not sure the UCLA connection helps us much. Ellie met Dash there, I gather, and Harvey. Dash met Mavis and Lance. And Lance and Mavis met each other. But it appears Ellie didn't know Dash knew Mavis—or Lance at the time. And Edelstein is way out in left field.'' She straightened the stack of books on her nightstand and wondered if she'd ever again feel free to cozy up under the covers with a good page-turner. ''How'd Lance fall down in the first place? That gimpy knee, I suppose.'' She paused, looking back down at the almanac. ''So Dash tries to bribe Lance to throw the Rose Bowl, or at least get a big point spread in Michigan State's favor. Lance can't—or won't, and UCLA wins by two, which must have thrown the oddsmakers for a loop. Lots of people lose a bundle and maybe Dash has to knuckle under to the mob—or at least to his father, Dukes Frascatti. Make sense?''

"As much as anything else about now," said Renie, pulling her sweatshirt over her head and putting it back on the right way. "So what 'family' was Oriana talking about on the back stairs with Dash? A real one, or gangsters?"

Judith tried to remember exactly what Oriana had said. "She mentioned blackmail, stabbed to the heart, and—what was it?—no sense of family. That sounds more like blood relatives than mobsters."

"In this case, maybe both." Renie ran a hand through her short brown hair. "I wonder what Oriana's maiden name was."

"Bustamanti," said Judith. "At least that's the name she sang under. What are you thinking of?"

"Well, they're both of Italian descent," Renie pointed out. "They could be related."

"They don't look alike," said Judith dubiously.

"Neither do we."

"True. Cousins, maybe?"

Renie shrugged. "Dash was in Italy. Maybe Oriana was singing there. Do you still get *Opera News?*"

Judith shook her head. "I had to give it up years ago as a luxury I couldn't afford, along with toothpaste and shoes." She gave her cousin a wry look. "Then, after I started the B&B, I couldn't listen to the Saturday Met broadcasts because of the weekend guests. I've got all my old copies, though, down in the basement."

"Let's look through them," suggested Renie. "It's a long shot, but we might find out something about Oriana in the international reviews."

Judith agreed, then suddenly bolted off the bed. "My God! Where is Oriana now? She never came down for breakfast!"

At a gallop, Judith and Renie headed down to the second floor. A multitude of grisly scenarios swam before her mind's eye: Oriana poisoned in her bed, Oriana strangled with the drapery cord, Oriana shot with a .357 magnum. The prospect of another murder, had been kept at bay. Yet any killer who had dared to strike once wouldn't hesitate the second time around. Ellie had suggested as much. Judith's heart was pounding as hard as her feet when they reached the hallway and heard the strains of the Habañera floating out from the near bathroom.

"Thank God!" breathed Judith, leaning against the door that led to Otto and Oriana's room. "She's never sounded so good!" As Judith let her shoulders slump in relief, the door creaked open, almost causing her to lose her balance. "Well!" said Judith softly, eyeing her cousin with a conspiratorial look honed to perfection by almost a half century of practice. "Well, well."

Otto was obviously elsewhere, no policeman sat on duty in the wicker chair, and Oriana was still singing her head off. The cousins tiptoed into the bedroom. The Brodies had been given the largest of the guest rooms, with a king-sized bed in a reasonable facsimile of First Empire design and a chest of drawers and dressing table to match. Judith took the precaution of locking the bathroom door while Renie immediately began rummaging as quietly as possible through the Brodies' luggage.

The pickings were scant, as might be expected for an overnight stay. Otto's brown leather suitcase revealed only shaving gear, a change of underwear, socks, slippers, a silk bathrobe, and a pair of orange and green striped pajamas. Oriana's eelskin bag contained black lingerie, a tiger-print negligee, black satin mules, and the clothes she'd worn the previous night. Disappointed, Renie shook her head at Judith, who was plundering Oriana's purse.

"Ah!" mouthed Judith, waving a medicine bottle and tapping at the label. Renie pointed to her eyes, indicating that she didn't have her glasses. "Nembutal, Oriana's prescription," whispered Judith, unscrewing the lid. She showed the capsules to Renie. "Easy to use."

Oriana launched into the Seguidilla. Judith extracted a small leather-bound appointment book and flipped through the pages. Sure enough, Otto was right—Oriana had a message or facial scheduled virtually twice a week. "Pam-

pered,'' said Judith under her breath, holding out the book
to Renie, who looked blank.

A sound in the hall froze both women in place. Judith
threw the appointment book back into the purse while
Renie gave the suitcases a shove in the direction where
she'd found them. In virtual unison, the cousins dove under the bed just as the outside door opened.

''Pipe down,'' muttered Otto as he trotted across the
shag carpet to the bathroom. ''Hey, pizza puss, are you
coming out or do I have to borrow the other can?''

Oriana let out one last high note and turned off the
shower. ''I have to put my face on,'' she replied in a
petulant voice. ''Go down the hall.''

In the darkness under the bed, Judith tried to make herself as small as possible, and in the process, bumped
rumps with Renie. Grimacing, they held their breath. Otto
was moving past the bed, toward the bathroom door. Beneath the flounce that covered the mattress and box
springs, the cousins could just make out Otto's sturdy
walking shoes.

''Come on, lasagna lips, we're blowing this joint. Get
your tail in gear.'' He rattled the doorknob in impatience.

''I thought we had to stay,'' Oriana called back to her
husband.

''We do. We won't. Let's hit it. I'm about to have a
heart attack.''

The clatter of cosmetic implements could be heard in
the bathroom. When Oriana spoke, it was in a strained
voice. ''What do you mean? Are you ill?'' Judith thought
she sounded faintly hopeful.

''I'm at death's door,'' he replied jauntily. ''Come on,
come on, my little cannelloni. The day is dying, and so
am I. Or will be shortly.''

''Dio mio!'' exclaimed Oriana, once again the impas-
sioned diva. ''You've locked the door!''

''Huh?'' Otto could be heard jiggling the little bolt.
''Didn't mean to,'' he muttered, flinging the door open
for his wife. Judith and Renie watched Oriana's bare feet

with their painted toenails pad across the carpet. "Hey," said Otto as they both moved out of viewing range, "you smell good! You even look good without all that goop. Maybe I better put off my heart attack for a half hour or so. How about it, my ravishing ravioli?"

"Otto!" gasped Oriana in horror. "This is a house of mourning! How can you think such lustful thoughts?"

"Lustful, my butt!" responded Otto as Judith and Renie cringed under the bed. The idea of being captive voyeurs to the Brodies' lovemaking dismayed both cousins almost to the point of revealing themselves.

But Oriana had taken command even as she stepped into a pair of Midnight Haze stockings. "Now see here, Otto, you'd better explain yourself. What's this about a heart attack and leaving the house? How do you intend to deceive Harvey and all those policemen?"

"Hell," said Otto, apparently no longer on the scent of passion, "Harvey couldn't tell if that fortune-teller died from a stroke or a snakebite! As for the cops, they'll be too worried about another homicide to cause any problems. All we have to do is get out of here and into a hospital. After that, it's a cinch—we wait until the doctors and nurses disappear like they always do when you're really sick, and we sneak off to the airport."

"The airport!" Oriana dropped her silk blouse, then bent to pick it up a scant six inches from Judith's left foot. "Why? Where are we going?"

Otto didn't answer right away. His feet passed by the bed en route to the window. "It's clouding over again. Looks like more rain, maybe even snow by tonight. How about Portugal?"

"Otto!" Oriana's voice was sharp, all affection gone. "What are you running from? Don't tell me you . . . you're implicated in this sorry mess?"

"Hey, relax, pizza puss." The walking shoes rejoined the sheer stockinged feet. "We're all implicated just by being here. I didn't murder the blasted woman, I swear it. But I don't want to get mixed up in some second-rate scandal, okay?'' He was talking much faster than usual, his words punctuated by the rocking of his shoes from heel to toe. ''Let's face it, I'm no spring chicken. I came home from California to get off the merry-go-round. All this murder investigation claptrap could give me a coronary, see? Who needs it?''

''Well . . .'' Oriana seemed to be wavering. ''I don't like the idea of running away. It might appear to be an admission of guilt.''

''Bull.'' Otto planted his feet flat on the floor, then let out a terrible cry. ''Aaaargh! Aaaaarghhh! Ooof!'' He crashed onto the bed, sending mattress and springs crunching down on Judith and Renie. They both shuddered from the sensation, silently cursing bumped heads, backs and bottoms.

Oriana danced in place while Otto hissed at her from the bed: ''Move it, get help! Aaaargh!'' Judith and Renie could feel him writhing above them.

The stockinged feet disappeared but apparently stopped to put on shoes. Then the door banged open and Oriana went into a bravura performance. ''Help! Help! My husband's having a heart attack! Help!''

Officer Price and Gwen were first on the scene. The CPR that Judith had suggested for Madame Gushenka was attempted by the policeman amid Gwen's wails of alarm, Oriana's full-throated lamentations, and Otto's piteous groans. The bed rocked and quavered, while more pairs of feet appeared beneath the flounce, including Joe Flynn's loafers.

''Get an ambulance!'' he shouted. ''Where's Dr. Carver?''

Mavis's voice cut across the din. ''He's out in the back yard consulting with that nosy neighbor about her varicose veins. Ellie's with him.''

Somebody, probably Lance, judging from the hurried but halting step, went out to use the upstairs phone. The bed had stopped jumping as Otto took to gasping in a manner most feeble. The beleaguered cousins dared to catch their collective breaths even as Joe's right loafer pointed straight at Judith's nose.

"Everybody out of the room," Joe ordered. "We need space for the ambulance drivers. Keep the stairs clear. Mrs. Brodie," he began, then was forced to raise his voice again over Oriana's latest howl, "Mrs. Brodie, you can ride with your husband in the ambulance."

"Caro mio!" cried Oriana, dropping to her knees. "Live for your little pizza!" Judith, admiring the red crepe pleated skirt that floated on the carpet, wondered if Oriana had assumed the role of Mozart's Donna Anna at the side of the stricken Commendatore.

"I should come, too," insisted a tearful Gwen. "He's my daddy!"

"What's happened?" The voice from the vicinity of the door belonged to Harvey Carver. "Let me examine him! Maybe it's poison!"

"We'll ride with them, Harvey," said Ellie, her voice more wispy than ever. "Oh, poor Uncle Otto! How sad!"

"Out!" bellowed Joe. "We'll see who goes where when the emergency crew gets here. It's an ambulance, not a bus." But before he could further sort out the babbling Brodies, sirens wailed in the distance. Judith offered Renie a heartrending expression: The 911 squads must all know the route to Hillside Manor by rote.

Beneath the flounce, various pairs of feet moved away. Only Joe's remained, still too close to Judith for comfort. Otto's voice had lapsed into little squawks, resembling a sick chicken. "Check the stairs and hallways," said Joe, presumably to Price. He shifted his stance, turning his attention to the man on the bed. "Hang in there, help is on the way."

It was, in the form of two efficient ambulance drivers who gently but swiftly transferred Otto from bed to stretcher. Judith stared quizzically at Renie: Renie shook her head; Judith nodded. Their understanding was perfect.

Otto was already in the hall, but Joe had moved only a few inches, apparently keeping out of the ambulance attendants' way. With a mighty heave, Judith scraped herself across the carpet and stuck her head up from under the flounce.

"It's a fake!" she cried. "Stop him!"

"What the hell?" Joe's green eyes went wide as he shook himself like someone waking up from a bad dream. "Jeeezus!"

Awkwardly, Judith angled the rest of her body out from under the bed. "It's a ruse," she said doggedly. "Otto is headed for Portugal."

Regaining his composure, Joe grabbed Judith's arm and hauled her to her feet. His astonishment was giving way to comprehension. "Are you sure of that?"

"Yes," asserted Judith, dusting herself off. "He told Oriana he didn't kill Wanda but he wanted to avoid a scandal. Frankly, I think he's just hoping nobody finds out that Wanda was his daughter."

Joe straightened Judith's sweater, then brushed a strand of hair out of her eyes. "You look beat," he said. "Did you sleep at all last night?"

"No." Judith fought down a desire to give in to the luxury of letting someone take care of her. The truth was, she'd forgotten how. The irony was that the only man who had ever taken care of her was Joe. "But I'm okay. I have to be," she declared, more to herself than to him. "Hey, do something! Otto's getting away!"

Joe responded as if someone had broken a spell. He moved easily but swiftly to the hallway, calling for Officer Price. With a faint smile, Judith watched him disappear. Was Joe just exercising his usual Irish charm, or did he still care about her? He'd always been the kind of man who could make a woman, even a casual acquaintance, feel she was special. Musing on the mystery of men rather than of murder, Judith wandered to the window where she saw the latest battle erupting on the front walk between the police, the ambulance men, and the Brodies. The small cry for help could have come from any one of them, she thought, leaning on the mahogany headboard.

It actually came from Renie. Judith jumped when she

realized that her cousin was still under the bed. Dropping down on the carpet, she yanked up the flounce. "What are you doing down there?"

Renie's brown eyes glared from her flushed face. "I was trying to be tactful. Then I got stuck. My sweatshirt's caught on a damned nail. I kept waiting for you and Joe to rip off your clothes and bounce up and down on top of me."

"No such luck," said Judith, exerting considerable effort to extricate Renie. "The only ripping of clothes is what's happened to your sweatshirt. Want to borrow one of Mother's housecoats?"

Renie wriggled across the carpet and sat up, scowling at the jagged tear above the elbow. "Damn. I should have run off to Portugal with Otto. I might have been seduced by life's exotic pleasures—like food and clothing." She worked out the kinks in her back and neck, then wagged a finger at Judith. "That was almost as miserable under that bed as the time we shared an upper berth on the Super Chief going to New York."

"You slept at the head, I slept at the foot, and we kept kicking each other." Judith shook he head in reminiscence. "Then you woke me up at four in the morning so I could see Cleveland. I almost killed you."

"I thought it was interesting," said Renie, picking lint off her charcoal-gray pants. "I'd never seen Cleveland before."

Judith sneered. "I still haven't. I refused to look." Reluctantly, she returned to the window. The standardbearers of right seemed to be triumphing over the representatives of wrong. At least the ambulance drivers had stopped trying to stuff Otto into the rear of their vehicle. "Right now," remarked Judith, heading for the door, "I'd rather see Cleveland than this bunch. Come on, coz, bind up your wounds. We're heading back down into the fray."

ELEVEN

TEN MINUTES LATER, a much-chagrined Otto returned to the house. Joe had all but resorted to physical force in prying Otto off the stretcher. Oriana had played her part to the hilt, a regal Isolde flinging herself on her Tristan; Harvey had threatened to sue; and Gwen had succumbed to hysterics. But Joe prevailed, much to the entertainment of the neighbors, including the Rankers and Gertrude, who watched the latest incident from the front yard. Dooley strolled by, making a halfhearted attempt to conceal himself behind the maple tree's massive trunk.

"Wow," he said to Judith, as Otto was finally hauled back inside, "you sure have a lot of excitement around here! It's better than the movies!"

"I may end up with the only X-rated B&B in town," Judith muttered. " 'X' as in 'ex-owner.' " She gestured discreetly at Lance who was following Mavis back inside the house. "There's your mystery man from last night. He hurt his knee playing for the Hollywood Stars. Remember the team?"

But Dooley was obviously remembering something else. "That's not the dude I saw."

"What?" Judith stared at Dooley, then at Lance's back. "It has to be!"

"Uh-uh." Dooley was emphatic. "It was that one, over there." He nodded toward the ambulance where Dash was comforting a still-hysterical Gwen. "They're both tall, sure, but the football guy is broader. I don't make mistakes like that. I'm learning to be a trained observer." He spoke with pride, his voice cracking in the process.

Judith didn't doubt him. Maybe Dash had walked funny because it had been cold outside and he wasn't wearing socks. Obviously, the back yard had been a crowded place. She wondered how Lance and his business associates had avoided running into Dash and whoever he had been meeting in the dark. But she had to put the question aside for the moment. Otto might be a pain, but he was still a guest. With a weary tread, Judith climbed the four steps to the front porch and went back into the house.

Otto was holding court in the living room, protesting police brutality with as much vigor as Mavis had exhibited the previous night. Not only did he demand to be visited by his personal physician and his attorney, but insisted on breaking into Judith's liquor supply. His ruse might have been in vain, but he wasn't surrendering without a struggle.

"While Otto gets blotto, let's check out those magazines downstairs," Judith said to Renie. "Joe just told me he's got some information coming up from L.A. any minute."

"The hit-and-run and the amnesia story?" Renie asked as they descended to the basement.

"I guess." Judith flipped on the light switch, revealing a new gas furnace, the laundry area with a hamper full of linens, boxes marked Christmas Decorations, Easter baskets—the whole gamut of life and times in a family home combined with a business enterprise. Judith kept the various kinds of outdated reading material in three cartons next to the freezer. She dug down deep, then shook her head. "These are Mike's old car magazines and *Sports*

*Illustrated*s. My *Opera News*es must be in that box over there.''

''Hey,'' said Renie, ''let's check out the *SI*'s, too. Maybe we can research Lance.''

''Speaking of Lance,'' said Judith, pulling out a foot-high stack of musty periodicals, ''he wasn't the one Dooley saw last night. Dash was outside, also meeting a couple of peculiar people.''

Renie looked up from a cover showing Verdi in a top hat and muffler. ''Do you suppose that's who called him during dinner?''

Judith considered. ''Could be. I wonder who?''

''His parole officers, maybe,'' suggested Renie with only token interest. ''Lordy, you've got a lot of these things. What years do you think Oriana was singing in Europe?''

''I'm guessing. She's got to be in her forties. So let's figure the late 1960s or early 1970s. If so, judging from what Joe said about Dash's history, he would have had to have been abroad either just before or after he was married to Wanda. Start with 1967.'' Judith returned to sorting out the *Sports Illustrated*s. ''Ah! A pro football preview issue for 1979! That was the first year Mike had a subscription.''

''We gave it to him for his birthday,'' recalled Renie. ''Your mother always hid the swimsuit issue.''

''*I* always hid it,'' said Judith. ''I didn't want Dan to nag me about my weight.''

''What a crock, especially from a guy who looked like the Goodyear blimp.'' Renie leaned over Judith's shoulder. ''Anything on Lance and the Stars?''

''They were picked dead last in the Western Division.'' Judith flipped through the lengthy spread that took up most of the issue. ''Here—'This year's Stars would be better off not coming out at all. Except for perenially tough nose guard Calvin Tweeks and the skittish wide receiver Lance Brodie, this cast of Hollywood has-beens should stumble off into the sunset.' Gee, no wonder they folded.'' She snapped her fingers. ''Hold it! What did Wanda say about the night going dark and the sky being empty? I'll bet she meant the Stars going kaput. And the crowd that went quiet—maybe there's a connection.''

"Could be. The Steelers were big that year,'' said Renie, joining Judith in perusing *SI*'s autumn of '79 collection. "Dallas, L.A., gee, Tampa Bay? Hey, here's a picture of Lance!'' She waved the magazine in front of Judith. "Look, that's him, up in the stands, on top of the hot dog vendor!''

Judith gasped. Sure enough, Lance Brodie, No. 88, had been captured by the camera falling into the wienie wagon while a stunned vendor and an astonished cluster of fans reeled against the seats of Alameda County Coliseum. The cutline read: "Out-of-Bounds Brodie finally went too far in the Stars' 35–3 loss to the Raiders last weekend. Brodie ran a down-and-way-out pattern that sent him flying first into the Oakland stands, and later into a Los Angeles hospital.''

The article featuring the photo was a summary of the week in the AFC. Renie read aloud, quoting the magazine as saying that Brodie's injury did not appear to be as serious as it was spectacular. The team owners, however, had taken the precaution of flying Lance back to L.A. in their private jet. Eagerly, Judith and Renie perused subsequent issues, but up through early December they found only one reference to Lance, again in a league round-up:

"Even All-Pro Calvin Tweeks looked helpless against the rampaging Chargers in a 45–7 rout in San Diego. Dwindling attendance and lack of interest in TV rights may dim the Stars forever next season. To add to the team's woes, Lance Brodie probably won't be back this year. Coach Pete Chakiris admitted last week that the capricious wide receiver's knee injury was more serious than first expected.''

"Lance must have retired then,'' said Judith. "Check out the Milestones column.''

But up through the Super Bowl, they found no mention

of Lance. Judith gave Renie a woeful look. "It was probably in the swimsuit issue."

"That's okay," soothed Renie. "We know he retired. Let's get back to Oriana."

But Mrs. Brodie proved much more elusive than her stepson. After going through the '67–'70 issues, the cousins could find no mention of her, at home or abroad. An inadvertent glance at her watch told Judith it was ten minutes past the noon hour.

"Lunch! Oh, good grief! I've got to feed this crew! Quick, let's check the freezer!"

While Renie raced upstairs to alert the guests that food was in their future, Judith hauled out frozen shrimp and pastry puffs. In her absence, restrictions on the dining room table had finally been lifted by the police. To the tune of can openers, clanging saucepans, whirling spoons, and microwave buzzers, Judith and Renie produced a satisfactory lunch of shrimp florentine en croute, sliced pears on a lettuce bed, and tin-roof sundaes. The entire family had gathered, though in a far different mood from the dinner party of the previous evening. Otto was still grumbling mightily if drunkenly, Oriana had grown testy, Lance seemed more morose than vague, Mavis smoked frantically, Ellie could hardly sit still, Harvey was sunk into gloom, Gwen's chatter was punctuated by exclamations verging on hysteria, and even Dash seemed on edge. When the doorbell rang, he almost jumped out of his chair.

Judith was on the phone in the living room, trying to convince her mother that it would be best for her to stay at the Rankers's, at least for a few more hours. Gertrude was not pleased by the prospect, asserting that the world had gotten to be a sorry place when a poor old crippled woman couldn't live under her own roof without a bunch of damned-fool murderers using her towels, her soap, her dishes, and, for all she knew, her Tums. Begging off after the second ring of the doorbell, Judith arrived in the entry hall at the same moment as Renie.

"Where's Joe?" Judith whispered, peering through the peephole and seeing a stranger on the doorstep.

Renie shot a cautious glance toward the dining room. "He and Price are using lunchtime to snoop around in the guest rooms. They just went up the back stairs."

Judith gave a little shake of her head, then opened the door. "Yes?"

A balding man with wary blue eyes stood splay-footed on the porch. He was of medium height and wore a plaid sports coat, maroon pants, and a rumpled open-necked shirt. The fine lines around his mouth indicated that he had probably experienced some happy times. The scowl that creased his high forehead showed that this wasn't one of them.

"Hillside Manor, right?" He made no attempt to shake hands. "I'm Lester Busbee."

Judith went momentarily blank, but Renie rode to her rescue. "Busbee? Oh, *that* Lester Busbee! We're so sorry about your sister! Come in, we weren't expecting you until late this afternoon."

"Those nitwits in that Cedar River hick town couldn't get the part for my car until Monday so I rented one," said Busbee, tromping into the house. "Who killed Wanda?"

Enlightened as to the newcomer's identity, Judith introduced herself and Renie, even as she steered Lester into the living room and out of hearing range of the lunching Brodies. "I'll get you something to eat," she said, "but I imagine you'll want to talk to the homicide detective first."

"What do you mean?" demanded Busbee, stopping in his descent onto one of the matching sofas in front of the fireplace. "Haven't they found the murderer yet?"

Judith assumed an air of dignity as she and Renie seated themselves across from Lester. "If they have, we haven't been told. After all, everybody here is under suspicion."

"I should hope so," said Busbee, reaching for the cranberry glass dish on the coffee table and stuffing a handful of mixed nuts into his mouth. "Anybody who'd knock off

Wanda would have to be a real creep. She was a good egg.'' The words came out a trifle garbled.

"I don't suppose," said Judith casually, "that you'd have any idea who might have wanted her dead?"

Lester reared back in surprise. "Me? Heck, I don't see that much of her. I've been living in Riverside until this last summer. All I know is that she came up here to visit her dad."

Judith stiffened and Renie twitched. "Her dad," echoed Judith. "How nice. Your dad, too?"

Lester was shoveling in more nuts. "Nope. Wanda's dad was our mother's second husband. We're half-brother and half-sister. My dad croaked a long time ago."

Judith's brain was engaged in trying how to best play Lester Busbee. "Your mother's still alive then, I take it? This will come as a terrible shock to her." Despite his lack of sentiment, Lester's presence underscored the impact of Wanda's death on her family. Judith mentally berated herself for so far having seen the tragedy only in connection with her B&B enterprise.

Lester cracked his knuckles, swallowed the last of the nuts, and gave Judith an ironic look. "The only thing that shocks Mom is what they hook her up to at the asylum. Come to think of it, they stopped doing that years ago."

The photo showing young Wanda with her mother at what Judith had at first guessed to be a hotel now made sense. No doubt the teenaged boy in the picture had been Lester, though the resemblance was marginal. Judith guessed him to be some four or five years older than Wanda. "I'm sorry," said Judith, feeling as if she and Renie had cornered the forgiveness market as far as Lester Busbee was concerned, "I didn't know she was . . . mentally ill."

Lester pointed a finger at the empty cranberry glass dish. "Nuts. Just plain nuts, has been ever since Wanda was born. Before, maybe. She thought she was traffic signs and streetlights and stuff. Must have grown up by a busy intersection. They took her away when she was being a four-

way stop at La Cienega and Pico. Brought everything to
a dead halt, all right.'' His scowl deepened, and he
cracked his knuckles as he spoke: "Mom and Dad were
divorced when I was two. My dad and his second wife
brought me up in San Bernardino. After Mom was hauled
off, poor Wanda got stuck with a foster family.''

Renie was staring at the design on the cranberry glass
as if seeking inspiration. "Why didn't Wanda's father raise
her?'' she asked innocently.

Lester shrugged. "He split, not long after they were
married. I guess he was from up here. Maybe he went
into the service, maybe he didn't want to be bothered with
a kid. Who knows? But Wanda finally tracked him down
two or three years ago, in Palm Springs, as a matter of
fact. Then he moved back here and she decided to go see
him. They must have hit it off better this time around.''

Judith and Renie avoided looking at each other. They
were also careful to keep their voices down, and hopefully
in the process, encourage Lester to follow suit. "You mean
she spent a lot of time with her dad?'' asked Renie, still
playing the round-eyed middle-aged ingenue.

Lester had found the mints on the end table. "She must
have.'' He gave another shrug and chomped away. "She's
been up here for a couple of months at least. When she
called me last week she said she and her dad had a big
surprise and wouldn't I like to drive up to help her cele-
brate?'' He dropped a mint on his pants, picked it up, and
popped it into his mouth. "So off I go, and some surprise!
Wanda gets whacked. How's her dad taking it?''

At that very moment, Otto exploded from the dining
room, yelling for Judith. "Where the hell is the rest of the
scotch? The bottle I just finished tasted like antifreeze!''

"He's drinking to forget,'' murmured Judith. "Excuse
me, Mr. Brodie, but that's all the scotch I have. The bottle
was, I think almost full.''

"So was your birdbath last summer,'' snapped Otto.
"What kind of a place is this, running out of scotch?''

Judith evaded the issue. "Mr. Brodie, I'd like you to meet

Lester Busbee.'' She paused, waiting for Lester to rise from the couch, and Otto to the bait. But though Lester got up and put out a wary hand, Otto didn't react as Judith had hoped. ''He's Wanda Rakesh's brother,'' she threw in.

This time, she was rewarded with the most fleeting of shocked expressions. Indeed, under any other circumstances, Otto's response might have been ascribed to dismay for a grieving relative. ''Sorry about all this murder stuff,'' he muttered, giving Lester's hand a perfunctory shake. ''Damned shame.'' Turning away, he started to trot back toward the dining room.

''Hey,'' said Lester, pointing at Otto's retreating figure, ''what did you say his name was?''

Judith all but smirked. ''Brodie. Otto Ernst Brodie.''

Lester charged around the coffee table, knocked the mint dish off onto the carpet, and dove after Otto. ''Hold it, Brodie!'' he cried, grabbing Otto's arm. ''You're Wanda's dad! Haven't you got more to say than 'Where's the scotch'?''

They were standing under the archway between the living room and the dining room. At the oval table, the other guests sat with mouths agape. Gwen actually screamed.

Dash jumped to his feet. ''Les!'' His greeting was uncertain.

''Ankles!'' Lester was still hanging on to Otto.

''Get this lunatic off me!'' Otto demanded, fixing his angry little eyes on Lance. ''He's mad as a hatter! Probably comes from a long line of cuckoos!''

Lester decked Otto with one blow. Gwen screamed again, Oriana howled, and Ellie made as if to faint. It was Mavis, not Lance, who flew from the table and locked her fingers in Lester's lapels.

''Keep your paws off my father-in-law, buster,'' she warned, looking him straight in the eye and jiggling him up and down.

''L-Lester, not b-b-buster,'' corrected her would-be victim. ''Cut it out, lady, I'll bet that little creep bumped off my sister!''

The little creep was groaning on the floor at Judith's feet, sounding far more realistic than he had when faking his heart attack. Harvey had rushed to his uncle's aid, sending the shaken Ellie off to fetch his medical kit.

"Step aside," he commanded in his most autocratic hospital manner. He leaned over Otto, who was squealing in pain and frustration.

Gwen was torn between defending her father and Lester's recognition of Dash, but opted for playing the dutiful daughter. "Daddy had a heart attack this very morning! How dare you hurt him!" she wailed, trying to wedge her considerable bulk between Lester and Mavis. "How dare you speak to Dash!"

"Dash?" A squirming Lester was trying to break Mavis's hold on his plaid jacket. In spite of himself, he grinned. "Dash, huh? Hey, I like that better than Ankles!"

Ellie had reappeared, clutching Harvey's state-of-the-art emergency case. "Ice," said Harvey, helping Otto sit up. "That's all he needs for now."

For once, Oriana assumed the role of selfless spouse, hurrying off with Renie into the kitchen. Otto was tentatively rubbing his jaw, malevolent little eyes cast up at Lester. "I'll sue your butt off! Where's my lawyer?"

Mavis shouldered Gwen out of the way. Refusing to relinquish Lester, she gave his lapels a sharp shake. "Simmer down, everybody! What's this about Wanda and Otto?" She yanked Lester closer until they were nose-to-nose. "Watch what you say. I'm making mental notes for KINE-TV."

For Lester, it was muscle over media as far as Mavis was concerned. "Hey, lady, I'm more than willing to talk! That's why I drove up here from Cedar River this morning. But give me a break! Let go, will you? You're fraying the threads!"

Mavis hesitated just long enough to remind Lester who was in charge, then released him. Harvey and Lance were helping Otto into an armchair in the living room. Armed with ice, Oriana ministered to her husband. Ellie stood by the armchair, holding Harvey's medical kit at the ready. Gwen and Dash sat down on the window seat while Judith commandeered a footstool. Renie appeared with the last of the shrimp florentine, clutching the plate with a possessive air. Lester started to sit back down on the sofa, thought better of it, and struck a pose in front of the fireplace. He cracked his knuckles, this time more gingerly, and was preparing to speak when Joe Flynn and Officer Price strolled into the living room. Seeing Otto about to explode, Judith intervened with rapid-fire introductions. Joe and Price responded with solemn handshakes and appropriate sentiments.

"Mr. Busbee is about to make a . . . clarification," said Judith, resuming her place on the footstool.

"What is this, Jude?" asked Joe under his breath as he nudged Judith over and sat down beside her. Judith ignored both his question and the pressure of his hip.

Lester's posture on the hearth suggested a racetrack tout imitating the lord of the manor. He smoothed back the long graying hair he'd trained to grow over the farthest reaches of his bald spot and hooked his thumbs in his belt. Satisfied that his audience was at full attention, he cleared his throat and launched into speech:

"Wanda was a good broad," he began, "as Ankles— excuse me, Dash—here can tell you. She was big-hearted, liked to have a few laughs, worked hard at her job, and was always there when you needed her. Wanda was somebody you could count on." Lester's blue eyes misted over as he dug deeper into his impromptu eulogy. "She was like a sister to me." He paused and sniffed. "Hell, she *was* my sister, half-sister, that is, but so what?" He turned vaguely defiant, as if he expected his listeners to split hairs over blood ties. "So what I want to know is, who killed the poor kid? I haven't been here half an hour and I already got my ideas." He glared at a hostile Otto, who would have sprung from his chair had he not been restrained by Lance and Oriana. "My money's on you, Otto Brodie! You're her dad, and I don't see any tears!"

Protests again erupted from the Brodie contingent. Lester let them run their course, then strutted a bit and cracked his knuckles. Judith winced. Next to her, Joe sat with a pleasant, if noncommittal, expression on his face. At the moment, he looked more like a guest at an informal gathering than a homicide detective.

"Well, well," said Lester after the latest tumult had died down, "you all seem surprised. Funny, I didn't think this was some big secret."

A fuming Otto renewed his bluster, but Joe emerged from his pose to cut him off. "It's not, Mr. Busbee. Wanda's parentage is a matter of public record. So is Mr. Brodie's marriage to her mother. We've confirmed all that with the authorities down south."

"Daddy!" Gwen threw her arms around Otto's neck. "How could you! Did Mommy know?"

"*I* didn't know," exclaimed Oriana. *"Dio mio!* I married Bluebeard!"

"Put a cork in it," muttered Otto, eyes narrowing as he took in Lester, lounging against the mantelpiece. "Okay, okay, I made a mistake about a hundred years ago! Big deal. It was a crazy fling, a Vegas J.P., a romp in the hay. I was young, she was a knockout." He stopped, running a hand over his naked pate. When he spoke again, it was in a deeper, more reflective tone. "Hell, she was a movie starlet. I was still a kid, playing the bigshot and making deals with defense contractors. I got caught up in that L.A. action. I didn't even realize Gloria was nuts until I found her out in front of our motel, making like a detour sign."

Oriana was holding her head in both hands, a study of the Wronged Woman. Gwen had backed away from her father's chair, her fingers clutching at Dash's shirt. Ellie was exchanging puzzled glances with Harvey while Mavis scribbled on a notepad she'd found in Judith's treasured eighteenth-century escritoire. Lance sat next to his wife on the sofa, eyes fixed on a guide to Midwestern birds which reposed atop the coffee table.

"This Gloria was Wanda's mother?" he asked in an uncertain voice. Taking the pervasive silence for assent, Lance shook his head and regarded his father with bewil-

derment. "She was your wife. And she was crazy as a"—
he paused, his gaze reverting to the guidebook—"loon?"

Gwen shuddered. "Then Wanda was our half-sister! How
horrible!" The comment could have referred either to Wanda's demise or her family connection. Judith wasn't sure.

"Gee," said Lance in wonder, "that's right. That's
weird!" He actually frowned, mulling over the enormity
of it all.

Otto took a deep breath and fingered his bruised chin.
"I told Minnie, before we got married. I'm no deceiver.
But we decided to keep it to ourselves. The thing was, I
didn't know about the kid." He gave himself a little shake,
quivering from top to toe, then turned to the distraught
Oriana. "I didn't tell you because . . . well, I sort of
forgot, and that's the truth. It happened so long ago."

A sudden silence fell over the room. The afternoon light
was thinning as the sun gave up its attempt to peer through
the gray clouds. At the front of the house, the evergreen
trees stirred in the wind and a flock of starlings fled the
branches of the big old maple. On the leaden waters of the
bay, a tugboat hauled a huge blue barge into port while
seagulls trailed behind like an honor guard.

It was Mavis who broke the spell, using her most direct
interrogative manner: "Who got the divorce, Otto? You,
or . . . this Gloria?"

Otto gave his daughter-in-law a baleful look. "She did.
In those days it was the gentlemanly thing to do, before
all this women's lib claptrap. Nowadays, everybody can
be at fault."

Mavis's tight features expressed disdain for such rampant chauvinism. Lester, however, had stopped cracking
his knuckles. "Hold it," he said, looking half amused and
half surprised. He started to laugh, a finger pointing at all
of them. "Wanda getting murdered is no laughing matter,
but if there's any joke here, it's on you. Gloria didn't get
a divorce. Mrs. Otto Ernst Brodie is alive and trying to
stop traffic in Pismo Beach."

TWELVE

THE DOORS TO the front parlor were closed, with Officer Price and two other policemen keeping watch on the bellicose Brodies. Lester Busbee had been sent out of harm's way, over to the Rankers's, where the ever-hospitable Arlene promised a late lunch in exchange for the latest news.

Judith had started a fire in the grate to ward off the gathering winter gloom. She sat at the little table with Joe and Renie, sharing mugs of hot chocolate and a big bowl of popcorn. Sweetums, making a rare attempt to get into his mistress's good graces, swished his scraggly tail against Judith's leg. It would have been a cozy January scene, had the topic of conversation not been murder.

"You two have done your homework," Joe said in admiration after the cousins had finished relating their most recent discoveries and suppositions. "Despite your skepticism, we've done ours, too. Most of what you figured checks out. The part about Otto's first wife not getting a divorce stumped me this morning. We assumed she had, but maybe in Mexico. But Lester's right, Woody just told me Gloria is residing at the mental institution in Pismo Beach as Mrs. Otto Brodie. The poor old girl has been there since March of 1943.''

Discreetly, Judith tried to extract a popcorn kernel from her back teeth. ''Wow, forty-six years! In other words, since right after Wanda was born. I suppose Otto could be telling the truth about not knowing Gloria had had a baby. She might have been too gaga to let him know.''

''That's possible.'' Joe sat back in the chair, hands clasped behind his head. ''It's time to have another talk with Otto. Do you really think he recognized Wanda when he came into the kitchen last night?''

''Last night.'' The words came out on a weary sigh. To Judith, Wanda's murder seemed to have occurred days earlier, maybe even weeks. For all that she was trying to keep to some sort of schedule in her role as hostess, Judith had lost track of real time. ''Yes, he may have,'' she replied, trying to visualize the confrontation between Otto and the alleged Madame Gushenka. ''Something certainly put him off. Then Madame . . . Wanda made some remark about 'seeing through people' which was more cryptic than I guessed at the time.''

Joe nodded. ''So maybe Wanda rigged all this to meet Otto. She initiated contact with Oriana, remember. That wrong number was no accident, and for all her outward sophistication, Oriana is a gullible soul. Lester says Wanda had seen Otto before, in Palm Springs. I suspect he's right.'' He got to his feet, stretching his neck muscles and warming his backside in front of the fire. ''The other question is, did any of the others know about Otto being Wanda's father?''

''Dash?'' suggested Renie, scraping out the last of the popcorn.

Joe considered. ''That would depend on when Wanda found out that Otto was her father. Let's say she finds out when she gets her birth certificate for her first driver's license. But there's a whole page of Brodies in the L.A.

phone book—yes, we checked—and God only knows how many in the area. So, being a typically flighty and/or lazy teenager, she doesn't pursue the matter. Lester indicated that she only tracked Otto down in the last couple of years."

"A.D.," said Judith, then clarified in the face of Renie's puzzled expression. "After Dash. But at the time of her marriage to Dash, she probably knew *who* Otto was, if not *where*. Dash's introduction to Gwen strikes me as being trumped up, too. Unless, of, course, he was just after her money." She picked up her mug, discovered the hot chocolate had grown quite cold, and set it back down on the table. "You know something, Joe," she said, giving him a sidelong look and a crooked smile, "Renie and I have been babbling like a pair of brooks. But you haven't told us a damned thing, other than what we've figured out for ourselves."

A less confident man would have had the grace to look sheepish. But Joe Flynn merely shrugged and gave Judith a wry smile. "This is business, Jude-girl, not show-and-tell. You're doing just fine with your amateur night performance. Don't screw us up—remember we have to go through procedures—and when we're done, we'll figure out which one of these yo-yos is the perp. Okay?" He stood on his tiptoes, leaning forward, hands behind his back.

It wasn't okay, as far as Judith was concerned. Joe's so-called professionalism rankled. He was dragging his feet, concealing information, acting as if he really didn't trust her, despite everything. Which, she realized, was nothing much, at least for the last twenty odd years. She was about to lash out at him when Renie, obviously sensing trouble, intervened:

"You said you were getting some data up from L.A. on the hit-and-run and the amnesia cases. Have you found any tie-in so far with Wanda or the Brodies?" Renie's voice had changed, taking on the more studied tones of her formal graphic design presentations in the city's most important corner offices.

Joe was taken aback by Renie's unexpected metamorphosis. "Okay," he agreed, "I can give you what little I've got. The Edelstein hit-and-run case was closed six months after the accident. There were no witnesses, no traceable skid marks, nothing. And Wanda never worked at Star of Jerusalem.''

"What about Harvey?'' asked Judith, trading wrath for hope.

"Harvey was at St. Peregrine's until he came to Norway General.'' Joe picked up a Hummel figurine from the mantel. "Wanda might have dated Edelstein, who knows? At any rate, L.A. can't find any connection between Edelstein's death and this case.''

"Then there *is* a connection between Harvey and Wanda,'' said Judith. "Assuming Harvey was at St. Peregrine's during Wanda's era.''

"She was there quite a while,'' agreed Joe. "Harvey was on the staff for at least ten years. The question is, was there any way Wanda could have found out that Otto was Harvey's uncle? Our operating room oracle isn't exactly the chatty, chummy type. I doubt he'd just casually mention his family connections to one of the nurses.''

Renie had also stood up, leaning on the back of her chair. "It's definitely not his style. Who's Rakesh?'' she queried, still in her board room voice.

Joe grinned, then carefully replaced the Hummel. "I thought you'd never ask. Omar Rakesh apparently was the only poor Arab in L.A. He was on welfare when Wanda met him in 1983. They were married the same year, divorced in '86. Omar folded his tent and moved to Montana.''

Judith and Renie exchanged frustrated glances. It seemed there was nothing to be gleaned from the Rakesh angle, either. "Okay,'' sighed Judith, "what about Dr. O'Doul and the amnesia case?''

Joe grew somber. "Remember the big plane crash at Dallas in '85? Jack and Cynthia O'Doul were aboard.''

He paused, as if offering a moment of silence for the deceased couple. "If Wanda thought the surgeon and the amnesiac were one and the same, she was working strictly on supposition. Nobody else in L.A. knows anything about it."

"Nobody?" Judith's voice was unusually sharp. "Who'd your people talk to? The chicken farmer? Or did he fly the coop, too?"

"No," snapped Joe, "they talked to members of the local amnesia association. They couldn't remember a thing."

Judith made an ominous rumbling noise in her throat. To be fair, the events chronicled in Wanda's newspaper clippings had happened some time ago. Nor was there any reason to believe they had the slightest connection to her murder. Yet Judith's logic told her otherwise: A woman whose sole purpose for coming north was to seek out her estranged father was unlikely to have brought along excess baggage.

"I'm going to question Dash again, too," said Joe, deliberately changing the subject. "If nothing else, I'll find out who he met in the back yard last night."

"Probably Mother," said Judith, staring into the empty popcorn bowl and wondering, as she always did, how Renie could eat so much and stay so aggravatingly slim. "Why don't I talk to Dash? Or to Otto, for that matter?"

Joe grimaced. "Are you after my job? I thought you got your degree in librarianship, not police science."

"I have more than one degree," Judith said with dignity. "You're omitting Milton's School of Mixology. Know how to make a Purple Weasel?" She saw Joe's exasperation, and for once, took heed. "I just thought that I might get them to open up more. People talk to me. Lord, do they talk!"

"I know." Joe sighed. " 'Judith Grover has never met a stranger.' That's how you were introduced to me, remember?"

Judith avoided his gaze, staring down at Sweetums, who was sprawled inelegantly next to her chair, making occasional twitches in his sleep. "Sure, I remember. It was the parish roller derby."

An awkward silence followed. Joe came over to Judith and put a hand on her shoulder. "Leave the investigating to me. Go take a nap. You're beat."

Slowly, Judith raised her eyes. Joe's face hovered over her, concerned and . . . what? She didn't know; suddenly she was too tired to think. But she refused to give in, to let him have the satisfaction of looking after her. Salve to his guilt, she decided, then wondered if he'd ever had any. Guilt had never loomed large in Joe Flynn's repertoire.

"I'm okay." She ran a hand through the holiday perm that was beginning to wilt. "Go interrogate your suspects. As long as you won't let these wackos go yet, I have to think about what I'm going to feed them. The Brodies are getting to be a very expensive proposition. It's a good thing I wasn't booked for tonight or any new arrivals would have had to sleep at the Ericsons. Who do I bill, Oriana or the chief of police?"

"KINE-TV. If Mavis tells all, their ratings will soar." Joe winked, then slipped out of the front parlor. Judith glanced at her watch, saw that it was after three p.m., and got up from the table. Sweetums twitched on. "I've got steaks in the freezer," she said to Renie. "Let's go get them and have another look at those opera magazines."

But Renie waved a hand at her cousin. "That's fine, but wouldn't it be easier just to ask Oriana when she sung in Europe? I expect she'd be flattered by our interest."

Judith considered briefly. "True. Okay, let's find her." She started for the door, then stopped, hand on knob. "I don't buy that hit-and-run story. Oh, I believe Joe when he says the case was closed and nobody knows anything. But Wanda brought those clippings for a purpose and I'm convinced it had something to do with Otto. Or at least with the Brodie family."

"Okay." Renie was willing to be convinced. "But what can you do that the local police and their L.A. counterparts can't?"

Judith walked across the room and banked up the fire. It was growing quite dark outside. Sweetums stretched, yawned, and spit up another hairball.

"That's what I'm trying to figure out," she said, bending down to mop up after her miserable cat. "Beat it, Sweetums, the meter's running overtime on your attempt at being a serious pet." Sweetums did not oblige, but instead curled up in front of the hearth, offering a passable imitation of a domesticated animal. "Dash might know some of the people Wanda worked with, especially further back. Lester might have some names, too. Maybe we could call some of them and ask why Wanda was so interested in Drs. Edelstein and O'Doul."

"Reasonable." Renie nodded approval. "I wish I'd seen those clippings. Who took them, do you think?"

"In theory, no one but Ellie could have seen them. In fact, the field's wide open. How do we know who saw that officer deliver the envelope, and how do we know that Wanda wasn't known to all of these people before she ever set foot in this house?"

Renie reflected, then inclined her head in assent. "You're sure the dates of the amnesia case and the gossip column coincided? What were they?"

"They didn't coincide, exactly—that's the point." Judith began picking up mugs and crumpled napkins while Renie gathered the empty popcorn bowl to her bosom. "The amnesia report was early in the week. Cynthia O'Doul, poor soul, returned from Europe a few days later. And her husband forgot to meet her plane. It was—I'm concentrating, I want to get this right—the third week of October, 1979."

"Okay," said Renie, "that makes sense. The link, I mean. Let me think," she continued as they emerged from the parlor, ignored whichever of the guests was haranguing the others in the living room, and went into the kitchen, "what significance could those two incidents have other than that Jack O'Doul suffered from a bout of amnesia?"

"I'm trying to remember the year itself. Our Christmas

turkey weighed twenty-eight pounds and my late husband three hundred and fifteen. We'd just been evicted from the bungalow at Five Corners, and Dan was trying to put together another restaurant venture. Mother bought a green eyeshade for her poker club. I remember that because it was the same year Uncle Al broke his arm on Halloween when he fell off the top of his toilet and had to—''

"October 1979!" cried Renie, losing her grip on the popcorn bowl, but catching it between her hip and the sink. "That's when Lance got hurt!" She set the bowl down and all but hopped around the kitchen. "Let's get Lance! We've got to find out if O'Doul was his surgeon!"

Judith stood stock still, looking not unlike a Maypole to her cousin's jubilant footwork. "Wait—what is it we want to know? We're dealing with Lance, not a real person. We've got to put our questions very clearly."

"Right." Renie stopped dancing. "How do we handle him? True of false? Multiple choice?"

Judith's reply was forestalled by the swing of the kitchen door. Oriana, clutching her white silk blouse around her neck, came shivering into the room. "Mrs. McMonigle, I must insist that you turn up the heat! Have you looked at your outside thermometer? It's dropped below freezing. I'm about to take a chill. I could get laryngitis!"

Suppressing the urge to say that they should be so lucky, Judith merely smiled politely. "Of course. It may snow any minute." From behind Oriana's back, Judith made urgent gestures at Renie. But when she came back from revving up the thermostat in the entry hall, she found Oriana railing at Renie, rather than Renie finessing Oriana.

". . . held like criminals, and worst of all, our privacy has been invaded!" Oriana whirled on Judith, pointing a well-manicured finger. "I must insist upon knowing why the police have been permitted to rampage through our belongings!"

Judith decided to let Joe and his crew take their lumps, deserved or not. "They probably have a warrant," she replied calmly. "I imagine they've searched our things, too. In fact," she went on pointedly, "a few items have disappeared from my bedroom."

Oriana was unmoved as well as unruffled. She did, however, quiet down a bit. "I wouldn't doubt it. Really, these policemen are like the KGB! I wouldn't be surprised if that Irish thug didn't resort to physical force! Though," she added, with a faint note of longing, "he does have nice eyes."

Judith pressed her lips together. It was Renie at the stove manning the tea kettle who launched the current inquiry: "What you need right now, Mrs. Brodie, is a nice hot cup of tea. It'll soothe your throat and calm your nerves. Tell me," she went on, almost as chatty as her cousin but not quite so genuine, "what is your favorite operatic role?"

Oriana finally stopped clutching at the neck of her blouse and sat down at the dinette table. She preened a bit, then smoothed back her coils of auburn hair. "Carmen, I suppose, though Princess Eboli is a great challenge. The eyepatch, you know. So seductive."

Talking about herself seemed to have a tranquilizing effect on Oriana. "Oh, very," said Renie as the cousins joined their guest. "Eboli has some beautiful music. In fact, I've always felt the Veil Song in *Don Carlo* and the Seguidilla in *Carmen* had a lot in common. Of course," she noted modestly, "I don't know much about opera except that I enjoy it."

"Bizet and Verdi were very different sorts of composers," Oriana pontificated. "The commonality you hear is Verdi's attempt to utilize a type of Moorish music in *Don Carlo,* while Bizet was working with the gypsy tradition. Though both operas are set in Spain, *Carmen* was not originally intended to be a grand opera, but was written instead for the Opera Comique in Paris. It was my debut role at La Scala in Milan." She gave a toss of her head, implying that the sole purpose of Bizet's masterpiece had been to serve as a springboard for her career.

Judith looked duly impressed. "How exciting! When did you sing at La Scala? Renie and I were in Italy in 1964."

Oriana was not so impressed. But at least, Judith noted with satisfaction, she seemed to be settling in for a cozy biographical interlude. "Oh, it was years after that! In fact, I was a mere girl at the time—it must have been 1974. It was the classic theater debut, just like the movies, with the understudy taking over for the ailing star. Grace Bumbry came down with bronchitis"—she paused, a hand at her bosom, as if to ward off the possibility of contagion even at so late a date—"and I was thrust onto the stage with very little rehearsal. I'd sung the larger roles in some of the provincial houses, but never in as prestigious a place as La Scala! Naturally, I was terrified!" Oriana's eyes grew very wide, summoning up the hallowed opera house filled with demanding music cognoscenti. "But fate was kind— I gave the performance of my life, and the audience went wild. Even the critics raved about the Ravishing Unknown from the Bronx."

Oriana seemed to be quoting from some long-ago review. The kettle on the stove sang its own little aria, and Renie got up to make tea.

"You're a New Yorker, then," said Judith, aware that Oriana had cultivated her speaking, as well as her singing, voice. No trace of accent had so far surfaced.

"Yes," said Oriana. "My father played the violin in a neighborhood symphony orchestra. We had very little money, but my parents scrimped and saved to give me singing lessons. Eventually, I went abroad to study."

Her story sounded plausible, though Judith knew that vocal studies in Europe usually weren't financed by a piggy bank. But where was the connection with Dash? Presumably, they'd been raised three thousand miles apart. As Renie poured tea, Judith juggled dates in her head. "Was your mother musical, too?" she asked, stalling until she could come up with a better question.

Oriana's laugh came from deep in her throat. "My, no! Contrary to popular myth, not all Italians can sing. Mama was tone-deaf. She was one of twelve children, and not one of them was allowed in the school choir. 'God will

be glad to let the Frascattis pray only once,' their parish
priest used to tell them." Seeing the sudden shift of both
Judith's and Renie's expressions, Oriana hastened to explain: "There's an old saying, 'He who sings prays twice.'
Perhaps you've never heard it."

"I have, somewhere," said Judith, a trifle vaguely. To
cover her surprise at Oriana's mention of Dash's real name,
she lifted the lid on the sheep-shaped cookie jar. "Drat,
it's empty. I should do some baking after all this . . . dis-
ruption is over."

Oriana was arranging herself into another graceful pose
in the dinette chair. "Yes, it's all too, too upsetting. I shall
be very glad to get home. Assuming, of course, the fumigators are finished."

"Is that stuff really poisonous?" Renie asked guile-
lessly.

Oriana drew back in her chair. "Noxious! How do you
think we get rid of the pests?"

Judith had been asking herself the same question, but
about the human variety. Renie, however, continued to
play the game, still in her guise of aging round-eyed ingenue. "What sort of pests?"

"Earwigs. They come in on the cut flowers." Oriana
turned grim. "And carpenter ants. The Brodie house is
very old." She cast her eyes up at Judith's high-ceilinged
kitchen, a memento of the Edwardian era. "It's almost as
old as this place. Our home in Palm Springs was quite
new, very high-tech." She sighed with regret just as Otto
stumbled into the kitchen.

"I'm doomed! It's the gallows for me! I can see the hang-
man now!" He leaned with each hand on either side of the
doorway, the picture of a bent, if not broken, man. "They
know all about Wanda. They even know about the cyanide!"

"*What* cyanide?" shrieked Oriana, hands raised in horror.

Otto shambled to the table where he flopped onto the
vacant chair. His bruised chin sagged on his chest. He
seemed oblivious to Judith and Renie, who were both riv-

eted to their seats. "Do you remember about a year and a half ago when you went to the fat farm for a week?" he asked his wife in a gloomy voice.

Oriana bridled. "It wasn't a fat farm. It was a health spa, solely for muscle and tone."

"Okay, okay, whatever. Anyway, my testy tortellini, it was the summer before this last one. I'd just come in from the golf course and here was this woman waiting for me. I'd never seen her before, right? Raul didn't want to let her in, but she told him she was family." He stopped, stared first at Judith, then at Renie, as if noticing them for the first time. "Hey, beat it, you two. This is a private conversation."

Fleetingly, Judith considered telling Otto she wasn't accustomed to being ejected from her own kitchen, but decided to save her breath. The Brodies would simply go elsewhere to talk, no doubt to their own room, where the eavesdropping possibilities were more limited without another session hiding under the bed. Leading the way for Renie, Judith headed for the back stairs. Their pause on the first landing drew only silence; Judith gestured for Renie to continue upstairs. The sound of ascending feet seemed to satisfy Otto, for he began to speak again:

"So this broad told me she was Wanda Brodie Rakesh, a nurse at an L.A. hospital, and that she was my daughter! I was floored. In fact, I told her to go, uh, chase herself. But she had a birth certificate, and my marriage license for the Vegas wedding with Gloria. I swear to God, pizza puss, I never knew a damned thing about any kid! You could have knocked me over with a feather!"

To Judith, plastered against the wall of the stairwell, the image evoked by Otto had its comic aspect. He was still talking, and Judith could imagine the grim-faced Oriana, listening with a jaundiced ear.

"She gave me a lot of guff about wanting to meet me after all these years, of not knowing where I'd gone before she was born, of tracking down the records and making some kind of search. She couldn't get a thing out of Gloria, who's nuttier than a squirrel's nest. She'd had no luck for a long time, then some blabbermouth patient from Palm Springs mentioned my name and that's how she found me." His voice had dropped, making it somewhat more difficult for Judith to hear. "She wrote three letters I never answered, all full of mush and gush about wanting to meet her pop. She was all steamed up on getting herself acknowledged, or some such swill, but I'll admit she didn't ask for money. *Then*. But when she finally showed up and got all sentimental—which I admit was beginning to put a lump in the old throat—the grabby woman puts the squeeze on me! She said I owed it to her, for having abandoned her and her mother! She wanted to set Gloria up in some swishy place with big ferns and her own set of streetlights! Bull, I told her, take a hike! We had a real row and she finally left. Good riddance, I said, and it was. At least I thought so at the time." Otto was sounding as if he'd cornered the market on self-pity.

"So that's why we went on that world cruise," said Oriana in a musing, if tart voice. "Well, well, Otto. I also assume that's why we moved to this rainy backwater."

There was a sheepish note in Otto's reply: "Hey, it was blackmail, extortion, a real squeeze play! I couldn't sit around and let the woman bleed me dry. Besides, this is my home. Don't knock it, fettucine face."

"Except that flight didn't prove to be the solution." Oriana sounded almost as if she were enjoying Otto's misery. "Tell me, did this Wanda person mention that her mother had neglected to get a divorce?"

There was a noticeable pause. Judith glanced up the staircase, where she could see Renie peeking around the corner of the second landing.

"No. I suppose she was going to spring that on me last night." His manner took a sudden sharp turn: "Or did she tell you when you were up to your snooty nose in putting this fiasco together?"

"Of course not." Oriana was disdainful. "She revealed absolutely nothing about herself, except for her successes as a fortune-teller. And I only gave her some basic, if damaging, facts about your dear family.''

"Such as?''

Another pause ensued. "I forget.''

"Like hell you do,'' growled Otto, sounding more like himself. "You were supposed to have her needle 'em, not get herself killed! I just wanted to have a little fun and make that bunch of parasites squirm.''

"What about the cyanide?'' countered Oriana.

"Oh, that!'' Otto sputtered a bit. "Well, see, after I recognized this Madame babe as Wanda, I slipped a little cyanide in my tea. I got it from the fumigators—Ralph, who owns Bugs Ahoy!, is an old pal. I told him it was a joke. So then I switched cups. Nothing to really hurt her, just to knock her out. I was sure she was going to blab everything right then and there. I should have just bribed her out in the kitchen but those two goofy dames were hanging around like the Bobbsey Twins. I guess I panicked. But there was only a teeny-weeny bit of cyanide. I know a lot about the stuff, I used it in the armaments business during the war. In fact, I was going to take it myself.''

"Otto!'' For once, Oriana's astonishment sounded genuine.

"Sure, to scare the hell out of that crew of vultures. Remember, when I threatened to fall down in the salad with a heart attack? Well, I'd planned on doing something like it later on, just to see how they'd react.''

"That's ridiculous! You saw how they behaved when you pulled that stunt this morning.''

"Yeah. I was disappointed, too. They all acted normal—for them.'' He uttered a deep sigh that floated out of the kitchen and all the way up to Judith and Renie. "But don't you see, the cops will figure I killed her. My own daughter! I might have wanted to get rid of her, but not permanently!''

"It doesn't look good,'' Oriana admitted. Judith wondered if it would have looked better to the would-be Mrs.

Brodie if Gloria weren't still around. "Your other children are bastards."

"Oh, sure, I know that," he said in an offhand manner. "I mean, they're a bunch of . . . oh, *bastards!* You're right," Otto remarked in wonderment.

"Gwen," said Oriana, presumably in greeting as a new set of footsteps entered the kitchen. "Do sit. There's tea."

"I couldn't," moaned Gwen, apparently in great distress. "They're giving Dash the third degree! Do you suppose the police use rubber hoses?"

"I hope so," muttered Otto, his chair scraping on the kitchen floor. "Come on, Oriana, let's go upstairs and try some of that thrusting and throbbing Gwen's always writing about."

"Otto!" exclaimed Oriana. "What an idea!" Her teacup rattled in its saucer. "Have you forgotten? I'm not your wife."

"Holy meatballs!" The pause which followed was accompanied by Gwen's nervous titter. Otto started to rant in a voice that made both cousins wince, then he slammed out of the kitchen. Judith could imagine the swinging door all but dropping from its hinges.

"Daddy!" cried Gwen, hesitating. "I must console him," she announced in noble tones, presumably to Oriana. What was left of the swinging door swung shut again.

Judith motioned to Renie, then started up the stairs. Oriana might decide to exit the kitchen from the rear. The cousins scrambled ever upward until they reached the third floor and Judith's bedroom. They were only mildly surprised to find Harvey Carver sprawled on Grandmother Grover's braided rug.

THIRTEEN

"DR. CARVER!" CRIED Judith, "are you all right?"

A sullen Harvey looked up at her from his awkward position on the floor. "Does it look like it? I'm having a spasm in my back."

"You're also having it in my bedroom." Judith spoke with bite, then felt immediately repentant. "I'm sorry, but guests aren't permitted up here. The outer door is clearly marked Private."

Harvey wallowed around on the old rug, then put out an importunate hand. "Help me up. I've got to walk this off."

Judith and Renie obliged, carefully hauling Harvey to his feet. The Brodie men struck Judith as unusually accident-prone; but then again, the Brodies were all unusual, period.

"Ah!" Harvey emitted a sigh of relief as he staggered around the room, one hand at his back. "That's not recommended treatment. But it works for me."

"That's great," said Judith dryly. "Would you mind explaining why you're up here, Doctor?"

Harvey straightened up slowly, tipped back his head, and flexed his knees. "The police let me in. They couldn't find you." His black eyes accused Judith of shirking her duties.

"So?" Harvey's I.Q. might be several notches higher than his cousin Lance's, but he was equally hard to draw out. "For what purpose did the police let you come into our private rooms?"

Harvey's thin lips tightened. Judith realized that he wasn't used to being held accountable for his actions. She assumed that, like all great surgeons, he thought he was God. "I don't see any reason to tell you, Mrs. McMonigle. It's between the detectives and me." His highly polished wingtips pawed at the rug like the hooves of an impatient pony.

Judith shrugged. "Lieutenant Flynn will tell me," she asserted with considerably more confidence than she felt. "The explanation had better put hair on my chest."

After a flash of anger, Harvey relented. "Very well," he replied in his sulky manner. "It had to do with my medical kit. When I took it back upstairs, I checked to see if I had any anti-inflammatory medication for Uncle Otto's chin. I sensed that things had been moved. I can't be absolutely certain, but there may be a couple of items missing. With a poisoner loose, I decided to search the house from top to bottom."

Harvey's story sounded a trifle lame to Judith. "Couldn't the police conduct the search?" she asked, glancing around the room but finding no sign of a wholesale scouring. The afternoon shadows had grown long and deep, and the threatening sky promised a snowfall.

"They don't know what to look for," Harvey replied defensively. "I'm not sure myself—I don't take a daily inventory." He dusted off his tweed jacket and smoothed his unruly gray hair. "I could be wrong, of course." The admission sounded unnatural. "Still, it doesn't hurt to take precautions."

"True." Judith was vacillating between belief and skepticism. She caught Renie's eye, saw her cousin curl her lip at Harvey's back, and looked away. She was standing by the dressing table, watching both the real Harvey and his mirror image. The first impression of a weasel hadn't been quite accurate, Judith decided: He was a more of a gnome, in some ways resembling a slender version of Otto far more than Lance or Gwen—or even Wanda—did. His long, sallow face had a melancholy quality and his black eyes seemed ever-vigilant. Now poised for his exit, Harvey was deterred by Judith's seemingly casual question:

"Tell me, Doctor, did you know Wanda Rakesh when she worked at St. Peregrine's?"

Harvey gave a little start. "I don't think so. She may have come after I left."

But Judith shook her head. "I gather she'd been there several years."

"Could be." Harvey shrugged. "At the risk of sounding arrogant, all nurses look alike, especially in the O.R. All you can see is their eyes. Most of us are too busy concentrating on our work to indulge in studying the staff." He was edging for the door, but Judith and Renie were closing in.

"You must have known Dr. Jack O'Doul," Judith said, aware of how dark the room had become as the lead-gray clouds settled in over the rooftops.

Harvey's face registered surprise. "O'Doul? Of course! He was chief of surgery at St. Peregrine's. A brilliant man. He was my mentor." For the first time, Harvey showed a shred of warmth. "Why do you ask? Did you know him?"

"In a way," Judith answered vaguely. "My mother-in-law used to be a nurse." That much was true, thought Judith, though Effie McMonigle had been strictly ob-gyn and had worked in Arizona. "His death in that plane crash was certainly a great loss."

Harvey looked properly solemn. "It was. Ironic, too." The black eyes flickered with some emotion Judith couldn't fathom. "I took the offer at Norway General because I realized I could never become chief of surgery at St. Peregrine's as long as Jack was there. I didn't want to, mind you, he was the ideal person for the job, but I felt I had to move up. Three months after I left St. Peregrine's, Jack was killed." He spoke with a certain amount of awe, as if he still couldn't believe it.

"What about Stanley Edelstein?" queried Judith. "Do you remember him from St. Peregrine's?"

"Stanley Edelstein?" Harvey mulled over the name. "There was somebody with a name like that," he conceded, "but it doesn't sound quite right. Edelmann, maybe, or Millstein."

Judith adopted a confused expression. She was aware that Harvey was again growing restive. She also realized that he wasn't used to talking so freely in front of others, especially strangers. "Odd . . . for some reason, I had the idea that Edelstein operated on Lance's knee." She'd only just thought of it, but having done so, decided it didn't qualify as an outright lie.

"No, no," said Harvey with a scowl. "That was Jack O'Doul. The Hollywood Stars' owners insisted that Lance have the very best."

Renie looked stunned. "But how could such an outstanding surgeon flub such a simple operation?"

Harvey hitched up his belt and gave Renie a scornful glance. "No surgical procedure can be called 'simple'. And even the best surgeons can have an off day. We're not infallible." He made the statement as if he were.

"Were you there?" Judith asked, as the glimmer of an idea danced in her mind's eye.

"No. Jack felt that since Lance was family, it would be better for me not to assist. Too emotional, you see." He paused as Judith flipped on a floor lamp and tried to imagine an overwrought Harvey Carver, flooding the O.R. with tears. "I remember talking to O'Doul afterward," Harvey went on, "and how upset he was. Jack told me he'd like to erase the whole thing from his mind. He apologized over and over to Lance and the other players and the team owners. He thought the failure was divine retribution for not renewing his Hollywood Stars' season tickets.''

"Poor man," murmured Judith a bit absently as she racked her brain for a way to worm further information out of Harvey. The idea that had begun to emerge pirouetted out of her mind's range. Somehow, the facts she was eliciting weren't falling into the proper pattern. At least not yet. She was about to inquire as to the exact nature of Lance's injury when they heard Ellie calling from the other side of the door.

"Harvey! Yoo-hoo! Are you in there?"

Harvey lowered his head, swung his arms, and charged for the door. "Coming. Did you find my brown socks?"

"Of course, dear," said Ellie, nodding across the threshold to Judith and Renie as she took her husband's arm. "I always find your things, don't I?"

"Not all of them," said Harvey darkly, as he cast a final glance over his shoulder at the family inner sanctum.

Judith quietly but firmly closed the door behind Harvey and locked it. "Wanda worked in surgery, remember? What do you bet Harvey *did* know Wanda?"

"Everybody knew Wanda," said Renie, falling into the armchair and looping one leg over the side. "I'm even beginning to feel like she and I were real close."

Judith had wandered over to the window, where she peered down at the Rankers's house. Gertrude must be champing at the bit to come home. She'd never been one for long trips even if the family could have afforded them on Donald Grover's salary as a high school teacher. Spending the night with Arlene and Carl had probably been a bit of a lark, if only to get a ringside seat at one of the couple's domestic brawls. But a second night out for Gertrude seemed in store, and Judith knew her mother would balk. The investigation was taking too long, there were too many loose ends, the police were dragging their feet. Or was it Joe?

Judith turned to Renie, who was nodding off in the chair. "Where are your kids?"

Renie jumped. "Huh? What kids?" She blinked rapidly. "Oh, *those* kids! Anne went to Port Royal for the weekend. Tom and Tony are skiing up at Mount Woodchuck."

"When's Bill due back?" Judith moved a few inches out of the draft that was coming in through the casement.

"Tomorrow night. I'm supposed to meet his plane at seven-forty. He's in Palo Alto." Renie yawned and shook herself. "Why don't you take Joe's advice and have a nap? I can start dinner. If we're doing steaks, there's no rush except to get baked potatoes ready for the oven. It's not even four yet. How about mashed carrots and rutabagas?"

"How about cardboard and Elmer's Glue? Nobody in the family eats rutabagas anymore except you and your mother, and you know it. I'd always hoped that when they said 'You can't take it with you,' God made an exception and let Grandma Grover bring along that ghastly recipe."

Renie's umbrage was halfhearted. "You don't like grilled lamb kidneys, either. Okay, how about green beans with bacon?" Before Judith could answer, Renie was on her feet, waving the arm with the torn sleeve. "You're avoiding the issue, coz. Why don't you lie down for an hour or so?"

Judith looked at the bed with yearning. Coming from Renie, the suggestion was more palatable than it had been from Joe. "I could rest my eyes," she said, quoting their grandmother, for whom that phrase had meant falling into a virtual coma. "It's starting to snow," Judith noted with another glance out the window. "No wonder it got so dark."

"Lord," groaned Renie, going to the other window to see for herself, "I hope we don't get marooned here with all these goofballs! Especially since one of them is a murderer." She paused, expecting an appropriate comment from her cousin. But Judith was standing motionless by the bed, a frown creasing her forehead. "I mean," Renie clarified, "it sounds incredible, but the fact is, we're giving food and shelter to a killer. If I gave it serious thought, I'd—''

"Dark!" Judith snapped her fingers. "That's it! How could Harvey find anything without turning on the lights?"

"What?" Renie, caught up in her self-induced horror show, gaped at Judith. "Oh! Well, it wasn't this dark when we came up here. Maybe Harvey had been rolling around on the rug for a long time."

"It looked to me like he was eating the rug." Judith glanced outside again as the Rankers's house began to disappear in the snow. "His story sounded fishy from the start. I'll bet he was looking for something else. Or maybe he was hiding something."

"The clippings?" suggested Renie.

Judith passed a weary hand across her forehead. "I don't know. In theory, he didn't even know we had them. And I can't imagine what else he'd think we had up here, which isn't a good premise anyway, since he'd need light to look for that, too. I think I just shot my own hypothesis in the foot." A bit clumsily, she hoisted herself onto the bed. "To hell with it. I feel like my head's made out of wood. Give me an hour, that's all I need. I keep thinking that if I stop pushing this damned thing, it'll never get solved. Am I nuts?"

"Yes," replied Renie with a shrug. "You have to be, to get by in this world." Going to the door, she sketched her cousin a wave. "Forget everything for a while. Go to sleep. Maybe Joe will build you a snowman."

Maybe, thought Judith as she rested her head on the pillows, Joe will build a case—against somebody, anybody, just to put an end to this mess. She kicked off her shoes, pulled up the comforter, and closed her eyes. But though she was utterly exhausted, sleep would not come. Instead, her guest list paraded across the bedroom ceiling, all of them looking guilty as sin. Even Lance, mused Judith, and all of them with a motive named Money. If, she reminded herself, just *one* member of the Brodie party—excluding Otto—had known who Wanda really was, the others might also have known. But which one? Dash was the most likely, and if he'd told Gwen, she would have told the world. But who *really* had the opportunity to poison Wanda? Ellie and Mavis had been in the kitchen when the coffee and teacups were being readied. Wanda had sat between Mavis and Otto at the dinner table. But any of the guests could have left their places—and some of them had. Maybe all of them. Judith, as well as Renie, had been in the kitchen most of the time.

But what if Wanda's bloodlines weren't the motive? Who knew that Madame Gushenka was really Wanda Rakesh, former circus performer turned registered nurse? Otto, who admitted he'd spiked Wanda's tea; Dash, who had been married to her, and might have been in on the game; Gwen, who could have seen a picture of Wanda in Dash's belongings; Harvey, whose memory for nurses could be a lie; Ellie, who must have had occasion to meet some of her husband's co-workers over the years; Lance, who might have met Wanda during his stay at St. Peregrine's; Mavis, who could have seen her while visiting Lance; and Oriana, who had been related to Wanda by marriage, could have known the victim in her real guise. The Brodie party shuffled and jived its way into the eaves. Judith turned over, pounded the pillow, and cursed aloud.

The rap at the door snapped Judith to attention. Peering at her watch, she noted that it wasn't quite four-thirty. Maybe Renie needed help after all. Or else fresh troubles had surfaced. "Come in," she called, sitting up.

It wasn't Renie who crossed the threshold, but Joe Flynn, looking more buoyant than Judith felt he had any right to do. "I see you took my advice," he remarked.

"Did not," mumbled Judith. "Renie drugged me with carrots and rutabagas." She felt for her shoes and ran a hand through her hair. "I wasn't asleep, I was cogitating."

Joe sat down next to Judith on the bed. "This is a nice room. Cozy. I didn't get a chance to study it when I was up here earlier calling you names."

"It was originally the servants' quarters," said Judith, wishing Joe had taken the armchair. "Before the First World War, my grandparents had a cook and a maid."

"My grandparents *were* a cook and a maid," Joe noted, taking in the bold yellow tulips of the wallpaper and the matching chintz curtains, pillow slips and comforter. "Grandpa Maloney cooked at the old Cascadia Hotel. Grandma was a maid there. That's how they met."

"I never knew that. I thought your grandfather was a streetcar conductor."

"That was Grandpa Flynn." Joe admired the Childe Hassam print of the Boston Common. "Whatever happened to the Grover money?"

Judith made a face. "There wasn't that much, really. It came from a sawmill, out at the south end of the bay. Grandpa got influenza in 1919 and his partner, Ole Pierson, fleeced him. Then Grandpa got better and tried to shoot Ole and ended up in jail. Grandma joined the Wobblies and got arrested for chaining herself to a totem pole. Naked. They were both released the same day. The neighbors hired a brass band to welcome them home. Ole wasn't invited."

Joe looked leery. "How come you've never regaled me with all this violent history until now?"

Judith shifted on the bed, inching away from Joe. "I didn't know about it then. Mother and Aunt Deb and Uncle Al and even Uncle Corky were sort of ashamed. But one night Renie and I got Mother gassed on Singapore Slings and she spilled the beans."

"I'll be." Joe was thoughtful, sitting on the bed with his fingers perched on his knees. "I always thought the Grovers were highly respectable."

"They were. They are. They—we—just sort of have things happen to us."

Joe nodded. "Sure. Like assault with a deadly weapon and exhibitionism and murder." He turned to Judith, started to say something, and stopped. Judith froze, wishing Renie would show up.

"Well?" Her mouth had gone dry.

"It's been a long time since I've been in your bed-room." Joe's tone was guileless, almost boyish.

"You were never in this one," retorted Judith. "I didn't live here back then." She made it sound like another century.

"True." Joe was still watching Judith closely, the gold flecks dancing in the green eyes. "There's something I have to tell you."

Judith braced herself, mentally and physically. "What?" Her tongue seemed to stick to the roof of her mouth.

Joe put a hand on her thigh. "It's taken too long for this, but . . ." He paused, frowned, and pressed her flesh ever so gently. "Well, I can finally tell you."

"What?" repeated Judith, cursing herself for fluttering from head to foot.

Joe's glance was unwavering. "The M.E. has given his report. Wanda had traces of cyanide in her system, but she died from an overdose of sodium pentothal. Harvey has reported a vial of the stuff missing from his medical kit."

Judith burst into tears.

For at least three minutes, Joe held Judith, letting the tears roll down her cheeks and onto his red and blue striped tie. At last, she began to gulp, then sniff, and finally erupted into a spate of self-reproach:

"I'm such a jerk! I can't believe I'm crying! I'm an ass!"

"Hey!" Joe gave her a sharp little shake, but kept her in the circle of his arms. "Listen," he said, his face almost touching hers, "you're a lot of things, but none of the above. What you are most of all—and I get the feeling you keep forgetting it—is human. I don't give a damn if you cry until Tuesday." He took a deep breath, as if his own emotions were getting the better of him. "Tell me," he asked, pulling back, but still holding on to Judith, "did you cry when Dan died?"

Judith's red eyes were defiant. "No. Not really."

"That's what I figured." He moved one arm away from her, using his free hand to rub at the back of his head. "Didn't you care? At all?" There was a trace of awe in his voice.

Silence filled the room. The snow was coming down in big, heavy flakes, already piling up at the windowsill. Judith leaned her head back and looked down her nose at Joe. "I cared. I even miss him sometimes. But the day he died, all I could think of was that I was free. Over the years, he'd managed to trample whatever feelings I had for him. Then, when he was gone, I cared about his memory." She shrugged, then turned flashing eyes on Joe. "I can lie and cheat and maybe steal, but I can't be a hypocrite. If you think I'm crying for Dan McMonigle, you're nuts!"

For once, Joe looked abashed. Absently, he caressed Judith's shoulder and studied the pattern of the braided rug. "I guess I always thought you were madly in love with him. He was one hell of a good-looking guy before he piled on the pounds."

That much was true, Judith had to admit. When it came to appearance, Dan had Joe—and most other men—beat six ways to Sunday. "Dan was tall, dark, and handsome before he became tall, dark, and then some." She slowly shook her head at the recollection. "No," she asserted, forcing Joe to meet her gaze, "I was never in love with him. And you're full of crap."

"Why?" asked Joe, looking blank.

"Because you know better," retorted Judith, reaching out to straighten Joe's tie and inspect the damage inflicted by her tears. "You wished I'd been in love with Dan. It would have made you feel better."

"No, it wouldn't." Joe spoke simply. Then the hand at her shoulder tightened, drawing her closer. "Have you forgotten what makes me feel better?" he asked, his mouth almost on hers.

Judith drew in a quick breath, started to shake her head,

and then let out a little squeak as the bedroom door opened.

"Ta-rum-pah-pah, ta-rum-pah—oh, rats!" exclaimed Renie. "Goodbye!"

"Renie!" screamed Judith. "Come back!"

"Jude-girl!" Joe sounded dismal, his arms still outstretched.

But Judith had managed to escape, half stumbling across the room. She yanked open the door, coming face-to-face with a chagrined Renie. "I'm sorry, I had no idea . . ." she began in miserable apology.

Judith waved her into silence. "Never mind. It could have been a horrible mistake." Of course it could, she lectured herself. She was exhausted, upset, in no frame of mind to make vital moral and emotional decisions. Where was logic? Where was reason? Where was her diaphragm?

Somewhat red in the face, Joe was on his feet, putting the finishing touches on his tie and smoothing back his hair. "Glad you're here, Renie," he said, sounding very formal. "I was just telling Jude-girl about the M.E.'s report. I spoke to Dash, too, and there have been some other interesting developments."

"How about a drink?" offered Judith brightly. "Is anybody in the living room?"

"Everybody," said Renie, deciding to let Judith and Joe play out their parts. "We can use the front parlor, instead. But we're running low on booze." Carefully, she led the way down the private stairs. "Shall I check with the Rankers, or can you send somebody to the liquor store, Joe?"

"Not really," he replied. "My men are all in uniform. Besides, driving out there must be pretty dicey already."

"The Rankers, then," said Judith as they descended the second flight. The kitchen was mercifully empty except for Officer Price, who was wearing an apron and rubbing shortening on a dozen large baking potatoes. "I'll go. I want to talk to Mother anyway."

Renie was momentarily distracted. "Woody, did you

poke holes in those potatoes?'' It appeared that Renie and Joe's assistant had established a certain rapport.

''Of course.'' Price looked at Renie with reproachful eyes. ''I help my wife make dinner all the time. Would you like my fondue recipe?''

''Cheese or beef?'' inquired Renie, then grinned at Officer Price. ''We'll do this later. Don't forget to ask me about my carrots and rutabagas.'' She gave Judith a mischievous look. ''He'll love it,'' she said, then went on before her cousin could protest. ''While you're next door, ask Arlene if she's got any chives—you're out. Then hurry back. I could use a stiff drink about now.''

''Okay,'' said Judith, going to the pantry and rummaging for her boots. ''Is everything under control here?''

Renie gave the kitchen a cursory glance. ''It is for dinner. Otherwise, I'm not so sure.'' She took a deep breath and leaned back against the sink. ''I had the radio on while I was thawing the steaks. The four o'clock news said there was new evidence in what they're calling the Fortune-Teller Murder. The broadcaster mentioned news clippings, but didn't specify what was in them.'' Renie's expression was wry.

''Mavis!'' cried Judith. ''How did she know about the clippings?''

But Renie shook her head. ''I wasn't listening to KINE. I had on that country and western station Bill's nephew, Kip, works for.''

Judith and Joe stared at Renie. ''But it had to be Mavis!'' insisted Judith, though the conviction wavered in her voice. ''If not, who?''

Joe was rubbing at the back of his head again. ''It's five p.m., and I'm off duty,'' he muttered, looking at the old school clock. ''Go get the booze.''

FOURTEEN

THE SNOW HAD grown finer and the wind had come up in the last half hour. Judith trod carefully across the back yard, hugging her down jacket close to her body. The footing was slippery, and she avoided the walkways, just in case the snow should camouflage any patches of ice. Blinking against the storm, she smiled: This magical world of white evoked so many memories, of hiking up the snowbound hill to Grandpa and Grandma Grover's on Christmas Eve; of laughing with Renie as they threw snowballs at each other's Swiss ski sweaters; of Joe in a tux, top hat, and flowing cape on New Year's Eve; of Mike on his first sled, with fear in his eyes and a yelp of pleasure on his lips. Judith heard her boots sink in the snow, but kept smiling. A moment later, she was on the Rankers's back porch, stamping off her feet and brushing snow from her lashes.

"Judith!" Arlene's welcome was as expansive as usual. Her red-gold hair was tousled and her smile was wide. "Come in! We were just going to have a hot toddy before dinner!"

Judith moved carefully into the kitchen which the Rankers had remodeled that summer. "So were we, but the Brodies drank all our liquor. Could you spare a fifth of something?"

"Carl!" Her husband's name bounced off the walls like a boomerang. To Judith, Arlene had two distinct voices: The one she used for her husband and children was frequently loud and strident; the other, which was reserved for friends and strangers, exhibited the most dulcet tones, a model of warmth and sensitivity. "Here, come into the living room, your dear mother is just coming down. She's been resting." Arlene stopped in the hallway between the kitchen and dining room. *"Carl!* Where are you?"

Carl had sneaked up behind Arlene and Judith. With a deft finger, he goosed his wife. "Here, my darling. May I help you?"

"Yike!" Arlene jumped, almost colliding with the telephone table. She whirled on her husband, who was laughing immoderately. "You're an animal! What will Mr. Busbee think?"

It was clear to Judith that the value of her own opinion had been lost in the mists of time and the avenues of affection. Carl's blue eyes danced in his craggy, handsome face as he patted his wife's bottom and went to the liquor cabinet. "Did I hear you say you could use some whiskey?"

But Judith had moved down the hallway to the arch which led into the beige and brown living room with its accents of emerald-green. Though both houses were basic 1907 saltboxes, their decor was markedly different. Simple contemporary good taste emanated from every room at the Rankers's, as opposed to Judith's eclectic style, with its often bold and sometimes cluttered appointments. But at least one piece in the Rankers's living room struck an unharmonious note: Lester Busbee sat in front of the TV, watching a golf tournament in some exotic place where it apparently didn't snow in late January.

"Hi, Mr. Busbee," said Judith. "Is everything okay?"

Lester looked up a bit groggily. At his feet was a half-

full bottle of beer. Next to the armchair, a six-pack carton
sat empty, mute testimony to Lester's method of passing
the time. "Huh? Oh, it's you, Mrs. McMonahan. I thought
you were an Eskimo. How far are we from Alaska?"

"It's at least a day on foot," Judith replied with a
straight face as she sat down by the television set and
discreetly turned off the sound. "Mr. Busbee, have you
someplace to stay tonight?"

Before Lester could reply, Arlene was on the spot. "Of
course he does, in Kevin's old room." She moved to Lester, noted the empty beer carton, and wagged a finger
under his nose. "Now, now, Lester, all that beer won't
make you feel any better. What you need is a hot meal.
Can you smell the pot roast?"

"But Arlene," Judith protested, "you're probably going to have Mother here again."

Arlene put an arm around Judith. "I hope so! She's such
a doll! We played cribbage all afternoon. She's in Mea-
gan's room. Now let me get your eggs and—"

"Not eggs. Booze." Judith pried herself loose. "Actually, I'd like to talk to Mr. Busbee for a minute. And
Mother, too, when she comes down."

"Well, of course you would," agreed Arlene as the
sound of something boiling over in the kitchen caught her
attention. "Good heavens, it's the carrots!"

Alone with Lester, Judith rushed to the point: "Are you
absolutely sure your mother divorced your father?"

Lester recoiled as if Judith had snapped a whip in his
direction. "What are you talking about?"

"It's simple," said Judith. "I want to know if Gloria—
your mother—was legally free to marry Otto Brodie. It
might not make any difference to you, but it certainly
would have to Wanda."

"Hell, yes!" He cracked his knuckles and scowled at
Judith. "My mom and dad split up when I was two. I
don't remember much about it except for a big fight and
then she'd bitch because my dad was late with his child
support or whatever they called it then. The fact is, Mrs.

Moynihan, I spent more time with my dad than I did with her. She was either hanging around the studios or working behind the desk at the auto court where we lived."

"I see." There was no question that Otto's marriage to Gloria was valid. She had given her name as St. Cloud, not Busbee, on the license, but Judith had the feeling her real name was something else. "What was her real name?" she asked.

Lester's eyebrows lifted slightly. "What do you mean? Gloria Ramona St. Cloud. The Wichita St. Clouds, she always said. She had it changed back after she divorced Dad. Then she called herself Gloria Brodie, when she wasn't calling herself a taxi or a fire hydrant."

Judith moved onto less certain ground as Carl appeared with three unopened bottles cradled in his arms. "Who do you think knew Wanda besides Otto and Dash?" she asked Lester.

Though his eyes were still fixed on the muted TV set, at least they were coming into focus. "Jeez Louise, I don't know most of those creeps myself except Ankles—or whatever he calls himself now. Wanda never talked about any of 'em. The big guy—didn't he play football for the old Hollywood Stars? Maybe he dated Wanda."

"I hope not," murmured Judith as visions of incest danced in her head. "Did she ever mention him? He was known as Lance 'Out-of-Bounds' Brodie in his playing days. In fact, he had knee surgery at St. Peregrine's."

"Is that a fact?" Lester cocked his head and cracked his knuckles, eliciting a grimace from Carl. "Wanda used to work on a lot of celebrities there. Cosmetic stuff, like boob implants and butt lifts. I think they call them something else at the hospital."

"Let's hope so," breathed Judith. But before she could pose her next question, Lester tugged at his ear and spoke up:

"Hey, wait, you mean *Lance Brodie!* Now I remember." Lester actually looked more or less alert. "There was something about the guy that bothered Wanda. His eyes, maybe. It didn't mean much to me at the time, but it bugged her because he had the same last name as her father. That must have been when she started trying to track old Otto down for real.''

Judith considered. Wanda had hazel eyes. So did Lance. And Otto. Perhaps she had recognized a resemblance between the patient and herself. It wouldn't have been that noticeable to anyone else, but coupled with the surname, Wanda's instincts could have risen up to goad her. "Do you think she talked to Lance about his father?" Judith asked.

Lester sucked on a dill pickle. "I don't know. It's usually pretty hard to talk to your patients when they're out cold." He smirked slightly at Judith, as if he'd come up with a witty riposte. "Give me a break, Mrs. McDoodle, that's all I remember about the jock. Or Crazy Otto, for that matter."

Judith tried another tack: "Does the name Stanley Edelstein mean anything?"

"Yeah. He was at St. Peregrine's. Or was he Wanda's dentist?" Lester frowned, then took a big gulp of beer. "There's something about him that sticks in my mind. Did he own a chicken ranch?" He waved the almost-empty bottle at Carl. "Hey, sport, got any refills?"

Carl gave Lester the same winning grin he exerted on temperamental advertising accounts. "Arlene's making hot toddys. Why don't we wait for her?"

Lester didn't seem too pleased at the idea, but gave in. Judith was leaning forward in the chair, feeling as if she were trying to grasp at some elusive object, like chasing guppies in a fish tank. "I don't think Edelstein raised chickens. Neither did Dr. Jack O'Doul, but there is a connection. This is important, Lester." She paused to let her words sink in. "What do you remember about Dr. Edelstein, Dr. O'Doul, and the chicken farmer?"

Lester took the last swig from his bottle. "O'Doul? He was that big-wheel surgeon who got killed in a plane crash, right? Or was that Edelstein?"

"It was O'Doul. And his wife, Cynthia." Judith kept very

still, her eyes never leaving Lester's mottled face. "Think, there must be something Wanda told you about them."

Lester thought. But his gaze had grown fuzzy again. "That was a long time ago, right?" He fumbled in the pocket of his plaid sports coat, then gave a little laugh. "I forgot. I quit smoking for New Year's. Carl, you got a cigarette?" Carl produced a pack and lighter. Lester lit up, inhaled deeply, and coughed twice. "Jeez Louise, I feel light-headed! Where was I?"

Judith gritted her teeth. "We were talking about Dr. O'Doul . . ."

"Oh, yeah, yeah." Lester nodded jerkily. "I didn't see much of Wanda for a while there, I was selling used cars in Studio City. But I remember she got all worked up over some deal at the hospital where a hotshot sawbones screwed up. Some kind of cover-up went on, I think. In fact, it was about the same time that she told me Lance Brodie had been at St. Perry's. Sure, it could have been O'Doul. Why not?" Behind a haze of smoke, Lester sat back in the chair, looking inordinately pleased with himself.

Judith was not so pleased, but held on to her patience. Lester wasn't telling her much she didn't already know—or could surmise. Unless . . . The idea that had been forming earlier in the day flitted through her brain, then evaporated. As for Lester, he was reclining in the chair, eyes closed, humming an off-key version of "Wake Up, Little Susie."

Judith wasn't going to get much more out of Lester for a while. Resigned to frustration, she started from the chair, but stopped when she heard the familiar clump of her mother's walker on the stairs. Carl winked at Judith and went into the hallway.

"Hey, sweetheart," he called, "you want a piggyback ride to the sofa?"

"Go on, you devil!" rasped Gertrude, though there was a coy edge to her voice. "You think because I'm old, I'm *easy?*"

Another series of clumps brought Gertrude into the living room. She was wearing a red tartan housecoat under a blue and white Norwegian sweater. Judith did not recall sending either garment over to the Rankers's.

"Well!" Gertrude's contempt was obvious as she spotted her daughter. "I'm not speaking to you. Take a hike!"

Startled, Judith fell back in the chair. "Mother, I'm sorry. We're stuck with the Brodies. They can't go home until one of them is charged with the crime. Or else they're all cleared. Joe says—"

Gertrude whirled around with amazing sprightliness, walker and all. "Joe! I know what that wolf in sheep's clothing says! Worse yet, I know what his kind *does!* And I thought you had more sense! Hussy!" Her face had gone quite pale, and a pulse throbbed along her jawline. Judith was more flabbergasted than angered. But Gertrude was banging away at the walker, moving with stiff-backed determination toward the sofa.

"Wait a minute, Mother," Judith pleaded. "I've lived like a nun since Dan died and you know it." She caught Carl and even Lester watching with interest; Arlene's red-gold head poked out from the door to the adjoining dining room.

"Some nun!" Gertrude sank down onto the sofa like a parachute crumpling to the ground. "Don't try to fool me, Judith Anne! I saw you two on that bed! It's a wonder I didn't have a stroke!" She grabbed at her chest as if to make sure her heart was still pumping.

"You *what?*" Judith was aghast. She spared not a glance for the rest of her audience. "How could you see such a thing?" The question was literal as well as figurative: Hillside Manor and the Rankers's house were close enough for window peeking, but the snow would have obscured Gertrude's vision. "Well?" demanded Judith, seeing her mother's set expression.

"I got two eyes, don't I?" Gertrude looked smug as well as outraged. "We borrowed Dooley's telescope. It's real powerful, even with the snow coming down. Arlene got it for me. She thought it might help me keep track of what was going on in my own house." Gertrude glanced out into the dining room where Arlene still lingered at the door. *"Some* people still care about old folks."

Judith put a hand to her head. What to pursue? It was a toss-up between her mother's ridiculous accusations and Arlene's blatant prying. "Telescope or not, you didn't see anything I wouldn't do in the front yard."

Gertrude snorted and turned up her nose. "Not in *my* front yard!"

Judith was weary of reminding her mother that, legally, Hillside Manor was not her domain. It was clearly time to throw in the towel. "Oh, never mind!" The liquor bottles clanked together as she rose. "I have to get back. Thanks so much," she said with a ragged smile for Carl. "Enjoy your dinner," she added to Lester. But he was snoring softly, splayed feet halfway across the carpet.

On the way out through the kitchen, she gave Arlene a frazzled shake of her head. "Mother gets notions. Ignore them."

"Well, of course she does!" Arlene beamed at Judith. "The main thing is, she cares about you so much. Isn't she a treasure?"

"If she were, I'd bury her," muttered Judith.

"Now, now," cooed Arlene, "she just enjoys fussing over you. Oh!" She stopped, blue eyes dancing. "I almost forgot, I must give you back those clippings."

"Clippings?" Judith blinked.

"Yes, the ones I took off your bed this morning when I came over to get that tartan housecoat. Your mother said the one you sent had too many cigarette burns in it. She wanted her blue sweater, too, and I didn't see you around anywhere, so I just used her keys and—oh! Here they are, I put them in this book by Guinevere Arthur so I wouldn't forget. Association, you know." Still smiling, Arlene handed over the purloined clippings, sticking them in the front pocket of Judith's jacket. "What do you think? The man with amnesia ran over that doctor and forgot he did it?"

To Judith, it was one theory that didn't bear even fleeting consideration. But she was too overwhelmed by Arlene's audacity to pursue the skewed hypothesis. "Arlene—did you tell anyone about those clippings?"

Arlene took on an injured air. "Why, no! I haven't seen anybody, not with this cold weather. Oh, I spoke to Mrs. Dooley when I borrowed the telescope, and I saw Gabe Porter across the street putting on his snow tires, and I guess I mentioned the clippings to one of those reporters. Such an earnest young man, probably just starting out. It's nice to help people make their way in the world, don't you think?"

Judith emitted a noise that was akin to a whimper, though the truth was, no harm had been done as far as the murder investigation was concerned. The newscast Renie heard hadn't mentioned what was in the clippings, no doubt because the radio station couldn't make head or tails out of Arlene's fragmentary information. Still, Judith was miffed.

"Why did you take the clippings?" she asked, wanting to hear how Arlene would circumvent the truth.

The blue eyes shimmered with the hint of tears. "For your mother, of course. She's over here stewing and fretting so. When I went to look for you in your bedroom, I saw them on the bed, and naturally I assumed they were your own mementos. I know how old people love to reminisce and I knew you wouldn't be having any spare time to look at them, so I brought them over here. Then I realized they had something to do with the murder. So I thought she and I could play detective when we got tired of cribbage. It perked her up," Arlene asserted with a compassionate little smile.

"I see." The convoluted explanation wasn't vintage Arlene, but it wasn't bad, either. Judith decided to let the matter drop. Except for Arlene's inquisitiveness and the occasional brawl, the Rankers had been steadfast neighbors and loyal friends for over twenty years. And, Judith realized, she herself had stolen the clippings first.

"That's one of Gwen's books?" Judith asked, pointing to the gaudy paperback. "Do you read them?"

Arlene's embarrassment was halfhearted. "She's really pretty good. As a writer, I mean. I was hoping I'd get to meet her, but I thought I'd wait and see if she killed that Wanda woman." She lifted a shoulder. "You know, it would make a difference in my opinion of her—and her novels."

Judith juggled the liquor bottles and picked up the paperback. *"Chastity's Belt Buckle.* Where do they get these titles?" Awkwardly, she flipped through the pages with one hand. "Hunh. It's set during the Civil War, among the North Carolina pro-Union insurgents. That sounds a bit deep for Gwen."

"Oh, no," insisted Arlene. "Chastity is a Confederate spy. She carries secrets inside the fake jewel on the belt of her riding habit. But of course she falls in love with one of the insurgents. All of Guinevere's books are based on real history. She's done the Hussite revolt, the Jesuits under Elizabeth I, the Wat Tyler rebellion—and then there are her contemporaries where she deals with real problems and issues, like epilepsy and the new poor."

Judith didn't try to conceal her astonishment. To compound matters, a cursory look indicated that Gwen actually used subjects and predicates and even displayed a certain amount of style.

"There's romance, of course," admitted Arlene. "And sex, to make the books sell, I suppose. Though the manager down at the bookstore at the bottom of the Hill told me she doesn't make a lot of money. She writes over a lot of readers' heads."

Including Gwen's own, thought Judith, and immediately recognized the unfairness of her reaction. "Can I borrow this?" asked Judith.

"Sure, I finished it last week. I've got some more, out in the bookcase."

"That's fine," said Judith, already wondering if she'd make it home with her load of bottles and *Chastity's Belt Buckle.* "I just want a sample. For now."

"Enjoy it." Arlene had gone to open the door for Judith. "My favorite is the Jesuit one, *Love's Prelate.* I think I lent it to Jeanne Ericson, but she never gave it back."

Judith made an appropriate remark, thanked Arlene for

everything, and began her cautious route back home. The snow was still coming down and the wind now howled between the houses. The garage and the toolshed at the back of the yard were all but obscured. Her foot slipped once, but she righted herself and had almost reached the back porch when a blurred figure streaked by, striking her left leg. Judith staggered and fell, clutching the liquor bottles against her down jacket.

"Sweetums, you wretch!" she shrieked, rolling onto the back steps in a manner not unlike a large padded pinwheel. The bottles were intact, Gwen's novel somehow wedged between them. At the door, Sweetums was clawing like mad, swinging back and forth on the screen.

Swearing under her breath, Judith crawled up the steps, set her burden down on the porch, and struggled to her feet. Her shins hurt, her shoulder felt jarred, and her teeth ached. But pain gave way to anger. Grabbing an old mop stick that probably dated from Grandma Grover's era, Judith took a swing at Sweetums. She missed, but the cat let out a menacing hiss, plopped onto the mat, and arched his back at Judith before taking off at a speed that tempted to break the sound barrier.

"Cat soup, cat stew, cat casserole, cat crepes," muttered Judith, tossing aside the mop stick and retrieving her belongings. "I'll kill that animal some day, I swear it!" Still muttering, she opened the door and stamped her way into the little back entry hall. Before she could blink against the bright lights of the kitchen, Sweetums raced past her, headed for the dining room.

"That poor cat," said Renie, calmly grinding pepper onto the raw steaks that she'd laid out on the counter. "How can you stand keeping him outside in weather like this?" Renie looked up from her culinary pursuit. "Gee, you look terrible! Did Lester chase you around the Rankers's living room?"

"Lester's unconscious." Judith started opening the liquor bottles even before she removed her jacket. "Go offer some of this to four so-called guests. If they don't want it—ha, ha—then pour it on Sweetums and I'll bring a match.''

''That nap didn't put you in a very good mood,'' Renie said with a touch of reprimand. ''Or was it my intrusion?''

Judith was stuffing *Chastity's Belt Buckle* and its contents inside her sweater. ''Skip it. I fell up the back steps. I also forgot the chives. Where's Joe?''

Renie was putting the bottles on a tray along with a bucket of ice and some glasses. ''He's in the front parlor with Woody. We made mulled wine while we were waiting for you. What was going on over there? Your mother giving you a bad time?''

''*My* mother?'' Judith looked at Renie in mock horror. ''She's at the Rankers's, knitting me a fleecy shawl and crooning over my baby pictures.''

Renie arched her eyebrows. ''Huh? Oh!'' she said suddenly, ''Falstaff's Market called while you were out and asked if you still wanted that roasting chicken for Sunday dinner. If so, will you pick it up or should they put it on a toboggan?''

''Drat, I forgot all about it. I asked Uncle Vince and Auntie Vance to eat with us. Maybe I should cancel. If it keeps snowing, they'll never get up the Hill anyway.'' She reached for the phone and started to tap out Falstaff's number, but heard Mavis's voice on the line.

''. . . ratings war with KWIP,'' Mavis was saying in her incisive manner. Business as usual, thought Judith, and started to hang up, but caught a snatch of another woman's voice at the other end of the line:

''. . . don't need a murder on top of that.'' Judith stood motionless, gesturing for Renie to keep quiet. The unknown woman was using well-modulated tones which suggested she, too, might be part of the electronic media. ''I still don't see why you didn't tell Lance the truth back then.''

''He didn't need to know,'' Mavis said flatly. ''Lance knows so little to begin with.''

''But his own sister!'' The second speaker sounded gen-

uinely appalled. Judith waved Renie to join her at the ear-
piece. "Mavis, sometimes you're *too* tough."

"I have to be tough, Kim, for both of us," Mavis said
grimly.

"I suppose," Kim replied in resignation. "At least
Wanda had a blameless reputation, except for those two
disastrous marriages."

"Anybody can make a couple of mistakes," Mavis allowed, sounding unusually charitable. "You're absolutely
certain she was still seeing Rico or Dash or whatever he
calls himself as recently as last summer?"

Judith and Renie were literally head-to-head, both of
their faces screwed up in concentration. "My hospital
contact is unimpeachable," insisted Kim. "Didn't I get
my start as a medical and science reporter?"

"Okay. Thanks, Kim. Good luck on the new talk
show." Mavis sounded faintly weary.

"Thanks. Good luck with . . . everything." There was
a pause at the other end. "Lance wouldn't do anything
dumb, would he?"

Mavis actually laughed, but it was a hollow sound. "I
told you, he didn't know anything."

There was another pause. "No. Of course he didn't. I
keep forgetting how dense Lance is."

"Don't forget," said Mavis in a warning voice. "Especially if you're ever asked to be a character witness.
Remember, my husband is as dumb as a rope," Mavis
declared, and hung up.

Judith waited a few seconds, then did the same. The
cousins eyed each other. Judith spoke first: "Well. So Mavis guessed."

"That Wanda and Lance were related?" Renie wrin-
kled her pug nose. "She may have known about Otto for
years. She's very shrewd, I'll give her that. It would have
been easy for her in her capacity as a reporter to check
the records in L.A."

"If Wanda noticed a resemblance between her own eyes
and Lance's, then maybe Mavis did, too." Seeing Renie's

blank look, Judith explained what Lester had told her within the hour. "Ordinarily, I suppose a patient's spouse wouldn't come into contact with an O.R. nurse. But Mavis is the type who'd grill any member of the staff she could get her paws on. Still, if she didn't tell Lance, would she confide in any other members of the family? Mavis isn't exactly buddy-buddy with her in-laws." Judith headed for the hallway to hang up her jacket, pausing to glance outside at the swirling snow. Movement at the edge of her vision caught her attention. There, on the porch that ran the width of the house, stood Mavis and Gwen, their attitude one of conspiracy. Judith took a deep breath and tiptoed back into the kitchen. "So I was wrong. Mavis and Gwen are outside, looking like a couple of sorority sisters."

Renie looked up from the cocktail napkins she'd been counting. "They probably are. The UCLA connection. I'm willing to believe anything about now."

"Including the fact that Dash did see Wanda after their divorce." Judith was feeling rather dazed, as well as stiff and sore from her tumble in the snow. "Never mind all that now, let's get going. I can hear the animals rattling their cages."

She could, in fact, for the Brodies were making angry noises out in the living room. The object of their ire almost toppled Renie—Sweetums was running for his life, seeking sanctuary in the basement. Judith ignored both the fleeing cat and the incensed Brodies, taking time to dig into her handbag for lipstick, blush and a touch-up to hide the dark circles under her eyes. After putting her black suede flats back on, she slipped out through the dining room and into the entry hall, then beat a hasty retreat into the front parlor. No one in the living room, including an embattled Renie, had noticed her. With a sigh of relief, she leaned against the door and shut her eyes. Her guests were barred, and Sweetums was outlawed. Judith wondered where Gertrude was training the telescope.

FIFTEEN

"WHERE ARE THE hors d'oeuvres?" asked Joe. He was sitting in the bay window which had once been an inglenook. His stockinged feet rested on an embroidered satin pillow; he held a pewter goblet in one hand and a Havana in the other. Woody Price was stirring the punch bowl with a cinnamon stick and humming along to a recording of Beethoven's *Eroica* symphony on the CD player Mike had given his mother for Christmas. The fire was burning merrily in the grate and the snow was inching up against the windows. The room smelled of wood smoke, pungent spices, and good cigars. Judith felt warm and protected and ridiculously happy. She laughed aloud at Joe's request.

"Nothing seems real," she said in wonder. Her dark eyes traveled around the cozy room, seeing the familiar surroundings through a mist of emotion. Somehow, it seemed right for Joe to be so casually ensconced in the window seat embrasure. For one giddy moment, it occurred to Judith that he belonged there. But she thrust the thought aside, and spoke of something quite different: "How can we be in here, snug as bugs, and out in that other room, a killer is complaining about my cat?"

Joe put his feet down and patted the vacant place next to him on the window seat. "Sit. We've made some progress."

"And some wine," put in Officer Price, handing Judith a goblet from the eighteenth-century set that had belonged to her grandmother. He smiled for the first time since Judith had met him, an engaging flash of white teeth set off by his dark skin and black moustache. The wine, she thought, or Renie's erratic maternal instincts had drawn him out.

"Thanks." Judith smiled back, then hesitated before joining Joe on the window seat. "Well?"

Joe exhaled a trio of smoke rings. "To begin with, Dash's buddies were a pair of bookies. He's up to his ascot in debt and needs money yesterday."

"Can Gwen bail him out?" inquired Judith, making sure she was seated as far from Joe as space would permit.

"We gather she's tried to help, but Gwen's royalties aren't exactly coming off of the *New York Times* bestseller list," Joe explained. "In fact, she's behind a payment on her condo overlooking the ship canal. Hence, a motive, or at least more of one, to eliminate Wanda. Assuming, of course, that Dash knew who Wanda's dad was."

"He might have," said Judith, relating the overheard phone conversation between Mavis and her L.A. connection. Joe listened with rapt attention, his green eyes fixed on Judith's face. She squirmed a little before adding the part about seeing Mavis and Gwen on the back porch. "Mavis must have come straight down from the phone in the upstairs hall. But I don't see her rushing to alert Gwen about Dash's continuing relationship with Wanda. Are we missing something?"

"A lot, probably." Joe drummed his fingers on his knees. "Murder makes strange bedfellows. For all we know, Mavis and Gwen hired Dash as a hit man to eliminate Wanda."

"Eliminating Otto would make more sense," said Judith, glancing out the window. At least three inches of snow already covered the ground. The planes and angles of the Ericson house looked like ski jumps. "Nobody gets any money as long as Otto's alive."

"Dash and Gwen aren't the only ones who need money," Joe went on. "Speaking of Mavis, she wasn't headed for KINE-TV last night, but for that pair of so-called business associates Lance has gotten mixed up with. They're putting the squeeze on him, and Club Stud could go belly-up at any minute. Mavis wouldn't like that for a lot of reasons, least of all because she'd hate to have to read that story off her cue cards. I don't think she took that .357 magnum along to protect her honor."

"I wondered," said Judith. "She wasn't dressed for work. I suppose Lance and Mavis blame the chain's woes on Calvin Tweeks's defection."

"Not entirely," replied Joe, going to the punch bowl for a refill. "Once Lance gets used to a routine, he functions almost like a normal human being." Joe sat back down on the window seat, this time a few inches closer to Judith. "But Mavis admitted that Lance hasn't been tending to business lately. He's been out of the office a lot, playing golf."

The door from the living room flew open, revealing a rattled Renie, clinging to a half-empty bottle of bourbon. "Holy cats! With any luck, that crew will all kill each other and you guys can arrest the sole survivor!"

Joe was unmoved by the news of the Brodies' collective distemper. "It's good for them. Gives them a taste of what jail is like." He caught Judith's glare and tried to make amends: "An elegant jail, of course, with superior food."

"Speaking of food," said Renie, pouring herself a stiff bourbon, "when shall I put the steaks on?"

Judith checked her watch. "Wait until six. Joe is filling us in."

As Renie and Woody sat at the little table in front of the fire, Joe quickly went over the ground he'd already covered. Judith listened closely to the details of the M.E.'s report, but the technical terms were lost on her. However, both she and Renie pounced on the essentials:

"How was the sodium pentothal administered?" asked Judith.

"Which poison actually killed her?" queried Renie. "The sodium pentothal or the cyanide?"

Joe tapped ash into a shamrock-shaped dish. "I talked to Otto again, as well as Dash and Mavis. The amount of cyanide Otto put in the tea jibes with the amount Wanda ingested. In fact, she didn't take as much as he gave her. And he's right, it wasn't anywhere near a lethal dose. But the sodium pentothal was."

"Don't tell me it was in the cream puffs!" Judith shrank back against the wall of the window seat.

But Joe shook his head. "It was administered directly into her bloodstream." He saw the startled expressions on Judith and Renie's faces. "That's right, it was injected, no doubt courtesy of Harvey's medical kit."

"You mean Harvey did it?" Renie exclaimed, inadvertently spilling bourbon on her battered sweatshirt.

It was Woody Price who answered while Joe tried to relight his cigar. "Not necessarily. Harvey says his case was rifled. If that's true, anybody could have done it. We checked for fingerprints, but it was clean—except for Harvey's and Ellie's."

"No," countered Judith. "Not just anybody could have done it. Doesn't sodium pentothal work very fast?"

"Usually," said Joe, the cigar glowing again. "But it depends on the person. I sure as hell wish one of you had stayed in that dining room to see who got up and moved around."

Judith made an effort to refill her goblet, but Woody Price rushed to the rescue. "What do the Brodies say?" asked Judith. "They must have noticed. At least Mavis would."

"They all noticed," replied Joe. "That's the problem. Harvey went to the john, Ellie and Mavis came out to the kitchen, Lance got up to keep his knee from going stiff, Dash went to the sideboard to get some brandy, Oriana dropped an earring, Gwen had to examine something in the china cupboard. The only one who didn't leave his place after the fortune-teller sat down was Otto—and he didn't have to, because he was knee-to-knee with his little Wanda.''

Judith stared into her goblet, Renie was scratching her pug nose, Price was mulling over the mulled wine, Joe had resumed blowing smoke rings. Or maybe just smoke, thought Judith with a flash of anger.

"This is progress?'' she burst out. Ignoring Joe's offended reaction, she plunged ahead. "Come on, we may know how, but we don't know who—or why. You want results? Here!'' She reached under her red sweater and pulled the missing evidence out from the waistband of her slacks.

"What the hell?'' Joe stared at the creased clippings. "Where did you get these? *This* time.''

Judith deliberately lifted her chin to show off her strong profile. "I don't think I'll tell you.''

"I'll tell you something,'' asserted Renie, joining the fray. "Where did I put those magazines?'' Her eyes darted around the room, coming to rest on the bottom shelf of the tea wagon. "When I went to the basement to get the steaks out of the freezer, I decided to have another go at the *Opera News*es. We had a much better idea of what to look for after we talked to Oriana.'' She paused as she bent down to get the magazines. "First, I found a review of her La Scala debut, January 11, 1974. Listen to this: 'Bustamanti's electrifying Carmen not only assuaged the disappointment of Bumbry's fans, but announced to the opera world that a new star is on the rise. The unerring pitch, the rich timbre, and the mature technique of her voice are astounding qualities in one so young. Under Maestro Sanzogno's baton, the dazzling understudy's lack of rehearsal time was hardly noticeable. The audience was so emotionally drained by Bustamanti's' vocal prowess that it could barely summon up the energy to applaud after each of her arias. However, the house erupted into a wild ovation at the opera's climactic scene when Don Jose dealt the fatal blow to his faithless Carmen. This auspicious debut has launched a career of international significance for the ravishing unknown from the Bronx, New York.' " Renie closed the magazine and regarded her listeners like a singer who has just finished an audition. "Sounds great, huh?"

"Too great," remarked Judith, but wasn't sure why.

"Then let me read on." Renie opened the second copy of *Opera News.* "Here we have Oriana in Brussels, six months later. 'The Azucena of Oriana Bustamanti was marred by troubles with pitch and breathing control. Her *Stride la Vampa* was horrific rather than horrifying. The laudatory reviews she received last winter at La Scala did not seem justified as far as Belgian opera-goers are concerned.' "

"Maybe Verdi wasn't the right repertoire for her," suggested Woody Price.

Renie had the third and last magazine in hand. "So it seems. Here's what they said about her Eboli in Vienna the following September. *'Don Carlo* is an operatic rarity in that Verdi wrote his best music for the mezzo-soprano rather than the soprano. But the composer's efforts were wasted on Oriana Bustamanti, who produced a series of harsh, undisciplined sounds that made her listeners wish she'd put the patch over her mouth instead of her eye.' Strong stuff, huh?"

"Savage," said Price.

"Ugly," said Joe.

"Suspicious," said Judith.

"How so?" Joe asked as the windowpane behind him shuddered in the wind.

Judith turned to Renie. "You know more about opera than I do, coz. But isn't La Scala a tough house?"

"Very," replied Renie. "The Milan critics are viscious." She looked at Woody for confirmation. "What's that other one in Italy, where they bring rotten fruit and vegetables to throw at the singers?''

''Parma,'' said Woody. ''Or is it Palermo? I've never been to Europe, but I'd like to go some day. Especially to Bayreuth, for Wagner.''

''For Chrissakes,'' exploded Joe, ''two years I've worked with you, Woody, and you turn out to be Boris-Freaking-Godolfsky!''

''Sorry, sir,'' murmured Woody with his usual stoic expression. ''My mother is very musical. She's a soloist with the Afro-American Free Methodist Church.''

''Never mind,'' grumbled Joe, with the air of a man forgiving the unforgivable. ''Okay, so those reviews are peculiar. So what? That was more than fifteen years ago.'' He leaned forward to take the magazines from Renie. ''How does any of this hook up with Wanda Rakesh?''

Judith was candid. ''I don't know. Except that Oriana and Dash are probably related, and Wanda used to be married to Dash. If you'd check his passport, I'll bet you'd find he'd been in Milan when Oriana made her debut.''

''We did check.'' Joe motioned at Woody. ''Look up those dates in your notebook.''

Price complied. ''She's right, sir. He entered Italy January 3, 1974. He crossed the border into France on February 26, then went to Spain April 10, and on to England two weeks later. He was brought back to the States for parole violation on May 5.''

Judith had gotten up and was pacing the room. ''That first review—there's definitely something odd about it. No, not odd, it's—oh, I can't put my finger on it.'' She picked up the issue and paged through until she found the article. The grandfather clock in the living room chimed six p.m. Judith closed the magazine and took a last drink from her goblet. ''Let's get the steaks on. I'll let whatever it is percolate in the back of my head.''

Out in the kitchen, Judith and Renie found Gwen refilling the ice bucket. ''Daddy's feeling much more relaxed,'' she said. ''He was so annoyed because his lawyer hadn't shown up. But Mr. Muggins was in Denver and only just got in before the snow started. Now I suppose he can't get up this hill.''

"Once it starts snowing on Heraldsgate, we're marooned," said Judith with a trace of gloom. It was all too true. Snow was a local rarity, falling perhaps once or twice a season, and some years, not at all. In a city of steep hills where the natives found snow a novelty rather than a challenge, few knew how to cope. Instead, the entire metropolitan area shut up shop for the duration. The total paralysis caused by two or three inches of snow never failed to make the national news, much to the amusement of East Coast and Midwestern inhabitants. "Snow tires and chains help, but not a lot," Judith went on in a morose voice. "It's too hard to get up the Hill. We were stuck here for five days last February.''

Gwen's china-blue eyes went wide with alarm. "Five days! Oh, no! I have a deadline to meet for my publisher! However will I manage?''

"Mike has a word processor upstairs," said Judith, opening the oven door and noticing that the smell of singed leather still lingered from Wanda's satchel. "Feel free to use it."

Gwen hugged the ice bucket to her bulging bosom. "Oh, I couldn't! I mean, I might not know the program you use. Oh, dear! This is too dreadful!''

Judith finished putting the steaks under the broiler and stood aside for Renie to drop the diced bacon into a kettle. "I borrowed one of your books from my neighbor," said Judith to the agitated Gwen. *"Chastity's Belt Buckle.* Tell me, do you think North Carolina's reluctance to join the Confederacy stemmed from the same people who supported the Union later on in the war?''

Gwen looked blank. "It's possible." The ice rattled against her chest. "I'm sure it was true of some of them. Or at least a few.''

Judith couldn't hide her puzzlement. "Maybe I put the question badly. What are you working on right now?''

Gwen brightened. "It's a contemporary, about a beautiful young graphics designer who falls in love with a handsome young homeless man. She finds him searching through the office garbage. I don't know whether to call it *Destiny's Dumpster* or *No Can of Her Own*. What do you think?"

"I can't," replied Judith, overwhelmed in more ways than one.

"Gee," said Renie, "that's . . . interesting. How are you researching your heroine's career?"

A bellow erupted from the living room. Otto was calling for the ice. Gwen jumped, but graciously answered Renie's question. "I do my homework. I've met some of the city's top designers. They've been ever so kind."

"Who?" asked Renie pointedly.

The blue eyes widened again. "Oh—the cream. They're the people behind the scenes," Gwen added loftily. "You wouldn't know them."

"But I *am* one," declared Renie, matching round-eyed stare for stare.

"Oh!" Gwen's hands fluttered over the ice bucket as if it were a fussy child. "Well! How exciting!" Otto's trumpeting voice grew even testier. "Excuse me, Daddy is getting a teeny bit restless. I hope he's not having another spell."

Watching the door swing shut behind Gwen, Judith reached for the aspirin. "If Otto isn't having a spell, I am. My legs hurt, my head aches, and my teeth are driving me nuts. I'll bet I need about four root canals and I won't be able to get to the dentist until the snow's gone."

"Gwen's a phony," said Renie as the bacon sizzled in the kettle. "Or am I being cynical?"

"You're being unsympathetic. To me," retorted Judith, swallowing the aspirin. "As for Gwen, you're right. Something's wrong there. According to Arlene, Gwen's books are not only well-written, but painstakingly researched. So who's her ghost writer?"

Renie tossed cut-up onion in with the bacon. "It could be anybody. We don't know who her friends are."

"But why?" puzzled Judith, opening a jar of green olives. "I know some writers work as a team and use a single name, but they don't make any secret of it. Who'd want to remain anonymous, do all the writing, and let someone else get all the glory?"

Renie turned thoughtful, a can of cut beans in one hand. "Somebody who is very shy, I suppose. Somebody who doesn't want to meet the public."

"Maybe. Or somebody who already knows the public too well." For a few minutes, the cousins toiled in silence, each lost in her own mental machinations. The potatoes were already done, the steaks were broiling away, the beans bubbled with the bacon and onion bits. Judith filled celery stalks with cream cheese and set them out on a serving dish with the olives. It would be a simple, yet satisfying meal, and as far as Judith was concerned, more than the Brodies deserved. She was momentarily pleased until it dawned on her that there was no dessert.

"They polished off the ice cream at lunch," fretted Judith, frantically searching the refrigerator. "What should we do?"

"Not to worry," said Renie, flipping a tea towel from a baking dish. "While you were upstairs dallying with Joe Flynn, Woody and I made apple crisp. The whipped cream is in that white bowl on the second shelf."

Judith gave her cousin a grateful look. "You're a peach—when you're not being an idiot." She picked up the celery and olives, along with a stack of plates, and headed out into the dining room. The silverware and napkins were already on the table, along with a fresh linen cloth from Belgium and the red azalea, which gave Judith a momentary shiver. Trying to ignore the fractious voices in the living room, she finished setting the table just as Oriana approached with quick, high-heeled steps.

"Are you ready to serve?" Oriana asked with a note of anxiety in her voice. "Otto is growing quite . . . unruly."

Otto wasn't the only one, Judith thought as she heard Mavis barking at Harvey and Ellie whining at Lance. "Five minutes," said Judith, aware that Oriana's makeup was smudged and her usual self-possession was frayed around the edges. "In fact," Judith said with sudden inspiration, "why don't you come into the kitchen, and we'll figure out who likes their steaks how?"

Oriana hesitated. "I'm not sure I know," she demurred.

But Judith just stood there with a smile on her face. At last, Oriana relented. Nudging Renie out of the way, Judith opened the broiler. "Right now, they all look rare. Who's for medium or well-done?"

"Otto prefers well-done. I like mine medium. So do Lance and Mavis. Harvey eats his practically raw. I'm not sure about the others."

"I'll pull the rarest for Harvey and put it on a warming plate," said Judith. She picked up a steak knife and plunged it into the thickest portion of T-bone. Red juices spurted out, and Judith nodded. "It's dead, but barely." She put the knife down and searched for her meat fork. "We can ask the rest of them or just go for medium. Now where is that blasted fork? Renie, did you see it?"

"The last time I saw your meat fork was five years ago when it was sticking out of your husband's behind," Renie said somewhat absently as she piled baked potatoes into an oval dish. "Don't you remember, Dan threw the Thanksgiving turkey out in the street because Aunt Opal didn't put enough sage in the dressing? You got mad and stabbed him in the butt."

"That's because the coward was waddling away." Judith gave Oriana a faintly embarrassed glance, then picked up the copy of *Opera News* which she'd left on the kitchen counter by the breadbox. "Guess what, we've been reading up on your career. It sounds as if you were a sensation in Milan."

Oriana's eyes narrowed as she reached for the magazine. "Give me that! How did you get hold of it?"

Judith held the copy at arm's length from the shorter Oriana. "It's mine. I save them. Don't you have your own?" she asked innocently.

Oriana's sultry mouth tightened and her entire body tensed. For a brief moment, she seemed on the verge of exploding. Then, quite slowly, her shoulders relaxed, her face assumed it's faintly arrogant yet provocative mask, and she gave a little toss of her head. "I certainly do. That issue chronicles how my star was born. La Scala was the most glorious night of my life. I sang like a goddess." A patronizing smile played at the smudged lips. Oriana lifted her chin, turned on her high heels, and floated out of the kitchen as if making a stage exit.

"What was that all about?" inquired Renie, draining the beans.

Judith had a strange look on her face. "Coz," she said, "you read those *Opera News* reviews aloud very well. But you didn't go quite far enough." She held out the magazine to Renie. "Look. The critique of *Carmen* from La Scala was submitted by none other than Arturo Allegro. Maybe Dash should have called himself Vocals instead of Ankles."

SIXTEEN

"HOLD IT!" YELLED Renie, almost dropping the beans as she scanned the signature at the end of the La Scala review. "Don't you dare go out in that dining room until you explain! Are you trying to tell me that Dash worked for *Opera News* under one of his other aliases?"

Judith had stopped at the door. "He admitted he used the name of Allegro at one time. His father, Dukes, was probably still alive then, and he had a lot of money. Maybe he even augmented the Bustamantis' piggy bank for Oriana's studies abroad. So here comes her big chance, Cousin Dash—or Artie or Ankles—is on hand, and together they connive at getting Oriana at least one rave review."

Renie's mobile face showed the workings of her brain as she digested Judith's theory. "How? By doping all the real critics? That's preposterous!"

"But bribing them isn't." Judith gave Renie a canny look. "Dash thinks big. This is the same guy who tried to buy a Rose Bowl. Would Milan strike him as any more of a challenge than Pasadena?''

"I don't know." Renie was still dubious, but open to persuasion. "I can't see every critic at La Scala being so venal."

"They only needed one. At least for American fans. It might have been muscle, not money. Or maybe the real critic got sick—Grace Bumbry did, so there could have been a rampant virus loose in Northern Italy that winter. In any event, our brash Dash filled in, and Oriana got the kind of prestigious review which would bring her other offers. Of course she couldn't pull something like that off again. That conversation I heard on the stairs makes sense now—Oriana mentioned 'blackmail' and 'sense of family.' I suspect Dash and Oriana cut a deal, and when she started getting other roles after her La Scala success, he got a chunk of her earnings. Now he wants more." Judith opened the kitchen door an inch and glanced into the dining room to make sure the Brodies hadn't yet trooped in to dinner. "But the giveaway was Oriana's comment about 'stabbed to the heart.' It called attention to Carmen's death scene, and that was the part of the review that sounded so odd. The listeners were so stunned by her magnificent performance—according to Arturo Allegro—that they couldn't even applaud. Except when she got stabbed and died, they went wild. I figure they didn't clap after her arias because she stank. But when she finally went sticks up, they roared with approval—or relief.''

Renie was leaning against the counter, still gripping the beans. "Could be." She looked bemused, her brown eyes roving up into the nether reaches of the high kitchen ceiling. But both her gaze and her thoughts came quickly down to earth. "So—as we said before, what does Oriana's phony review have to do with Wanda?''

Judith, hearing the Brodies start a stampede for the dining room, gave an impatient shrug. "I don't know. The only obvious crime is lousy reporting. We're only guessing about the bribes. Maybe Wanda knew the truth. Oriana wouldn't have liked that.''

''But Oriana would have had to been able to recognize Wanda as Madame Gushenka,'' Renie pointed out.

''She might have seen pictures,'' said Judith. ''We've got to talk to Dash again after dinner. But right now we've got to *serve* dinner. Let's hit it.''

Renie dutifully brought out the beans and potatoes. Over the wrangling of the Brodies, Judith was trying to parcel out the steaks. Joe lounged at the door of the entry hall, hands in his pockets; Woody Price was right behind him, standing like a totem.

''Got enough for a pair of working stiffs?'' inquired Joe.

''What?'' Judith leaned forward to catch his words and was rewarded with a slap on the bottom from Otto. ''Hands on the table,'' she snarled, forgetting her role of gracious hostess.

''Hey, toots,'' said Otto to Judith in a voice blurred by drink, ''you wanna play Throb and Thrust?''

''Shut up!'' Oriana's uncustomarily uncouth command cut across the table. ''You're disgusting!''

''Daddy's under stress,'' put in Gwen, giving her father a cloying look. ''He's not a well man.''

''Daddy's full of hooey,'' declared Mavis.

''Daddy's full of *scotch*,'' Lance corrected his wife in a serious voice. ''I've never seen him drink anything called hooey.''

''He would if it were eighty proof,'' muttered Harvey, slitting his baked potato as if it were an abdomen.

''Hush!'' hissed Ellie. ''Uncle Otto does look a bit peaked.''

Only Dash remained silent during this exchange, his attention focused on his plate. Judith managed to avoid further molestation from Otto, and finally escaped back into the kitchen with Renie, Joe, and Woody at her heels.

''There's enough for all of us tonight,'' she assured the others. ''But you'll have to wait for the steaks. I couldn't get more than eight under the broiler at once.'' She started to remove the T-bones from a platter on the counter when the phone rang. Renie answered it, but quickly handed it over to Judith.

The caller identified herself as Norma Paine. ''Judith,'' she said in an incisive manner, ''you know Wilbur and me. We're SOTS.''

''Of course you are, Norma,'' said Judith, acknowledging the nickname for parishioners of Our Lady, Star of the Sea Roman Catholic Church. ''Your youngest went through parochial school with Mike.''

''Yes, that was our Brian. Now, Judith, this is nervy of me under the circumstances, but I know from the news that the Brodies are still at Hillside Manor. We live next door to them, and we wondered if there was anything we should do about their house while they're . . . away?''

Judith frowned into the receiver. In a way, she was surprised that there hadn't been other inquiring calls about the Brodies. But perhaps Arlene's Broadcasting System had been more efficient than its chief oracle would admit. ''I'd have to ask them, Norma,'' said Judith. ''They're having dinner right now. Offhand, I'd say that if they needed anything, they'd have called you or one of the other neighbors. All the same, I'll ask Mrs. Brodie.''

An odd little sound that was half cough, half snort came through the line. ''Oriana Brodie isn't the domestic type. I don't think she's ever cooked a meal, let alone cleaned house or done the laundry. They have help, you know,'' Norma Paine declared as if it were a disease. ''Of course it's not for me to say, but I'd like to know how any woman can spend so much time taking care of herself and yet come home looking worse than when she left.''

''She should ask for her money back,'' Judith remarked with half an ear. Her attention was as much on her companions as on Norma Paine: Renie had taken over the steaks, Woody was opening more beans, and, amazingly, Joe was making béarnaise sauce in the blender.

''Some people think she's getting more than her money's worth already," Norma Paine said in her caustic voice. "Only Oriana Brodie could go off for a facial and come back with a hickey."

Judith's attention swerved fully around to Norma Paine. "Really?" She signaled for Joe to shut off the blender. "Goodness, Norma, you're not implying that—"

"Certainly not!" burst out Norma Paine. "She probably doesn't go to a licensed cosmetologist, that's all. I'd be the last one to tell tales. All I'm trying to do is be neighborly. Do you think the Brodies will be home soon? The fumigators are gone."

Thinking that the fumigators worked faster than the police, Judith cast a gimlet eye at Joe, who was happily sprinkling tabasco sauce into the blender. "I'll give them your message," Judith said noncommittally. "Thanks for calling. See you in church." She turned to the others, just as Joe was sampling his béarnaise from the tip of his finger. "Gather for gossip. Plus, we've got an interesting theory, all of which star Oriana Bustamanti Brodie."

The four of them sat at the dinette table, listening to Judith's theory on Oriana's La Scala debut. Joe was skeptical; Woody was flummoxed.

"That's an outrageous piece of deceit," declared Woody, looking personally offended, "especially for a performance at La Scala." He spoke the opera house's name in a reverential voice.

"It's not impossible, I suppose," allowed Joe, with visible reluctance. "No one at the magazine would link Arturo Allegro with Oriana, given his various AKAS. The problem is trying to tie it in with Wanda."

"That could be solved with the Dash connection," Judith pointed out. "He was obviously trying to get money out of Oriana. But if Oriana knew who Wanda was, she might have tried to silence her to keep from being exposed as a musical fraud and all-around laughingstock. Either she would have come up with the money to keep Dash quiet—or, having murdered one person already, done Dash out of his cash and done him in instead."

"But how did she do it?" asked Joe. "She was at the other end of the table. The only time she got up after Wanda arrived was to retrieve her earring. I'm assuming she didn't crawl all the way under the table to get it."

Woody was still looking stupefied. "I can't believe that critics at La Scala could be bribed. It's an outrageous concept!" His voice conveyed more emotion than the cousins had yet heard him express.

"Let's just say that part is open to speculation," said Joe. "We could find out, but it'd take some digging to get those old reviews out of the papers from Milan. As for Dash getting his hands on the money, he had two other options," he went on, rearranging the everyday silverware at his place. "He could sponge off Gwen and hope she got more money from her books, or plead with her to put the arm on old Dad."

"He had a third option," Judith observed. "If he knew Wanda was Otto's daughter, he could have tried to win her back. Maybe that's why he was seeing her again."

Joe's eyes slid in Judith's direction. "And she turned him down the second time around?"

Judith thought she heard an innuendo in Joe's voice, and spoke too sharply: "Why shouldn't she? He'd been a cad the first time." She saw the muscle in his jawline tighten and recanted: "I mean, he *probably* was, knowing Dash."

Joe said nothing. The foursome was silent for a few moments. The snow swirled in a white fury at the kitchen window above the sink. The wind moaned; the old house creaked. Except for the now-muted buzz of the Brodies in the dining room, the mortal world had grown very quiet. No cars attempted to climb the Hill, no airplanes braved the storm, no whistle of ferries heading into the slip disturbed the winter night. Perched on the side of Heraldsgate, Hillside Manor and its neighbors closed their doors against the storm.

It was Renie who broke the silence. "Gee, those steaks smell good! I'm starved! What did that big Paine, Norma, want?"

Judith told them. "Obviously, an affair is suspected. But even if it's true, I doubt it would have any bearing on this case. Unless Oriana was having it with Wanda."

Joe grinned. "So that's where Oriana spent all her time instead of getting toned and tuned. I wonder who the poor dope is?"

"Oh, no!" exclaimed Judith. "It couldn't be!"

"What?" asked Renie.

"Never mind." Judith shook her head, then got up to turn the steaks. "It was just a nutty idea that went through my mind."

"I'm open to nutty ideas," insisted Joe. "We don't seem to have any other kind in this case."

Judith closed the broiler oven door. "Lance. That's my nutty idea."

"He's that, all right," agreed Joe. "Golf dates. Gone from the office too much. Not tending to business. Who else but Lance would be dumb enough to play games with his father's wife?"

"Except that it turns out she isn't," objected Woody.

"But Lance wouldn't have known that," Renie noted, with a glance of longing at the stove.

"It might explain the inhaler," said Joe. He saw blank expressions on the others' faces. "The Nembutal. Oriana has always been the most likely culprit there. The sleeping capsules belonged to her, she had ample opportunity to dump the stuff in the inhaler before they got here. Even if it hadn't been for that mangy cat of yours, Jude-girl, Oriana probably could have convinced Otto he was having some kind of allergy attack by bedtime. So Otto sleeps like a log and Oriana trots off with Lance to horse around."

"Where?" demanded Renie. "And what about Mavis?"

Joe shrugged. "The logistics I leave to Oriana and Lance. Or at least to Oriana, Lance being on the two-digit end of the I.Q. scale."

"We're speculating," Judith admitted. "And even if

we're right, what does it have to do with Wanda? We keep coming back to that. It drives me crazy, because I have the feeling we're missing something really important.'' With her hand still encased in her oven mitt, she pointed at Joe. ''What are you doing, besides drinking and eating and making béarnaise sauce? Isn't it time to come up with hair follicles and fingernail parings?''

''I told you,'' responded Joe, a bit defensively, ''I'm off duty. At least for a couple of hours. The truth is, we've reached a dead end. If it hadn't been for this storm, I'd have had to let all these people go after the M.E.'s report came in. But as long as they're here, so am I. And Woody. All we can hope for is that the murderer makes some slip— or tries to kill again.''

''Oh!'' Judith paled. ''Don't say things like that! Do you want me to sleep standing up with Dooley's bow and arrow?''

Joe made a face. ''Don't be a goose. You and Renie are safe. If anybody is in danger, it's one of those loonies in the dining room. Besides, I've still got two men on duty outside.''

Judith was aghast. ''Freezing to death?''

''They're going to stay at the Dooleys'. That paper boy is all agog. I think he's a recruit for our young people's police auxiliary program.''

To Judith, it seemed as if the entire neighborhood had gone into the hostelry business. She had visions of marquees popping up all over the Hill: Rankers's Restful Rooms, Gossip As You Like It. Dooleys' Drop-Inn, Have We Got a View for You! And then Hillside Manor, its tastefully carved sign worn away by the weather, drooping on rusted chains, the walkway overgrown with nettles and weeds.

Her reverie was broken by the doorbell. ''Get the steaks out and dish up,'' she told Renie. ''It must be Arlene or Carl.''

But the newcomer was a short, stout, bespectacled man of about sixty, dressed in a camel's hair coat, a black fedora, and a tan cashmere muffler. He was carrying a pair of skis, and there was frost on his thick eyebrows.

"Oliver Wendell Muggins," he said as his breath came out in little white puffs. "I'm here to see Mr. Otto Brodie."

"On skis?" asked an astonished Judith.

"Certainly on skis," retorted Mr. Muggins. "How else could I get here? Where is my client?"

Otto's bellow from the dining room saved Judith from giving an answer. "Is that you, Muggins? Get in here, you pompous old coot! I'm practically on death row!"

Judith helped Mr. Muggins put his skis and poles next to the hat rack, then winced as big clumps of snow fell from his boots onto the entry hall floor. The lawyer handed her his hat, muffler, overcoat, and gloves as if she were the parlor maid.

"Finally!" cried Otto, with his knife and fork poised over the last of his dinner. "What do you mean, running off to the Rockies when I'm in such a terrible fix?"

Having put away Mr. Muggins's outer apparel, Judith hurried to get an extra chair from the front parlor. "Have you eaten?" she whispered as the attorney sat down with great dignity.

"I haven't had time," he said with a look of mild reproach for his client. "I came as quickly as I could."

"I'll get you some dinner," Judith offered, and was rewarded with a curt nod.

In the kitchen, Joe and Woody were already digging into their steaks. Without ceremony, Judith grabbed the plate that Renie was carrying to the table. "It's for Muggins," she said, rushing back into the dining room.

Otto was already in full spate, but at least he seemed to have sobered up a bit. Judith deposited Mr. Muggins's plate on the table, received a grunt in exchange, and hurried out of the room.

"You twit!" shrieked Renie. "That was my dinner!"

"Eat mine," said a frazzled Judith.

"I can't. Yours is too well-done. I'd just as soon eat a pair of old boots."

"Go get Muggins's. He's already ruined my parquet floor with them. Here," insisted Judith, dividing the food on her plate in half, "force yourself."

Appeased, Renie sat down. "Who is Muggins any-way?"

"Otto's attorney." Judith glanced at Joe. "Are we in for trouble?"

"Could be," sighed Joe. "How'd he get here? A four-wheel drive?"

"Skis," said Judith. "Last February, the city barri-caded Heraldsgate Avenue and turned it into a ski run."

"I know," Woody said gloomily. "My wife sprained her ankle when she crashed into Dino's Deli at the bottom of the Hill."

"It was a nightmare for the traffic patrol," recalled Joe, adding more sour cream to his baked potato. "The city had lent its snow removal equipment to one of the suburbs and they didn't find it until May."

"The 'burb or the snow removal equipment?" inquired Renie. "Frankly, the fewer 'burbs, the better. They're all full of transplanted Californians anyway. As for our winter weather equipment, it consists of one beat-up truck, two shovels, and a bucket of sand," she went on with some heat. "Bill says that the trouble with this town is that its collective mentality is predisposed to . . ."

Judith's attention wandered off from civic attitudes and Bill's opinions. So many strange incidents plagued the murder investigation: Oriana's phony debut; Gwen's ghost-written novels; Dash's gambling debts; Lance's failing business venture; Otto's first marriage; Dash's links with Gwen, Ellie, Mavis, and Wanda; Oriana's alleged affair; Harvey's residency at St. Peregrine's . . . Time was run-ning out. Judith knew it; Joe had admitted as much.

Judith pushed her half-eaten dinner at Renie. "Go ahead, finish it. I've got to go upstairs and make a phone call."

Three pairs of suspicious eyes followed her out of the kitchen. Fueled by determination rather than food, Judith ascended the back stairs with a quick step. Inside her bedroom, she locked the door and went to the phone beside her bed. It was a separate line from the phones on the first and second floors, with an extension in Mike's room. Gertrude denounced the telephone as a nuisance and had refused to allow one in her own inner sanctum. Instead, she used Judith's.

The 213 area code operator gave Judith the number for St. Peregrine's in Los Angeles. Hoping for a slow Saturday evening in the hospital's operating room, she was put through to a nurse with a musical Oriental accent.

"This is Lieutenant Grover, Homicide Division," Judith announced in her most businesslike voice. "We're investigating the death of one of your nurses, Wanda Rakesh."

An intake of breath reached Judith's ear from thirteen hundred miles away. "We heard of that this afternoon. It is very sad. Ms. Rakesh was fine nurse."

"Then I'm sure you'll be glad to learn we're making progress in apprehending her killer," Judith said, deciding that one big lie deserved another. "We'd like to talk to someone who worked with her earlier in her career, say from 1975 or so."

There was a slight pause. In the background, Judith could hear a doctor being paged over St. Peregrine's intercom. For a moment, she visualized the scene as Wanda must have known it, with the nurses' station, the operating theater, the recovery room, the ebb and flow of patients, orderlies, interns, and anxious friends and relations.

"I am only here one year," said the lilting voice. "Let me ask."

On hold, Judith reclined on the bed. The nurse was off the line for what seemed like quite a while. Judith's teeth still hurt, and now her shoulder was beginning to ache. She watched the snow falling steadily at the dormer window, and her eyelids began to droop. She was actually asleep when the exotic accents of the Far East again reached her ear.

". . . retired last June. That's Edna Stover in Santa Monica. The number is . . ."

Judith scrambled for the pencil she'd dropped. "Repeat that, please."

The nurse obliged. Judith thanked her in a faintly foggy manner, rang off, and shook herself. She'd have to keep alert if she intended to solve the murder case, she lectured herself sternly. At the very least, she'd have to remain conscious. Judith sat up, both feet flat on the floor, and prayed that Edna Stover, retired R.N., wasn't given to carousing on Saturday nights.

Ten minutes later, Judith was dancing down the stairs. The pieces of the puzzle had finally come together. If Sweetums had been anywhere in sight, she would have kissed him.

SEVENTEEN

"WHERE'S JOE?" JUDITH asked as she all but flew into the kitchen.

Renie looked up from where she was kicking the cupboard door beneath the kitchen sink. "I'm sick of answering that question. He and Woody went to the Dooleys' with the other policemen. Joe wanted to check things out there. Hey," she exclaimed, staring at her cousin, "what's wrong? Who have you been talking to?"

Judith started to explain, heard a roar from the dining room, and held up a hand. "Wait until Joe gets back. I don't want to go through everything twice. And why are you beating up my woodwork?"

The roar, presumably from Otto, died down. Renie turned on both taps, which sputtered, trickled, and then gushed. "Aha! Now they're okay. Did you remember to wrap your pipes?"

Judith's excited expression turned to chagrin. "Damn! Mike must have forgotten the one on this side

194

of the house. I'll go do it. I should start the car up, too.''

But before Judith could get her jacket, Otto and Mr. Muggins came through the kitchen door. ''Where's that cop?'' Otto demanded. ''Muggins here says he has no right to keep us. If we're not out of here in ten minutes, he's filing a complaint. Or a writ. Or something.''

''He can file his nails, as far as I'm concerned,'' Judith retorted, seeing Muggins bristle. ''See here, Mr. Brodie, don't blame me. Lieutenant Flynn will be back any minute. How do you plan to get off the Hill anyway? Did your lawyer bring eight more pairs of skis?''

''Folderol,'' said Muggins. ''The police have snow tires and chains. They're quite capable of transporting Mr. Brodie and his family to their homes. How, young woman, do you think they chase criminals in this kind of weather?''

''I'd like to think any criminal with an ounce of sense wouldn't be outdoors,'' said Judith, then realized that she had one under her very roof. It also occurred to her that it was imperative to keep all of the Brodies and their ilk locked inside Hillside Manor. But it wouldn't do to say so. ''Excuse me, I'm a bit on edge,'' she said with a self-deprecating smile. ''While you wait for Lieutenant Flynn, could you eat more dessert?''

''More?'' Otto's nose twitched like a pig snout. ''Let's start with *some*. We haven't had any yet. Got any cream puffs left over?''

''No,'' said Judith, shooting Renie a caustic glance. ''My cousin has made a lovely apple crisp. But she has this fatal flaw in her personality where she likes to make things but keep them a secret.''

''I forgot,'' Renie admitted. ''I got to eating my dinner . . .''

''My dinner,'' breathed Judith, removing the tea towel from the baking dish. ''Get the whipped cream, stupid. And coffee.''

Renie snapped to attention, then turned into a whirl of activity. Momentarily mollified, Otto and Muggins withdrew. An abject Renie apologized profusely, explaining that she'd been in the act of making coffee and tea when she'd discovered the pipes were acting up.

"When in doubt, blame it on my plumbing," muttered Judith, loaded down with the first servings of dessert. "Why not? Dan always did," she added cryptically.

Five minutes later, the Brodies were stuffing their faces with apple crisp and speaking to each other in almost civil tones. Joe and Woody had not yet returned. Judith was about to head outside when Dash sauntered in from the back stairs, a legal-sized document in his hands.

"This has got to be a joke, right?"

"What is it?" Judith asked, looking up from the drawer where she'd been rummaging for her ski mask.

"Old Otto's will. Here." He cavalierly handed the document to Judith, who was joined by Renie at the cupboard.

The last will and testament of Otto Ernst Brodie was short, but not so sweet. It was duly signed, witnessed, and dated two weeks earlier, and left his entire estate to his dog, Booger. "Where did you get this?" Judith asked, aghast.

"In Muggins's inside overcoat pocket," Dash replied, shameless over his theft. "He couldn't carry documents around in a briefcase on skis, could he?"

Judith and Renie were huddling over the will. "It may be a joke, all right," said Judith, "but if Otto had died instead of Wanda, Booger would have had the last laugh. Or bark, as the case may be." She refolded the single sheet, but didn't give it back. "By the way, Mr. Subarosa, why did you lie about not having seen Wanda since the divorce?"

For the first time since Dash had come under Judith's roof, he lost his aplomb. The debonair manner evaporated, the handsome if dissipated face crumpled, and his shoulders slumped under the Italian jacket. But he struggled for a shred of dignity and met Judith's probing gaze head-on. "Why do you think? For Ellie's sake, what else?"

"Ellie?" Judith was faintly incredulous, but deep down, she felt it was an unfair reaction.

"Sure." His composure was returning. "I didn't want her to think I had any part in Wanda's death. It was bad enough that I had to chase after Gwen, but admitting that I did it for my ex-wife would have made me look like a real creep."

"You knew who Gwen was before you met her?" Renie asked as, in the background, Otto bellowed for tea.

Dash was unperturbed by the question. "Yeah, I knew. Once Wanda found out who her old man was, she did her homework on the whole family. She had a notebook full of stuff. But nothing firsthand, except for her run-in with Otto. I already knew Lance—and Mavis''—he winked a bit lewdly—"and since Gwen was the only single one of the bunch, we zeroed in on her."

"Why not Ellie?" asked Judith.

Dash gave an odd little shake of his head. "I didn't know she was *my* Ellie. Wanda wasn't interested in the in-laws. She just wanted to shake up the family and expose Otto as a lousy husband and a rotten father. Then she could get him to acknowledge her, and maybe come up with some cash for her troubles. And Gloria's. It wasn't Wanda I was surprised to see here, but Ellie." He looked bemused. "Wanda and I had what they call an amicable divorce. She was, as Lester said, a good egg. I was glad to help her."

"For a cut, no doubt," said Judith with a touch of asperity.

Dash didn't take umbrage at Judith's comment, but waved his hand around the kitchen. "You work for free, dark eyes? We all have to eat."

"True," Judith agreed, feeling just a little bleak over her own prospects of putting food on the table. "Did you know that Wanda's parents weren't divorced?"

"Sure." Dash was once again his chipper self. "But I couldn't tell anybody, could I? How could Oriana reimburse me if she wasn't married to Otto?"

Suppressing the urge to retort that Oriana could sing for her supper, Judith uttered a sigh of resignation and handed the will back to Dash. "You'd better return this to Muggins's overcoat before he finds out it's missing. I wonder if Otto was going to tell the family about it last night."

"They'd have all wished they'd brought along an extra set of underwear if he had," said Dash, taking the will and strolling back out of the kitchen.

Judith and Renie stared at each other. "So Wanda knew about a lot of things," said Renie.

Otto was bellowing for tea again from the dining room. "She knew too much, I can tell you that," replied Judith, putting on her down jacket and boots. "Get that tea out there before Otto busts a gusset. And let's hope it's not laced with something nasty this time." She made one last effort at searching for her hooded ski mask, then swore aloud. "Mike must have taken mine along with his, blast his hide. What's he doing, wearing them both at once over at Priest Lake?" She pulled on a white angora cap and grabbed the tea towel from the counter, tying it around the lower half of her face.

"What are you doing?" asked a startled Renie. "You look like a burglar. Want me to get you a sack marked 'Swag'?"

"I'm protecting my teeth. This cold is killing them." Judith checked the square knot in the tea towel to make sure it wouldn't slip. Her voice was faintly muffled as she dug in her purse for her car keys. "If Joe gets back before I do, don't let him budge an inch. And by all means, don't let Muggins smuggle any of these people out of the house."

"I'll get Sweetums to stand guard," promised Renie. "Be careful out there. I'll bet it's icy underfoot."

After her earlier outing, Judith needed no further words of caution. Stopping first to get some heavy rags from a drawer in the pantry, she descended the back porch stairs with care, blinking against the relentless snow. At least another inch had fallen in the last hour. Her footprints between Hillside Manor and the Rankers's house were already virtually obscured. But the wind had gone down, even as the temperature fell further below the freezing mark. Judith rubbed her gloved hands together and tucked the tea towel inside the collar of her jacket.

At the side of the house by the kitchen, she peered between the viburnum and rhododendron bushes in an attempt to locate the exposed pipes. The snow-covered surroundings disoriented her, but the light from inside revealed the object of her search almost in a direct line from the window. Working as quickly as her numb hands would permit, she wrapped the pipes in the rags she'd brought, then saved one for the garden hose faucet by the dining room. She was frankly annoyed with herself: In all the years she'd been married to Dan, she'd always remembered to wrap the pipes and faucets before Thanksgiving. But this year, caught up in her new business venture, she'd asked Mike to do it on his long Armistice Day weekend.

"Half-assed," she muttered against the tea towel. "When do they grow up?"

Twisting around the new white camellia bush she'd planted the previous spring, Judith glanced up at the dining room window. The Brodies were polishing off their apple crisp and Oriana was actually laughing. It occurred to Judith that the reason for Oriana's smudged makeup might have less to do with anxiety and more to do with Lance. Trying to keep out of sight, she watched her guests with a newly-enlightened pair of eyes. Otto had his back to her, the pudgy creases of his bare neck showing above his collar. Judith's gaze moved slowly around the table. So, she thought with a shiver, that's what a murderer looks like . . .

Not that any of it seemed real. It had been less than twenty-four hours since Wanda Rakesh had died, just a few feet away, with her hand outstretched toward the azalea blossoms. Since that moment, Judith's whole world had been turned upside down. Her livelihood had been threatened, her home had become an armed camp, her mother had been sent into temporary exile, and Joe Flynn had waltzed back into her life, acting as if he'd never missed a beat in the first place, let alone almost a quarter of a century. Judith's meager dinner jumped up and down in her stomach. It was no wonder, she told herself: Between the emotional upheaval and the physical exhaustion, even a choice cut T-bone would revolt.

Feeling the snow caking on her gloves and her feet turning numb in her boots, Judith started to move away. For a fleeting, frightening split second, she thought she saw the murderer turn to look straight at her. The chill that went through her body had nothing to do with the cold weather. Judith dove away from the window, catching herself on the drainpipe that ran between the dining room and the kitchen. Breathing much too hard under the tightly-secured tea towel, she fought for composure. Only the carrying sound of Renie's voice, inquiring about coffee refills, restored Judith's nerve. Shaking off the unexpected sense of panic, she proceeded back along the side of the house, down the snow-covered walk, and into the garage.

Her steel-blue Japanese compact sedan looked reassuring under the yellow glow of the garage lights. As she slipped into the driver's seat, her gloved hands clumsily sought the ignition key in her pocket. The engine didn't respond on the first try. It only sputtered the second time around. Judith waited, checking out the instruments on the dashboard which stared blankly back at her. On the third attempt, the motor responded, kicking out a plume of blue smoke from the exhaust. She rolled down the window and kept her foot lightly on the accelerator, wondering if she dared try to put the car in reverse and ease it out of the garage just enough to feel what kind of traction existed under the snow.

It was, she decided, probably not a good idea, even with winter tires. Instead, Judith sat behind the wheel, fiddling with the gauges. She had just put a tape into the stereo when a shadow in the rearview mirror caught her eye. Wrestling the tea towel down to her chin, she leaned out the window, peering through the snow in an effort to see who had come out into the back yard. Renie, maybe, making sure she was all right. Or Arlene, on the prowl for her neighborhood news report. Even Dooley, playing detective.

But the figure that moved stealthily, yet relentlessly, toward the garage was not friendly. Within a scant yard of the car's trunk, Judith recognized that same chilling face she had seen through the dining room window only minutes earlier. Her mind raced; she swallowed hard. What if she was wrong? What if the murderer was someone else? But there was no mistaking the open animosity on the face that loomed above her as she shut off the engine.

"Hi," she said with a weak smile that barely reached her nose. "What are you doing out here?"

"How did you figure it out?" growled Harvey Carver, his bare fists clenched tightly at his sides. He wore no coat, only a thick cable-knit sweater over dark slacks.

"Figure what out?" Judith asked innocently. "Harvey, what do you know about cars?"

His left hand shot out and grabbed the tea towel around Judith's neck. "Don't toy with me! I hate it when people laugh at me! How dare you put on that nurse's rig to taunt me! You're like all the rest, especially my rotten relatives!"

Judith felt him jerk on the towel, making her head bob forward. "I'm not taunting you!" she insisted, and only then realized the significance of his accusation. The white angora cap, the white tea-towel masking the lower part of her face, the impression evoking Wanda as surgical nurse, Wanda as Madame Gushenka, Wanda as the symbol of all that had gone wrong in Harvey's life . . . No wonder he must have thought she had dressed in such a way to mock him. Judith felt her limbs tremble. "I just came out here to fix the pipes and start my car. You didn't happen to look at the thermometer on your way . . ."

Harvey gave another sharp yank on the towel. The square knot Judith had so carefully tied not only didn't yield, but grew even tighter. "Shut up! You might be better-looking, or wittier, or more likeable than I am, but you're not smarter! See this?" He thrust his other hand through the open window, revealing a curious-looking little implement that reminded Judith of a turkey timer. "Do you know what that is?" The black eyes glinted with what Judith at first took to be malice, and then realized with increasing horror, was actually pleasure. "It's a kind of syringe, like they use for TB tests. Only this one is loaded with sodium pentothal." He leaned into the window, a crooked grin making his sallow face look particularly ghastly in the yellow light of the garage. Judith tried not to give in to the terror that had overtaken her. Yet she dimly recognized that she was fighting a losing battle, not just against Harvey, but herself. All the reserves of strength she'd stored up over the years seemed to have deserted her. Why, a small, weak voice in the back of her brain asked, did I ever think I was so damned tough?

Harvey was rattling on, the grin still plastered on his distorted face. "They'll find you at the wheel of your stupid car, overcome by carbon monoxide fumes. They won't even bother with an autopsy, not under the circumstances. *Poor Judith McMonigle*, they'll say, *the grieving widow couldn't stand seeing her beloved bed-and-breakfast go down the drain! Maybe she killed the fortune-teller herself. Who knows? Or did that imbecile of an Irish cop turn her down?*"

"Now wait a minute!" shrieked Judith. Harvey had gone too far. Goaded into fury, she jerked away with an explosive sideways lunge. The tea towel was ripped from Harvey's grasp. He reached inside the car to grab Judith, but she was already pounding on the horn with one hand and pressing the levers to the power locks for the automatic doors and windows with the other. As the deep wail of the horn cut through the quiet night and the windows began to roll up, Harvey let out a terrible stream of curses. Just as he started to pull his hands out of the way, Judith snatched at his right thumb. Bracing her feet on the floor of the car, she gave a mighty yank, pulling Harvey's arm back inside. The automatic window pinned him just below the elbow. It was hard to tell which noise was louder—the car horn which Judith continued to press, or Harvey's painful screams.

The pastoral peace of the winter night had come apart, not only with sound, but light. People were shouting in the back yard and driveway, running feet, impeded by snow, tramped up from the house, flashlights wavered from what seemed like a dozen hands, and out of the chaos, Judith saw Joe Flynn, assuming a shoot-to-kill stance at the rear of the car.

"Freeze! It's the police!" he shouted to Harvey, who was still shrieking in agony. "Spread 'em!"

As she craned her neck, Judith's shoulders slumped in relief. "Gosh," she whispered to herself, "I wish Joe'd said that to me."

EIGHTEEN

GERTRUDE REFUSED TO come home until Joe Flynn was gone. "It's bad enough to have a homicidal maniac loose in my own house, but that Irish pervert is too much. Either he goes, or I stay at the Rankers's," she rasped over the phone. "*Some* people put old folks first."

"Not me," breathed Judith away from the mouthpiece as she looked at Joe. But her voice evoked patience itself when she directed her attention back to her mother. "Renie and I are just filling the police in. It may take a while, and it's already after ten o'clock. I'd hate to have you come out in this weather and break something."

"Ha!" snorted Gertrude, as Arlene made soothing noises in the background and Carl told his wife to put a sock in it. "You'd like to see me laid up in some ratty nursing home with a broken hip so you could cavort around like a floozy!"

"Broken *lip,*" mouthed Judith to Joe, Renie, and Woody.

But her mother wasn't done yet. "Well, don't worry about me," huffed Gertrude. "That nice Mr. Busbee is staying over, too, and we're going to play four-handed pinochle."

"What a coincidence," said Judith. "That's what Renie and I are going to do with the police."

"I'll bet my butt you are," said Gertrude, and slammed down the phone.

Judith wasn't fazed by her mother's tart tongue. She was too exhilarated by the events of the past few hours to let anything impinge on her sense of self-vindication. The grandfather clock struck ten: It had taken Judith less than twenty-four hours to identify the killer of Wanda Rakesh—and of Dr. Stanley Edelstein.

Harvey had been placed under arrest, not for murder, but for aggravated assault. Arrogant to the end, he had gone off to police headquarters vowing that he'd be acquitted of any wrongdoing, let alone homicide. Ellie had fainted from the shock, but when she left with the rest of the Brodie party, she was leaning on a gallant Dash. Gwen was pouting, bringing up the rear with Mavis and a limping Lance.

"Cheer up," Judith had heard Mavis say in what had been intended as a confidential voice, "there's a book in it. I can write it in five days. You get a really good title with some class this time."

Gwen had paused on the threshold, the snow drifting onto the porch. "I know!" she had exclaimed, transformed by her creative juices. "How about *Crime and Punishment?*"

Mavis had barely glanced at her dupe. "Try again," she had said, and helped Lance down the steps. "Lean on me," she'd ordered her husband, then had grabbed him by the coat. "I mean that in two ways, literally and figuratively. You got it?"

Lance had stared blankly at first, then with dawning comprehension. "I guess I'd better start tending to business, huh, Mavis?"

"Right," she'd told him. *"Our* business." Then her customarily hard features had softened, and to the surprise of Judith and Renie, she had kissed Lance. "It's a good thing you're beautiful, because you sure are dumb. And at least you wear socks."

Otto and Oriana had been the last to leave, waiting for Muggins to ski off down the hill, his muffler flying and his fedora miraculously stuck to his head.

"Hey, hotcakes," Otto had called to Judith from the front walk, "you want to make this an annual event? The entertainment stinks, but the grub's pretty good!"

"Don't call me, I'll call you," Judith had said cheerfully. "You haven't seen the bill yet."

"Dio mio!" Oriana had exclaimed, hugging her mink coat close and teetering dangerously on her high heels, "wait until he sees the bill from Muggins for the divorce!"

Otto had turned to Oriana with a stunned expression. "Wait a minute, my vivacious vermicelli, you can't divorce me! We're not married!"

Oriana had giggled, slipped in the snow, and collapsed against Otto, a picture of the kittenish Zerlina hoodwinking her poor Masetto. "Of course we're not! You're going to divorce *Gloria.* Then we can have a huge wedding and we won't have to invite Harvey. He always was a wet blanket."

In Judith's mind, Harvey Carver had been a lot more. He had, she reflected with sadness, been a brilliant surgeon who no doubt had saved many lives during his prestigious career. But he was a twisted man, eaten up by envy and insecurity. Lance, coming downstairs for the last time, had stopped to look Judith straight in the eye. "I'm sure glad they arrested him," he had said. "I always knew he did it. I never forgot about Spot."

Somehow, Lance's insight had not amazed Judith as much as it should have. "Did Harvey trip you at breakfast this morning?" she had asked.

Lance had considered briefly. "I think so. He did mean

stuff like that to me all the time. Funny, though, I kind of liked him. But he was sort of crazy, like a''—Lance had paused, then scratched at his side under his coat—''bed-bug,'' he'd concluded, causing Judith more alarm than amusement.

And then they were all gone, even Joe and Woody. Arlene had rushed in, having observed the last act of the tragedy through Dooley's telescope. As for Dooley, he'd raced over to Hillside Manor just in time to see Harvey being handcuffed and read his rights. Other neighbors had gathered, but to Judith's relief, the media had kept away. Deterred by the steep hill, they had headed instead for police headquarters downtown.

In the lull that had followed, Judith and Renie had fixed themselves stout drinks and collapsed in the blessed quiet of the living room. They barely had time to put their feet up when Joe and Woody returned, their official duties complete with the booking of Harvey. No sooner had they arrived than Gertrude had called, expressing her aversion to Joe. Now the fire was blazing merrily in the grate, Judith had hung up the telephone, and Renie was pouring beer for Joe and peach seltzer for Woody. Sweetums was asleep on the mantel, looking not unlike a stuffed trophy. Idly, Judith wondered why Harvey hadn't done something worthwhile, like giving her cat the same treatment he'd reserved for Spot.

''I'm surprised you came back,'' said Judith, then became aware that she hadn't intended the double entendre.

Apparently, he didn't notice. ''The paperwork can wait,'' he said, loosening his tie and taking off his shoulder holster with the snub-nosed .38 special. ''Despite the lesser charge, bail has been posted at five hundred thousand dollars. Ellie can probably raise that much by Monday—if she wants to.''

''Is there any doubt?'' asked Renie from her place on the sofa by Judith.

Joe raised an eyebrow. ''Are you kidding? The way she and Dash were looking at each other, I don't think either of them will be wearing socks for at least a week. I wonder," he mused, tasting his beer, "if Ellie can reform him."

"Men don't change," said Judith. "They just adapt. They're like little kids testing parents. Dash will get away with whatever Ellie allows. It all depends on how much they care for each other. Harvey almost got away with murder."

Joe and Woody exchanged knowing masculine glances, but offered no critique of Judith's philosophy. Instead, Joe spoke specifically of Harvey: "He would probably never have even been arrested if he hadn't been rash enough to try the same method on you that he used on Wanda." The green eyes twinkled. "I'm willing to be a good sport, though, Jude-girl. I suppose you figured all this out beforehand."

"Of course I did," Judith replied, sitting back on the sofa with her arms folded across her chest. "If you hadn't been lollygagging around with your subordinates at the Dooleys', I would have told you everything before Harvey tried to put out my lights."

The twinkle faded. "You're a sharp cookie," Joe said, setting the beer mug down on the coffee table, "but I don't see how you managed to pin the murder on Harvey so fast."

Judith made a tapping gesture in the air. "As simple as 213, that being the area code for Los Angeles. I called one Edna Stover, a retired nurse from St. Peregrine's Hospital. She helped put all the pieces in place."

Joe was still dubious. "How?"

Judith allowed herself to bask a bit in her own glory. "Edna worked with Wanda in the surgery unit. She wasn't on the team that operated on Lance, but Wanda was, and so was Stanley Edelstein. Afterward, Wanda told Edna that *Jack O'Doul hadn't been himself in more ways than one*. She said it in such a way that Edna not only remembered her exact words, but was puzzled as to what Wanda meant." Judith's dark eyes rested in turn on each of her listeners. "All along, it seemed obvious that O'Doul and the amnesiac were one and the same, which was why Wanda had kept those clippings. What was the explanation? Edna said Dr. O'Doul had never suffered from amnesia before or after that time, and she'd known him for over twenty years. But there are drugs—usually anesthetics used in surgery—which produce temporary amnesia. The question was, who gave Dr. O'Doul that drug? The only logical answer was Harvey Carver."

As Judith paused for breath, Woody shook his head. "I see how Harvey might have done it, but *why?*"

"Because he hated Lance, especially his perfect body and athletic prowess," replied Judith. "He always had, I think, ever since Lance came along and uprooted Harvey as the child of the house. His parents were dead, and I'll bet Minnie, if not Otto, doted on Harvey. Then Lance was born and Harvey took second place, then third by the time Gwen arrived. There must have been all sorts of slights along the way, like the one about Harvey's playhouse being torn down to make a basketball court for Lance. But Harvey was always smarter than his cousins, and he went off to medical school at UCLA and excelled at his studies. But who comes on his heels and grabs the glory? Lance, whose only skill is catching a football. Harvey must have been galled all over again."

"He's pathetic, really," remarked Renie. "Is that why he botched Lance's operation?"

Judith rearranged the cushions at her back. "Of course. To make matters worse, Dr. O'Doul—who stood in Harvey's way professionally—told him he couldn't assist with the procedure because he was 'family'. I doubt that Harvey gave a hoot about family, and his professional pride was probably wounded. So he got a double revenge by taking over for O'Doul and wrecking Lance's knee. Who would recognize him in his surgical rig? At least that's how he figured it, and it's true that people see what they expect to see. Harvey and O'Doul were about the same size, even the same type." She turned to Renie: "You actually mistook O'Doul for Harvey in that snapshot at the hospital. The leprechaun, as we called him, was O'Doul—Edna told me. She was in the picture, too.''

''Was the other doctor Stanley Edelstein?'' asked Renie.

''No. He was an anesthesiologist named Polk. No connection that Edna knew of.'' Judith paused, rearranging the sofa cushions at her back. ''So the operation is a failure, but the patient lives—as a has-been—and O'Doul gets a blot on his escutcheon. As for not wanting to remember the surgery, we only have Harvey's word that O'Doul said that. What's more likely is that O'Doul didn't remember the procedure because he couldn't—he wasn't there.''

Joe picked up the beer mug, noticed the ring it had left, and mopped away the moisture with a cocktail napkin. ''It's a great theory, but at this point, we could use more concrete proof. Where does Edelstein fit in?''

''I'm guessing that Edelstein and Wanda both realized something was amiss,'' said Judith. ''Somehow, Edelstein put a scare into Harvey. Maybe he threatened to expose him, maybe it was blackmail. Harvey cherished his professional reputation above all else, even love. In fact, I suspect he mistook respect *for* love. Harvey had to get rid of Edelstein. Edna Stover told me that St. Peregrine's surgeons operated at other hospitals under special circumstances. If the records still exist, I'll bet Harvey was at Star of Jerusalem about the time Edelstein was run down.''

''You're doing a lot of guessing and betting,'' Joe noted with a dour expression. ''Juries don't buy that.''

Judith made a gesture of dismissal. ''Of course not. Nobody will ever pin Edelstein's death on Harvey. But he did it. And, you may recall, he left L.A. soon afterward. He was ambitious, yes, but I think he was also afraid.''

Renie was hoarding the dregs of her drink; Carl's liquor loan had been exhausted. ''He had several years of feeling safe up here. What a shock it must have been for him to see Wanda!''

''*Was* it a shock?'' queried Woody. ''Or did Harvey find out she'd be here?''

Judith shook her head, which was beginning to feel very heavy. "I honestly don't think any of the Brodies knew Madame Gushenka was Wanda Rakesh until she came through the door. Except for Dash, Oriana was the only one to have any contact with her. But Oriana knew nothing about Otto's first marriage. Otto says he hadn't seen Wanda since Palm Springs, and I believe him. I think Wanda was playing a waiting game. She'd already discovered that an appeal to Otto's better nature was wasted, though she might have had better luck playing on his sentimental streak. But Wanda wouldn't know that. She felt Otto owed both her and her mother a lot, probably more than mere money. Realistically, though, that was all she could try to get out of him. So she conspired with Dash to dig up some dirt on all of them and hatched her plot, using her old fortune-teller skills and playing on Oriana's gullibility."

"What about those so-called predictions she made to other locals?" asked Renie, refilling Woody's glass with seltzer.

Judith gave her cousin a dry little smile. "I asked Arlene when she was here this evening if she knew anything about Madame Gushenka. She didn't. If Arlene Rankers hasn't heard of it, it never happened. Wanda was just padding her résumé."

"And Oriana fell into her trap," mused Joe, putting his feet on the coffee table despite Judith's disapproving gaze. "Except that when it sprung, it caught Wanda."

"I'm puzzled," confessed Renie. "How did Harvey—who insists he never notices nurses—and I believe him, he's too self-absorbed—recognize her? And how did he administer the poison? He was at the other end of the table, between Oriana and Gwen."

"Wanda outsmarted herself with that disguise," answered Judith, resting her head on the back of the sofa and realizing that her teeth didn't hurt anymore. "Those veils over her hair and face produced the same effect as a surgical mask and cap—exactly what happened to me tonight in my outdoor getup. When Harvey and Wanda worked together, he was used to seeing only the top half of her face anyway. That's how he'd remember her. She might have been better off coming as herself.'' She stopped for a moment as Joe got to his feet and leaned down to stoke up the fire. The big living room was drafty; the front parlor would have been more cozy. But Judith had chosen to sit in the larger of the two rooms, as if to reclaim it from the Brodies. ''I don't know how much of her spiel came from Oriana and how much from Wanda,'' she said in a flagging voice. ''A little of both, I suspect. The dark sky and the crowd across the ocean was Lance and the Hollywood Stars, which could have been Wanda's own contribution. The second princess, who was saved by the prince with the sharp sword, must have referred to Ellie marrying Harvey, sword being equated with scalpel or knife. That would be Oriana's input, since Dash didn't realize who Ellie really was. Maybe the pen and cord bit, too, which had to be Gwen and Mavis.''

''Huh?'' It was Renie, looking blank.

''Pen—instrument used for writing. Cord—as in microphone, a device used for transmitting the voice in television.'' Judith gave her cousin a condescending glance. ''Crank up the cranium, you're falling behind. I don't believe Oriana never read Gwen's books. She's the type who'd eat them up. And while she's not exactly the resident genius, Oriana's not stupid. She may have guessed that Gwen had to be collaborating with somebody. As for Madame Gushenka's other allusions, a lot of them had to do with Gloria and Wanda and Otto. And to avoid suspicion of collusion, Dash wasn't spared either. Of course the dark and rainy night was Harvey and Stanley Edelstein. Those words alone would have spelled Wanda's doom.''

''But Harvey wasn't her target,'' Joe pointed out.

''Right,'' agreed Judith. ''He was an afterthought. Once she was face-fo-face with him, she couldn't resist trying out her theory. She wasn't just a good egg, but a good nurse, and it must have outraged her to think what a rotten trick Harvey had pulled, not only on such a respected surgeon, but a patient who turned out be her half-brother.'' She frowned, thinking how foolish Wanda had been, how her arrogance had almost matched Harvey's. Had she really believed that a man who had killed before wouldn't try again? The stakes were the same. Wanda should have known that Harvey would stop at nothing to protect his precious reputation.

Wonderingly, Renie shook her head. ''She didn't take his cunning into account, I guess. Maybe she thought she was safe, surrounded by so many people. Dr. Edelstein had been alone and caught off-guard.''

''That's true,'' said Judith, sinking further down into the sofa. ''As for *how* Harvey killed Wanda,'' she went on with a glance of reproof for Joe, ''it might have been easier to figure if you'd told us where the sodium pentothal had been administered.''

''You never asked,'' replied Joe with his ingenuous expression.

''I shouldn't have had to,'' admitted Judith. ''Harvey left the table during dessert, presumably to use the downstairs bathroom, but instead he went upstairs where he'd left his medical kit. He put the sodium pentothal in the little tinelike syringe. It's very small.'' She shuddered at the recollection of the lethal device in the palm of Harvey's hand. ''I imagine he planned on killing her later, when the session was over. But Otto's cyanide knocked her out, giving Harvey a perfect opportunity. I'm sure he thought he was so smart he could even manipulate fate. What was more natural than that he should rush to Wanda's aid, feel for her pulse, and announce that she was dead? Except that she wasn't. Yet.''

''Oh!'' Renie's eyes were wide. ''He put the little prong thing on her neck! No wonder he didn't try CPR!''

''That was a mistake on his part,'' said Judith. ''He should have gone through with the charade. I can't say I was suspicious at the time, but it bothered me, which is why I asked him about it.''

''Harvey didn't dare move Wanda,'' said Joe, digging

a fresh Havana from the pocket of his shirt. "She might have shown some signs of life. It was essential that everyone should think Wanda was dead before Harvey ever got to her." He looked down his cigar at Judith on the opposite sofa. "Right, Jude-girl? How am I doing?"

"Not bad," she murmured, and suppressed a yawn.

"I'm surprised that the medics didn't see the marks from the tine," remarked Woody. "Kinsella is especially sharp."

"What kind of marks are they?" Renie asked with a grimace for Judith and her would-be fate.

"Four tiny red pinpoints," replied Joe, taking his first puff on the cigar. "I'm excusing Kinsella's oversight because Wanda was wearing all those damned bangles. Either he didn't see the marks in his preliminary examination, or he thought she'd scratched herself on her jewelry."

"So," Renie mused, pouring the last of her ice into the potted cyclamen on the coffee table, "Harvey tried a diversion by claiming his medical kit had been rifled. Obviously, he wiped it clean on purpose so only his and Ellie's fingerprints showed. But why was he rolling around on Judith's rug?"

Joe grinned from behind a cloud of gray smoke. "He could have been there all day if you two hadn't gone upstairs. I figure he realized that was the one place where he'd be noticed. Oh, he told my men about the case being plundered, but I think he wanted a neutral audience to see him in action, making the big search. If you'd found him poking around the kitchen, it wouldn't have made an impression, right?"

"Maybe not." Judith took a deep breath. "Hey, I think he overdid that bit."

Woody cleared his throat in a self-deprecating manner. "I'd like to know, Mrs. McMonigle, if you have a theory on who took the satchel and put it in the oven?" He avoided Joe's glance, lest his superior demonstrate displeasure at the deference to Judith.

"I don't know," she replied candidly. "It could have been any of the people who knew Wanda way back when. Except Dash. I think that photo of him with Wanda was left on purpose to implicate him. So it would come down to Harvey, Otto, or even Lance, though I don't really think he remembered her at all. If I had to put money on it, I'd go with Otto. He was in the kitchen before dessert, he might have noticed she had no purse with her then, and figured it had to have been stashed in the kitchen or the pantry." She turned to Renie. "You had flour all over yourself, not to mention the trail you left on the floor. It wouldn't take Einstein to figure out that the hiding place was the flour bin. And somehow, putting the satchel in the oven sounds like something Otto would do."

The gold flecks in Joe's eyes glinted. "You're right on all counts. Otto admitted it. Sorry, Woody," he apologized to his subordinate, "I forgot to tell you that bit. It seems Wanda had a notebook chock full of background on all of the Brodies. Otto didn't have time to read it, so he burned it in the fireplace. He could put the notebook in his pocket, but he couldn't be seen with the satchel, so he shoved it in the oven."

Renie clapped her hands once in remembrance. "Of course! He was the only one sitting by the fire after it had started burning again. I remember that, because I was talking to Lester on the phone, and when I repeated Wanda's name, Otto—" She stopped and put a hand over her mouth. "That's right, he seemed to be charging at me, like a small boar. That must have been the first time he realized somebody besides him knew who Madame Gushenka really was."

"He couldn't do much about it, though," remarked Joe, "which is why he backed off."

"Do you really think he'll leave his money to, ah, Booger?" Woody asked, trying to conceal his disgust at Otto's revolting nomenclature.

Judith rolled her eyes. "If he doesn't change that will, I'll expect to read about a poisoned Doberman in the neighborhood weekly. Cyanide, no doubt. But don't think Oriana will go through with the wedding until Booger gets disinherited.''

"What about the telephone eavesdropper?" asked Renie. Seeing Judith's blank expression, she amplified. "You know, when Dash went to pick up the phone and somebody else was listening in upstairs?"

"I forgot about that," said Judith. She thought for a moment, fighting the weariness that was taking over her entire body. "Gwen and Oriana were gone from the table." She turned her hands palms up. "Either of them might have wanted to know who was calling Dash—for very different reasons, of course. Take your pick." Judith slumped back on the sofa again. "I've got a question of my own," she said, looking at Joe from under drooping lashes. "Does Harvey really suffer from muscle spasms?"

Joe reclined among the cushions, cradling his beer in one hand and the Havana in the other. "Who knows? Who cares? All I want now is enough real evidence to convict him. Face it, Jude-girl, your testimony is going to be crucial. It'll be your word against his. He'll deny everything he ever said to you out in the garage. Harvey's a prominent citizen, with a lot of fancy letters and titles after his name. You are only a . . .'' He faltered, having the grace to look not at Judith, but the glowing end of his cigar.

"I'm a blameless widow, supporting my young son and aged mother." Though it was an effort to keep her eyes open, she forced herself to stare at Joe until he stared back. "Don't worry about it," she said in a faintly fuzzy voice. "I don't mind if Harvey speaks for himself." She fumbled at the pocket of her slacks.

Joe all but yanked the cigar out of his mouth. "What?"

Three pairs of eyes bored into Judith. "Here," she said, flipping a cassette onto the coffee table next to Joe's feet. "I put this into the stereo just before Harvey showed up. By mistake, I pushed the record instead of the play button. Those thick gloves, you know. The whole thing's on tape."

"Holy Mother!" exclaimed Joe, picking up the cassette with wary fingers. "But this may not be admissible in court."

"Oh, yeah?" Judith gave him an odd, off-center smile. "Then hand it over to Mavis, have Dash bribe the judge, lock my mother up with the jury. I've done more than my share. I'm *tired.*"

To prove her point, Judith promptly fell asleep.

The world was a dazzling white, the sun almost overhead in the clear blue sky as Judith and Renie trudged up the hill to eleven o'clock mass at Our Lady, Star of the Sea. Six inches of snow had fallen before the storm finally blew out over the bay, and the temperature hovered just above twenty degrees. A lone car with chains started down the avenue, stalled, and attempted to reverse. No buses were running, several snowmen already stood guard outside their creators' homes, and only a few random sidewalks had been shoveled. So far, there wasn't a sign of a municipal sanding crew. The city was living up to its reputation of being both unable and unwilling to cope with winter weather.

"I'm stiff," Judith admitted, fitting her boots into the footprints which had gone before them. "I almost wish I'd woke up so I could have gone to bed."

"We tried to move you around so you'd be comfortable," Renie said, watching a dozen sparrows attack a bird feeder on the other side of the street. "Do you know you slept eleven hours straight?"

"Eleven hours crooked," Judith corrected. "The phone woke me. Who was it? Mother?"

"Only the first three times." Renie struggled slightly in Gertrude's borrowed galoshes. "The other fourteen calls were from the press and would-be guests."

Judith turned a bit too quickly and had to grab the already unsteady Renie. "You mean people want to stay at Hillside Manor after all this mess?"

The cousins both went down, tumbling into a utility

pole. ''Sure they do,'' Renie sputtered, wiping snow from her mouth. ''I told you, notoriety is the best form of advertising.''

''Gee.'' Judith scrambled to her feet, giving Renie a hand. ''I can't believe it. That's amazing!'' They resumed their hike. ''But I bet I won't get into the guidebooks,'' Judith remarked with a trace of gloom. They kept walking, with Renie making a little whistling sound as they reached level ground. At the corner, they turned toward the church, its single Gothic spire crowning the crest of Heraldsgate Hill.

Up ahead, other parishioners were making their way on foot to Star of the Sea. Judith put a hand on her cousin's arm, forcing Renie to halt. ''Tell me—did Joe say anything about that annulment?''

''No.''

''Did he say anything about *me?*''

''No.'' She saw the disappointment flood Judith's face and patted her cousin's hand. ''He left a note, though.''

Judith brightened. ''A note? What did it say?''

Renie was indignant. ''How do I know? It was for you. Do you think I'd read it?''

''Yes.''

Renie shuffled her ill-fitting galoshes. ''It said 'Give me six months. Joe.' That's all.''

Judith cocked an eye at Renie. ''What does that mean? I've already given that jerk over twenty years!'' She plunged ahead, this time deliberately stomping along in virgin territory, churning the snow beneath her boots.

''There was one other thing,'' said Renie, fighting to keep up. ''He wanted to see a picture of Mike.''

Judith stopped in her tracks. They were in the shadow of the church spire, and the air suddenly felt very cold. ''Well? Did you show him one?''

''Sure. Mike's high school graduation portrait. He hasn't changed all that much since then.'' She spoke lightly, but kept her eyes on Judith's face.

A half-dozen fellow SOTS called out greetings as they

went into the church. Judith managed a halfhearted wave in return. "What did Joe say?"

"He wanted to know why Mike had red hair."

"Oh." Judith stared down at her snow-caked boots. "What did you tell him?"

Renie's gaze didn't falter. "That Effie McMonigle was a redhead, of course. What else could I say?"

Judith bit her lip, then nodded. "Nothing." The church bells tolled the hour, the sound floating out over the crest of the hill. "Come on, we'll be late." The cousins moved as fast as they could, slipping to one side, sliding to the other. Giggling like girls, they joined the stream of people in the vestibule.

"Judith!" cried Norma Paine, her wide nostrils flaring. "The Brodies are back home! Did that awful nephew really kill the fortune-teller? What did he try to do to *you?*" She had swooped down on Judith, with Wilbur tagging along like a mascot.

Cornered by the holy water font, Judith realized that quite a crowd was gathering, eager expressions on their faces, a swarm of questions on their lips. "Not now," she said with a friendly smile. "Later, at coffee and doughnuts." With a mixture of disappointment and understanding, the SOTS began to drift away, toward the church proper.

"Coffee and doughnuts," murmured Renie. "Sounds good to me. I had breakfast over three hours ago."

"It doesn't sound as appropriate as what we served up night before last," said Judith, making the sign of the cross.

"I wouldn't know," Renie responded as the organ thundered forth with the opening chords of the entrance hymn. "I didn't get any."

"You didn't deserve to," Judith said, tiptoeing toward the side aisle. "Face it, coz," she whispered, "we didn't serve mere cream puffs, we gave the Brodies their just desserts."

Church or not, Renie kicked her with Gertrude's galosh.

Judith grinned, genuflected, and slipped into the first vacant pew. As the priest, Father Hoyle, three altar servers, and Carl Rankers in his role as lector proceeded to the altar, Judith said her prayers. She had a great deal to be thankful for on this bright, brisk January morning. A strange sense of exultation mingled with humility consumed her. She had relied upon her own resources to protect life and livelihood. For now, the world seemed a better place just because she was in it. The feeling would pass, as all such euphoria did, but Judith would savor it as long as possible.

It wasn't until the congregation stood for the gospel reading that Judith happened to glance across the church. There, in the mellow light from the old, exquisite stained-glass windows, she saw Joe Flynn. He saw Judith. Discreetly, he held up six fingers. Judith held up only one.

But she smiled.

CHECK INTO THE WORLD OF MARY DAHEIM

WHAT COULD BE more relaxing than a well-deserved respite at Hillside Manor, the charming bed-and-breakfast inn set atop Heraldsgate Hill? Well, for Judith McMonigle Flynn, the ever courteous proprietress, hand-to-tentacle combat with an irritated octopus might, on occasion, seem like a quieter pastime than running her beloved inn.

Daily worries for Judith include whether she'll be able to pay the utilities bill, whether she'll be able to keep the inn at full capacity during the busy season, whether her supply of hors d'oeuvres will satisfy her guests, whether her crotchety mother will keep out of the way, but most importantly, Judith always worries where that next body will turn up . . .

It's not that she goes out in search of murders to solve—after all, she doesn't deliberately try to compete with her husband, Homicide Detective Joe Flynn, on his own turf—it's just that murder and mayhem seem to find her. And what's a gal supposed to do?

Grab her ravenous and reliable cousin Renie and hit the trail after the latest killer, before this energetic and entertaining hostess is put permanently out of business.

JUST DESSERTS

A WIDOW OF three years, Judith McMonigle decided to convert her family home into the charming—and therefore destined to be successful—Hillside Manor bed-and-breakfast, which will provide her with a steady income (she hopes) and a place to live for herself and her not-so-gracefully aging mother, Gertrude. In business for just over seven months, Judith suddenly wishes she hadn't gone out of her way to accommodate the Brodie clan . . . except for the fact that the corpse in her dining room, which may put her out of business, also brings the local police onto the scene. . . .

"She's pretty good at what she does," remarked Judith in an undertone. "I wonder if Oriana thinks she's getting her two grand worth?"

Over the flutter of unsettled noises, Madame Gushenka was speaking again: "Far off, bleak, isolated. A handsome bird in a concrete cage." Her voice rumbled into the very depths of her chest, then suddenly brightened. "There is music, too. Such pretty notes! Or are they? Greed, deception creep onto the stage." The tone had changed again, now overtly sinister. "Wrongs not righted, the past swept under cover, while over the ocean, a crowd roars, then goes silent. Disaster strikes! The night goes black, the sky is empty, hush . . . hush . . . ssssh. . . ."

The last utterances had slowed, then began to fade away. Judith and Renie almost banged heads trying to press closer against the door. They were steadying themselves when they heard the crash, the screams, and the sounds of chairs being overturned, crystal shattering and china breaking. Even as Judith fumbled for the kitchen light switch, the dining room sounded as if it had erupted into a stampede. Renie threw open the door.

The illumination from the kitchen showed a scene of utter confusion, with everyone clustered around the head of the table. Lance was struggling with something or someone, Ellie was whimpering and clutching at Harvey, Gwen was verging on hysterics, Oriana was deathly pale despite her makeup, Otto was swearing like a sailor, Dash was trying either to help or to hinder Lance, and Mavis was shrieking for order.

"The lights!" called Judith, and was amazed when Oriana immediately obeyed, bringing the chandelier up to full beam. Gwen stared at the blaze of shimmering crystal as if hypnotized and Lance stepped back, revealing Madame Gushenka, sprawled facedown on the table, one hand on the cards, the other clawing at the azalea's vivid blooms. Her black hair spilled onto the Irish linen, and the brilliant veils seemed to have wilted like weary petals.

"She's out like a . . . light," said Lance, peering up at the chandelier.

"It must be a trance," Oriana said, but her usually confident voice was uncertain.

"Get back," Harvey ordered, assuming his best operating-theater style. "Give the poor woman room to breathe." As the others, including the distraught Ellie, moved away, Harvey felt for a pulse, first at the wrist, then at the neck. His sallow face sagged as his search for a vital sign grew more frantic. "My God," he exclaimed. "She's dead!"

FOWL PREY

JUDITH AND HER cousin Renie are heading north to British Columbia and the Hotel Clovia for a pre-Thanksgiving getaway. But when an addled and impoverished popcorn vendor is murdered along with his foul-mouthed parakeet, a local policeman's suspicions land on the visiting Americans, Judith and Renie. Meanwhile, the cousins suspect one of the "Sacred Eight"—a strange collection of showbiz glitterati gathered at the historic hotel. And unless Judith and Renie can find the murderer among the glitzy group, their goose will be cooked!

Renie was about to respond when the cousins both heard another noise, this time very faint—and very near. Their eyes darted to the bathtub where the shower curtain was pulled shut. With the poker again held aloft, Judith stood at one end of the tub while Renie guarded the other. Renie yanked at the curtain, revealing a cowering Mildred Grimm.

"Well, Mildred, first you show up half-naked in the middle of the night, then you come to take a shower with your clothes on. What gives?" asked Judith, putting the poker down.

"You'd never understand," whined Mildred, gingerly climbing over the mahogany surround.

"Could we try?" asked Judith, keeping her exasperation at bay.

Mildred stepped out of her low-heeled pumps, which apparently had gotten wet in the tub. "You wouldn't believe me," she said, not looking at either cousin.

"You'd be surprised what we'd believe about now," remarked Judith, as the trio emerged from the bathroom, went out through Renie's bedroom, and into the sitting room. "We presume this handiwork is yours, not the police's?" Judith made a sweeping gesture with one hand while replacing the poker with the other.

"Yes." Mildred drooped, a pitiful thing in her baggy blue sweater and pleated skirt. "I'm sorry, I would have put everything back if I'd had time."

Renie was already straightening the sofa cushions. "Sit down, we'll have a drink, we'll talk. What were you looking for, Mildred? More library cards?"

Whatever color Mildred possessed drained away. She collapsed onto the sofa like a rag doll. "How did you know?" she gasped.

"We were there," said Judith, closing the drawers on the end tables.

"Yes." Mildred sighed. "I saw you. But I didn't think you saw me."

Renie was at the phone. "What will you have, Mildred?"

Mildred opened her mouth, started to shake her head, then reconsidered. "A martini. Very dry. With a twist."

"Drat." Renie replaced the receiver. "No dial tone. I'll run downstairs and give the bar our order." She was gone before Judith could say "scotch."

With only one cousin confronting her, Mildred seemed to revive a bit. "I tell you, it's not believable."

"Let me decide," said Judith, sitting in the armchair opposite Mildred. "You owe us an explanation. You broke into our room, you ransacked our belongings. We could have you arrested.''

''I know.'' Mildred's face crumpled again. ''But that will probably happen anyway. Only on a more awful charge.''

''Of what?'' asked Judith, but the catch in her voice told Mildred she already knew.

The close-set blue eyes welled up with tears. ''Murder. Bob-o was killed with my gun.''

HOLY TERRORS

CATERING THE ANNUAL brunch and Easter egg hunt is enough of a hassle for bed-and-breakfast hostess Judith McMonigle. Add to that, murder by a scissors-happy fiend in a bunny suit and the return of her ex-beau, Lieutenant Joe Flynn, and Judith is up to her elbows in some serious unsolicited snooping . . .

Joe's casual air masked his tenacious professionalism, just as the well-cut tweed sports coat camouflaged the spreading midriff Dooley had mentioned. His receding red hair was flecked with gray, yet his round face retained its freshness, despite over two decades observing the seamiest slices of life. At his side stood Woodrow Price, a uniformed officer on the verge of thirty and his next promotion. A stolid black man with a walrus moustache, Woody Price had displayed a hidden reservoir of talents during his previous adventure at Hillside Manor.

But it wasn't Woody Price's serious dark gaze which held Judith mesmerized at the back door. Rather, Joe Flynn's green eyes, with those magnetic flecks of gold, turned her faintly incoherent.

"You're early," she blurted. "It's still two weeks to go. But who's counting?" Judith giggled and mentally

227

cursed herself for sounding like a half-baked teenager instead of a poised middle-aged widow.

Joe's mouth twitched slightly, showing the merest hint of his roguish smile. "This is business, not pleasure. I've yet to bring Woody along on a date." He put a highly buffed loafer over the threshold. "May we?"

Judith actually jumped. "Oh! I didn't mean ... Sure, come in, I just heard about what happened up at church ..."

Gertrude's rasping voice crackled from the kitchen: "Is that Joe Flynn?" She didn't wait for confirmation. "Where's he been for six months? One lousy cribbage board and a box of chocolates won't buy this old girl! There was a caramel in with the creams, and it wrecked my partial plate! Get that bastard out of my house!"

As always, it was useless for Judith to argue over the legal rights of ownership to Hillside Manor. "Mother," she pleaded over her shoulder, "you know why Joe hasn't called on us since Thanksgiving. That was the bargain. Now he's here about Sandy Frizzell's murder."

"Baloney!" snarled Gertrude, wrestling with her walker as she tried to get up from the dinette table. "Joe's here because you got your hair dyed like a two-bit hussy! Out!" Her thin arm flailed under cover of a baggy blue cardigan. "Beat it, and take your chauffeur with you!"

"Mother!" Judith was aghast. "Don't be so ornery!" Agitated, she rushed to Gertrude's side. "Settle down. Do you want to be arrested for impeding justice, you crazy old coot?"

While she was still seething, Gertrude's voiced dropped a notch. "Justice, my foot! If there were such a thing, Joe Flynn would have spent the last twenty-odd years in prison for breach of promise! But you, you gutless wonder," she raged on, wagging a bony finger in her daughter's face, "you just rolled over and married Dan McMonigle! Is that justice, I ask you?"

DUNE TO DEATH

HAVING FINALLY MADE it to the altar, bed-and-breakfast hostess Judith McMonigle and Detective Joe Flynn head out for their overdue honeymoon. Settling into a cozy, costly cottage on Buccaneer Beach it seems like a dream come true. However, their newly wedded bliss is shattered when a dune buggy accident puts Joe in the hospital in traction and Cousin Renie shows up to keep Judith company. And to make a bad situation worse, the landlady shows up garroted to death in their living room . . . and Judith is on the case!

A soft mist had settled in on the MG's windshield when Judith and Renie reached the parking lot. The air was cool and damp, but the wind had died down. It was almost ten by the time they returned to Pirate's Lair. To Judith's relief, the house was dark, but she had remembered to leave a light on in the garage. The faint sound of music could be heard drifting from the We See Sea Resort next door. Judith decided they should build a fire in the cottage's stone fireplace. The cousins gathered wood and kindling to bring inside. Judith noticed that more boxes seemed to be missing from the garage. She gave a mental shrug—if Mrs. Hoke were moving her

229

belongings, that was fine—as long as she didn't keep popping into the house itself. Maybe, Judith thought with a wry smile, she'd taken home a crate of dulcimers.

Renie was already in the kitchen, flipping on the lights. "Have you opened the damper yet?" she asked, heading for the living room.

"No," replied Judith as Renie switched on a table lamp by the beige sofa that sat across from the fireplace. "Let's make sure we do it right. I wouldn't want to set off the smoke alarm."

The words were hardly out of her mouth when Renie set off her own alarm. A piercing scream brought Judith vaulting around the sofa and across the floor. Renie stood frozen, the kindling clutched in her arms like a newborn baby. At her feet was Mrs. Hoke, long arms and legs at awkward angles. At her side was the bright pink kite the cousins had tried to fly in vain that afternoon.

And around her neck was the long, strong string. Her face was a ghastly shade of purple and the gray eyes bulged up at the cousins.

Judith and Renie knew she was dead.

BANTAM OF THE OPERA

AS TIME GOES on, the bed-and-breakfast continues to do well, gaining a reputation that keeps Judith hopping for most of the year. In fact, Hillside Manor has begun to draw some high caliber celebrities, including obnoxious opera star Mario Pacetti, who threatens to eat Judith out of house and home. Judith's attempts to satiate the significantly statured songster seem of minor significance once the threats on his life draw his attention away from his next meal—which could possibly be his last. . . .

"Hey, Jude-girl," Joe called after his wife. "Where's my gun?"

Judith gnashed her teeth. During her four years of widowhood she had forgotten how men, even sharp-eyed homicide detectives such as Joe Flynn, couldn't find a bowling ball in the bathroom sink. Suppressing the urge to tell her husband to look in the vicinity of his backside, Judith opened her mouth to reply. But Joe had spotted the holster and was grinning with the pleasure of discovery.

"Hey, how'd it get there?" he asked in surprise.

"Gee, I don't know, Joe. I suppose it grew little

231

leather feet and walked, meanwhile tossing socks and shirts every which way. Are you taking that with you?'' It was Judith's turn to evince surprise.

But Joe shook his head. "No need. I'll ditch it in the closet. Or what about that little safe you've got?''

Judith rarely used the safe, but considered it an excellent repository for Joe's .38 special. "It's in the basement, behind the hot water tank. I think.''

"Right.'' Joe was filling his shaving kit; Judith headed out into the little foyer which served as a family sitting room. On her left, the door to Mike's room was closed. On her right, the door to Gertrude's former room stood ajar. As if, Judith thought with a pang, it was expecting Gertrude Grover to return at any moment. Judith consoled herself that by Monday she might have some good news for her mother. If the Swedish carpenter's estimates were relatively reasonable and his schedule wasn't too busy, Gertrude might be home for Christmas. Of course Judith must discuss it more fully with Joe, but not now, with his departure at hand.

She had just descended the short flight from the third floor when she heard a tremendous crash and a piercing scream. The sounds emanated from the front bedroom. Judith raced down the hallway and pounded on the door.

"Mr. Pacetti! What is it? What's wrong? Mr. Pacetti?'' Judith's heart thumped along with her fists. Fleetingly, she wondered if her insurance agent had already increased her coverage as she'd requested the previous day. It was a callous thought, she realized, since Mario Pacetti might be in a lot more trouble than she was.

A FIT OF TEMPERA

Judith and Renie are headed for their family's backwoods vacation cottage for some much needed R&R. But shortly after they've unpacked their bags they find out that someone has painted their world-renowned neighbor, artist Riley Tobias, permanently out of the picture— and has artfully managed to frame Judith for the crime!

"Let me make some coffee," Judith suggested, then remembered that the fire had gone out. "Or some pop? A drink? Ice water?" She grimaced slightly at the thought of chipping chunks off the ice block.

But both Kimballs declined the offer of beverages. Indeed, Ward was on his feet, fingering his beard and gazing out the window. Mount Woodchuck stood watch over the forest, the clouds dispersed along the river valley.

"I think I'll head over to see Iris," Ward said, touching Lark's shoulder. "The law should be gone by now, and if not, I'd like to hear what they've found out. If anything. Lark?"

His daughter shook her head. "I told you, I'd rather not play out a farce with Iris. She doesn't like me any more than I like her."

Ward Kimball sighed with resignation. "As you will, dear heart. I'll amble over there. I shouldn't be long." He sketched a courtly little bow and was gone.

"Come on, Lark," Renie urged, "have a beer. A sandwich? A couple of hot dogs?"

Judith heard the hunger pangs and made a face at Renie. "Don't force food and drink on people, coz. Not everyone is a Big Pig."

But Lark said she would like a glass of wine after all, if the cousins had any. They didn't. She settled for a beer. Judith and Renie joined her, trying to be companionable.

"I suppose," Judith mused as she sat down next to Lark on the sofa, "that Riley never married Iris because his first bout with matrimony was so unhappy."

To the cousins' surprise, Lark laughed. "No, it wasn't. Riley just didn't like the idea of the institution. Not when he was young, anyway. It wasn't part of his philosophy then. He was into Kerouac, and all those British Angry Young Men. But he changed. Riley matured late, but fully." She held her bottle of beer as if it were a case of jewels.

Renie cut to the heart of the matter. "Then why didn't he marry Iris?"

Lark's laughter took on a jagged edge. "He didn't love her." The beautiful, unworldly face turned from cousin to cousin. For one brief moment, Judith could have sworn that Lark Kimball was not only seeing but studying her hostesses.

"Did he tell you that?" Renie, as usual, had sacrificed tact.

"Of course he did. Why should he love her?" Lark sounded defensive. "She's well connected in the art community; she's supposedly glib, handsome, and articulate. Useful, in other words. But she's also a rapacious conniver. It didn't take him twenty years to figure that out."

"Yes, it did," retorted Renie. "They were still together when he died."

"That's only because he couldn't figure out how to get

rid of her.'' Lark's voice had risen and her face no longer looked so unworldly. Indeed, she was blushing, and her jaw was set in a hard line. "Riley needed some time to tell her how he felt. How *we* felt.'' She flounced a bit on the sofa. "He wasn't merely my teacher, he was my lover. And we intended to be married. As soon as he told Iris to go to hell.'' Lark Kimball sat back on the sofa, now smiling serenely.

MAJOR VICES

JUDITH AND RENIE would rather be boiled in oil than cater the seventy-fifth birthday party for their batty Uncle Boo Major, the billionaire breakfast mush magnate. But fortunately, their duties keep them in the kitchen and away from most of their contemptible kin—that is until the birthday boy is found blown away behind the locked den door. And now a plethora of wills is popping up all over the place making everyone suspect, Judith and Renie included.

Pandemonium broke out in the den. Aunt Toadie whirled on Jill, trying to tear the will out of her hands. Derek embraced his daughter, which wasn't easy, since he had to fend off his aunt's clawing fingers. Holly fanned herself with her hand and leaned against one of the radiators. Aunt Vivvie beamed—and fainted again. Judith called for Mrs. Wakefield and the smelling salts.

It was Renie, however, who showed up. "What the hell . . . ?" she muttered, encountering the chaotic scene.

"Derek won," Judith said in her cousin's ear. "Jill found the will."

"Well." Renie stared at Aunt Vivvie, who was lying on the parquet floor and making little mewing noises.

"Did you say smelling salts? I think she's coming around."

Renie was right. Vivvie was not only conscious, but also smiling, if in a trembling, anxious manner. "Oh, my!" she gasped out, allowing Judith to prop her into a sitting position. "Oh, my, my! Bless Boo! My son is so deserving!"

"Bunk!" shouted Toadie. "Let me see that will! It must be a phony!"

With an air of victory, Derek waved a hand at his daughter. "Let her read it, Jill. Let everybody read it. I always knew Uncle Boo loved me best." His off-center smile revealed his gold molar, making him look vaguely like a pirate.

Toadie snatched the document from Jill's grasp. She read hurriedly, then sneered. "This thing is three years old! He wrote this just after Rosie died. Do you really think he didn't make another will?" Toadie crumpled the legal-sized paper and hurled it at Derek. "I should make you eat that, you swine!"

Trixie's blond head bobbed up and down like a puppet's. "That's right, Mummy! Uncle Boo promised *us* his money! And the house! And . . ." Trixie took a deep breath, her cleavage straining at the deep ruffled neckline.

". . . *everything!* Let's go through those other books!"

Chaos reigned in front of the open bookcase. Shoving, pushing, and otherwise stampeding one another, the four Rushes, including a rejuvenated Aunt Vivvie, vied with the two Grover-Bellews. Books began to fly from the top shelf. Her librarian's sensibilities inflamed, Judith called a halt.

"Wait!" she cried, practically vaulting over the desk. "Stop!" To her amazement, the combatants did, staring at her with varying degrees of curiosity and hostility. Swallowing hard, she made a calming gesture with her hands. "I have an idea. There's a better way to find that will than to tear this place apart. Would all of you agree to a truce and to appointing Renie and me as neutral searchers?"

Aunt Toadie's face turned mulish. "We would *not*. Why should we trust you two?"

MURDER, MY SUITE

EVER SINCE JOE Flynn walked back into Judith's life and finally married her, Judith has begun to breathe a little easier. Life is good for Judith, who loves being surrounded by her devoted husband, her delightful son, her bosom buddy of a cousin, Renie, and even, in a rare tender moment, her mother. That is, until life takes a devilish turn when gossip columnist Dagmar Delacroix Chatsworth descends on Hillside Manor with a flurry of lackeys and her yappy lapdog Rover, who seems to think he owns the joint. But Judith is ever the professional, gritting her teeth and bearing the barrage, even when things become fatally frenetic....

Judith was at a loss. She abandoned guessing at Dagmar's veiled intentions. "You certainly cover everybody's peccadilloes. Do you ever get threatened with lawsuits?"

For a brief moment Dagmar's high forehead clouded over under the turban. "Threatened?" Her crimson lips clamped shut; then she gave Judith an ironic smile. "My publishers have superb lawyers, my dear. Libel is surprisingly hard to prove with public figures."

The phone rang, and Judith chose to pick it up in the

living room. She was only mildly surprised when the caller asked for Dagmar Chatsworth. The columnist already had received a half-dozen messages since arriving at Hillside Manor the previous day.

While Dagmar took the call, Judith busied herself setting up the gateleg table she used for hors d'oeuvres and beverages. At first, Dagmar sounded brisk, holding a ballpoint pen poised over the notepad Judith kept by the living room extension. Then her voice tensed; so did her pudgy body.

"How dare you!" Dagmar breathed into the receiver. "Swine!" She banged the phone down and spun around to confront Judith. "Were you eavesdropping?"

"In my own house?" Judith tried to appear reasonable. "If you wanted privacy, you should have gone upstairs to the hallway phone by the guest rooms."

Lowering her gaze, Dagmar fingered the swatch of fabric at her throat. "I didn't realize who was calling. I thought it was one of my sources."

"It wasn't?" Judith was casual.

"No." Dagmar again turned her back, now gazing through the bay window that looked out over downtown and the harbor. Judith sensed the other woman was gathering her composure, so she quietly started for the kitchen.

She had got as far as the dining room when the other two members of Dagmar's party entered the house. Agnes Shay carried a large shopping bag bearing the logo of a nationally known book chain; Freddy Whobrey hoisted a brown paper bag which Judith suspected contained a bottle of liquor. Another rule was about to be broken, Judith realized: She discouraged guests from bringing alcoholic beverages to their rooms, but a complete ban was difficult to enforce.

The bark of Dagmar's dog sent the entire group into a frenzy. Clutching the shopping bag to her flat breast, Agnes started up the main staircase. Freddy waved his paper sack and shook his head. Dagmar put a hand to her turban and let out a small cry.

"Rover! Poor baby! He's been neglected!" She moved

to the bottom of the stairs, shouting at Agnes. The telephone call appeared to be forgotten. "Give him his Woofy Treats. Extra, for now. They're in that ugly blue dish on the dresser."

Judith blanched. She knew precisely where the treats reposed, since she had discovered them earlier in the day, sitting in her mother's favorite Wedgwood bowl. Anxiously, Judith watched the obedient Agnes disappear from the second landing of the stairs. Rover continued barking.

"I thought the dog was a female," Judith said lamely.

Dagmar beamed. "That's because he's so beautiful. Pomeranians are such adorable dogs. Rover is five, and still acts like the most precious of puppies. Would you mind if he came down for punch and hors d'oeuvres?"

Judith did mind, quite a bit.

AUNTIE MAYHEM

JUDITH AND RENIE are taking in the London countryside for an unharried weekend at a real English manor. However, they find the weekend anything but relaxing with Aunt Petulia, Ravenscroft House's aged mistress, holding court to her many relations. Then a box of sweets poisons Aunt Pet. Now Judith and Renie are up to their American necks in a murder most British.

Judith and Renie both recognized the neighborhood; some of the Grover ancestors had lived there in the late nineteenth century. "But you spend weekends at Ravenscroft House," Judith noted.

"Oh, yes," Claire replied with a tremulous smile. "At least some. London makes me nervy." To prove the point, Claire looked as if she were on the verge of an anxiety attack.

Renie was nodding. "We've got a cabin in the woods, about an hour outside of town." She referred to the ramshackle structure that had been built a half-century earlier by their fathers and Grandpa Grover. "Of course it's sort of falling down. We don't go there very often."

Claire put a hand to her flat breast and leaned back in the chair. "Oh! I know! These old houses are so stress-inducing! The heating, the electrical, the plumbing!''

"Actually," Renie murmured, "we don't exactly have plumbing. Or electricity or heating. The outhouse is collapsing, too."

Claire sympathized. "Outhouses! My! We call them outbuildings. But I know what you mean about repairs. Such a challenge! Judith—may I call you that, I hope? Thank you so. Margaret said you renovated your family home. The one in the city. Into a bed-and-breakfast. I shall hang on every word. I swear."

Judith assumed a modest air. "I'll do my best. Hillside Manor had some serious problems, too." Fondly, she pictured the Edwardian house on the hill, with its fresh green paint and white trim, the bay windows, the five guest bedrooms on the second floor, the family quarters in the expanded attic, and the enclosed backyard with the last few fruit trees from the original orchard. There was a double garage, too. And the remodeled toolshed where her mother lived. Gertrude Grover had refused to share a roof with her son-in-law. She didn't like Judith's second husband much better than her first one.

"It *was* a challenge," Judith finally said, thinking more of coping with Gertrude than of the renovations. "It's expensive. I had to take out a loan."

Claire's high forehead creased. "My word! A loan! Charles should hate that!''

Trying to be tactful, Judith made an effort to put Claire's mind at rest. "I'm sure my situation was different. I'd been recently widowed and had no savings." Dan McMonigle had blown every dime on the horse races or the state lottery. "My husband wasn't insurable." Dan had weighed over four hundred pounds when he'd died at the age of forty-nine. "We had no equity in our home." After defaulting on the only house they'd ever owned, the McMonigles had lived in a series of seedy rentals, and had been about to be evicted when Dan had, as Judith put it, conveniently blown up. "In fact," she went on, feigning serenity, "I had no choice but to move in with my mother. That's when it occurred to me that it didn't make sense for the two of us to rattle around in a big old house. My son was almost ready for college.''

"How true!" Claire positively beamed, revealing small, perfect white teeth. "That's precisely what I've told Charles. Why maintain a second home with so many expenditures and taxation? Why not turn it into something that will produce income?"

"Exactly," Judith agreed. "The main thing is to figure out if you're going to run it or let someone do it for you."

Claire's smile evaporated. "Oh, no. The main thing is Aunt Pet," she insisted, her rather wispy voice now firm. "First of all, she has to die."

NUTTY AS A FRUITCAKE

WITH ALL THE comings and goings around the bed-and-breakfast, Judith finds it comforting to know that, should her aging mother require her assistance—beyond the meals she serves her every day and the errands she runs—Gertrude is right on the property, living in the converted toolshed. Although Judith and Gertrude have their moments, this mother-daughter relationship is an affectionate one, depending on how you look at it. . . .

"They're questioning the neighbors," Naomi said in a breathless voice. "First, Mrs. Swanson, then the Rankerses, and finally, me. Nobody else is home—except your mother."

"*My mother?*" Judith gaped at Naomi, then jumped out of the car to look down the driveway. She saw nothing unusual, except Sweetums, who was stalking an unseen prey in the shrubbery.

"They're questioning her now," Naomi added, backpedaling to her own property. "Don't worry, Judith. I'm sure she'll be treated with respect."

That wasn't what concerned Judith. With a half-hearted wave for Naomi, she all but ran to the toolshed. There wasn't time to think about the awful things Gertrude could say to the police, especially about Joe Flynn. Judith yanked the door open.

Patches Morgan was standing by the tiny window that looked out onto the backyard and the Dooleys' house. With arms folded, Sancha Rael leaned against a side chair that had originally belonged to Judith and Dan. Gertrude was sitting on her sofa, smoking fiercely, and wearing a tiger-print housecoat under a lime-and-black cardigan. She glared as her daughter came into the small sitting room.

"Well! Just in time, you stool pigeon! What are you trying to do, get me sent up the river?"

Judith's mouth dropped open. "What? Of course not! What's happening?"

With his good left eye, Morgan winked at Judith. "Now, now, me hearties, this is just routine. But," he continued, growing serious, "it seems that certain threats against Mrs. Goodrich were made by Mrs. Grover. You don't deny that, do you, ma'am?" His expression was deceptively benign as he turned back to Gertrude.

Gertrude hid behind a haze of blue smoke. "I make a lot of threats," she mumbled. "It's my way. I can't remember them all."

Judith stepped between Gertrude and Morgan. "Excuse me—who told you that my mother threatened Enid?"

Morgan's good eye avoided Judith. "Now, I can't be revealing my sources, eh? You know that anything we might regard as a threat has to be investigated when there's a homicide involved."

"It was years ago," Judith said, then bit her tongue. "I mean, it must have been—*I* don't remember it. Either," she added lamely, with a commiserating glance for Gertrude.

Sancha Rael stepped forward, a smirk on her beautiful face. "This threat involved a family pet. It had something to do with"—she grimaced slightly—"sauerkraut."

Gertrude stubbed her cigarette out. She shot Morgan and Rael a defiant look.

Judith didn't know whether to grin or groan. She did

neither. "Look," she said to Morgan, "this is silly. I can't believe you're wasting the city's time interrogating my mother. Does she look like the sort of person who'd take a hatchet to somebody?"

Morgan eyed Gertrude closely. "In truth, she does," he said. "Where were you Wednesday morning, December first, between seven and eight-thirty A.M.?"

SEPTEMBER MOURN

JUDITH HAS AGREED to run a high school chum's bed-and-breakfast for a few days. So off she goes with cousin Renie for B&B sitting in the rustic splendor of Chavez Island. But when one odious blowhard tries to horn in on their dinner one night, Renie beans him with a china dish and moments later he takes a deadly tumble down a flight of stairs. Now Judith must find the real killer and prove coz Renie innocent.

Hodge bristled. "Lips that touch liquor will never touch mine."

Defiantly, Renie took a big swig of bourbon. "You can count on it, Burrell. I wouldn't touch you with a ten-foot pole."

"Let's all calm down," Judith urged, as she counted the simmering prawns. There were an even dozen. Divided by three, that made four apiece. Renie wouldn't be happy to share.

"We're having dinner for two," Renie asserted. "Beat it."

Though appalled by her cousin's attitude, Judith knew she had to side with Renie. "It's a rule," she insisted. "Mrs. Barber doesn't do dinner."

"Mrs. Barber isn't here," Hodge countered. "H. Burrell Hodge is." He wedged himself between the table and the matching bench. "Ah! Do I smell garlic? H. Burrell Hodge is fond of garlic!"

"Guess what?" Renie said, placing a knee on the bench next to Hodge. "I'm not fond of rude people who try to steal my dinner. You're not eating our pasta, but you might end up wearing it. Am I being clear?"

Hodge glared at Renie. "You're very maddening," he averred, picking up the silverware that had been intended for Renie. "H. Burrell Hodge doesn't give in to silly threats from mouthy women who drink too much. Where are my prawns?"

"That does it!" Renie was enraged. She snatched up the heavy blue-and-pink plate and cracked it over Hodge's head. The plate broke. Hodge let out a howl of pain. Clutching his head with one hand, he made a fist with the other.

"Damn your hide! I'm reporting this to the authorities! You assaulted me! I'll sue!"

Judith was staring at Hodge in horror, but the unrepentant Renie had gone to the cupboard to get another plate. "I'll use a skillet next time," she snapped. "Did you think I was kidding about the prawns? R. Grover Jones doesn't kid about *food*!"

WED AND BURIED

JUDITH MCMONIGLE FLYNN'S son Mike is getting married and the Hillside Manor B&B is packed to the rafters with relatives. However, the joyous occasion is dampened for Judith when she spies a tuxedo-clad gent tossing a bridal-gowned beauty off the roof of a nearby hotel. Judith's determination to find the killer could put some stress on her own marital bliss with policeman husband Joe, but she's not about to take a honeymoon from amateur sleuthing until she's gotten to the bottom of the homicidal hanky-panky.

"I feel awful," Judith declared after they had driven around the block four times to find a parking place and waited ten minutes for a table. "I think it's the heat."

Joe was scanning the long list of microbrews that were written in various shades of colored chalk above the bar. The Heraldsgate Pub was crowded as usual, but Judith and Joe had been lucky—their table was at the far end of the long, narrow establishment, and, thus, not quite in the center of noise and bombast.

"The heat?" Joe replied rather absently. "Maybe." The green eyes finally made contact with Judith. "How about the corpse? You pegged the wrong one, Jude-girl.'' A faint smile touched Joe's mouth as he started to reach for her hands.

Abruptly, Judith pulled back. "Hey! I pegged *somebody*! You're ticked off because I knew there was a dead person at that hotel. You thought I was hallucinating.''

Joe's grin was off-center. "You're having one of your fantasies. Nobody was pushed off a roof. The dead man didn't die from a fall. He was stabbed.''

Judith gaped. "Stabbed? With a knife?''

Joe was noncommittal. " 'With a sharp instrument' is the way we put it. No weapon was found. Dr. Chinn says he'd been dead about forty-eight hours. He'll *know* more after the formal autopsy.''

"Stabbed,'' Judith echoed. Then the rest of what Joe had said sank in. "What do you mean? 'Whoever he is'?''

Joe shrugged. "Just that. The guy had no ID. He looked to be about thirty, just under six feet, a hundred and forty pounds, not in the best of health, signs of poor nutrition. But you're right about one thing—he was wearing a tuxedo.''

Judith's eyes sparkled. "So he was the man I saw on the roof.''

SNOW PLACE TO DIE

JUDITH MCMONIGLE FLYNN is more than ready to hang up her oven mitts, but her effervescent Cousin Renie needs help catering the telephone company's annual winter retreat. Judith gives in because the pay is good, never thinking that there would be a killer cooking up mischief on the premises. But when Judith and Renie discover the frozen garroted remains of the previous company caterer, they know that they are on the trail of a killer who would like nothing better than to put the two cousins in the Deep Freeze.

"When do you make your presentation?" Judith asked, forcing herself out of her reverie.

"Friday," Renie answered, no longer placid. "I told you, it's just for a day. Can't Arlene Rankers help you throw some crap together for these bozos? Bring her along. You'll be up at the lodge for about six hours, and they'll pay you three grand."

"Arlene's getting ready for her annual jaunt to Palm Desert with Carl, and . . . *three grand*?" Judith's jaw dropped.

"Right." The smirk in Renie's voice was audible. "OTIOSE pays well. Why do you think I'm so anxious to peddle my pretty little proposals? I could make a bundle off these phone company phonies.''

''Wow.'' Judith leaned against the kitchen counter. ''That would pay off our Christmas bills and then some. Six hours, right?''

''Right. We can come and go together, because my presentation should take about two hours, plus Q&A, plus the usual yakkity-yak and glad-handing. You'll get to see me work the room. It'll be a whole new experience. I actually stay nice for several minutes at a time.''

Judith couldn't help but smile. Her cousin wasn't famous for her even temper. ''How many?'' she asked, getting down to business.

''Ten—six men, four women,'' Renie answered, also sounding equally professional. ''All their officers, plus the administrative assistant. I'll make a list, just so you know the names. Executives are very touchy about being recognized correctly.''

Judith nodded to herself. ''Okay. You mentioned a lodge. Which one?''

''Mountain Goat,'' Renie replied. ''It's only an hour or so from town, so we should leave Friday morning around nine.''

Judith knew the lodge, which was located on one of the state's major mountain passes. ''I can't wait to tell Joe. He'll be thrilled about the money. By the way, why did the other caterers back out?''

There was a long pause. ''Uh . . . I guess they're sort of superstitious.''

''What do you mean?'' Judith's voice had turned wary.

''Oh, it's nothing, really,'' Renie said, sounding unnaturally jaunty. ''Last year they had a staff assistant handle the catering at Mountain Goat Lodge. Barry Something-Or-Other, who was starting up his own business on the side. He . . . ah . . . disappeared.''

''He *disappeared*?'' Judith gasped into the receiver.

''Yeah, well, he went out for cigarettes or something and never came back. Got to run, coz. See you later.''

Renie hung up.